"A STURDY PLOT AND KEEN SATIRICAL POINT . . . in the spirit of the season, Hess is as generous with her affection as she is with her wit." —*New York Times Book Review*

"THE SCALES TIP HEAVILY toward jollity in *O Little Town of Maggody* . . . its tenacious characters will grow on you." —*Wall Street Journal*

"A GIFT IN ITSELF . . . will please fans of humor as well as those of whodunits." —*Arkansas Democrat Gazette*

"FAST, FUNNY, AMIABLY SARDONIC A MARVELOUS TRE

"ANOTHER UPF BACKWOODS."

"ONE OF HESS'S FUNNIEST MYSTERIES." —*Tower Books Mystery Newsletter*

"HYSTERICAL . . . A PERFECT HOLIDAY STORY, filled with rollicking jokes and a lot of laughter. Just the tonic against the hum-drum of the season." —*Ocala Star-Banner*

Other books by Joan Hess

The Maggody Series

MALICE IN MAGGODY
MISCHIEF IN MAGGODY
MUCH ADO IN MAGGODY
MADNESS IN MAGGODY
MORTAL REMAINS IN MAGGODY
MAGGODY IN MANHATTAN

The Claire Malloy Series

STRANGLED PROSE
MURDER AT THE MURDER AT THE MIMOSA INN
DEAR MISS DEMEANOR
A REALLY CUTE CORPSE
A DIET TO DIE FOR
ROLL OVER AND PLAY DEAD
DEATH BY THE LIGHT OF THE MOON
POISONED PINS

Joan Hess

O Little Town of Maggody

An Arly Hanks Mystery

AN ONYX BOOK

ONYX
Published by the Penguin Group
Penguin Books USA Inc., 375 Hudson Street,
New York, New York 10014, U.S.A.
Penguin Books Ltd, 27 Wrights Lane,
London W8 5TZ, England
Penguin Books Australia Ltd, Ringwood,
Victoria, Australia
Penguin Books Canada Ltd, 10 Alcorn Avenue,
Toronto, Ontario, Canada M4V 3B2
Penguin Books (N.Z.) Ltd, 182–190 Wairau Road,
Auckland 10, New Zealand

Penguin Books Ltd, Registered Offices:
Harmondsworth, Middlesex, England

Published by Onyx, an imprint of Dutton Signet,
a division of Penguin Books USA Inc.
Previously published in a Dutton edition.

First Onyx Printing, November, 1994
10 9 8 7 6 5 4 3 2 1

 REGISTERED TRADEMARK—MARCA REGISTRADA

Printed in the United States of America

BOOKS ARE AVAILABLE AT QUANTITY DISCOUNTS WHEN USED TO PROMOTE
PRODUCTS OR SERVICES. FOR INFORMATION PLEASE WRITE TO PREMIUM MARKETING
DIVISION, PENGUIN BOOKS USA INC., 375 HUDSON STREET, NEW YORK, NEW YORK
10014.

To the wickedly witty Dorothy Cannell,
who started it all with a single observation

ACKNOWLEDGMENTS

"Where do you get your ideas?" is this writer's least favorite question. However, I'm going to be in serious trouble if I don't announce for all to read that the idea for this book came straight from Dorothy Cannell. In the spring of 1992, Dorothy, her husband, Julian, Sharyn McCrumb, and I explored Hannibal, Missouri—a town not oblivious to its most celebrated hometown boy. "It's too bad Maggody doesn't have a famous son," Dorothy sadly opined in her melodious British accent. The conversation blossomed, and long before we arrived in Peoria, Sharyn had named Matt Montana and concocted the majority of the lyrics of his award-winning song (Dorothy and I contributed as best we could, but Sharyn is truly knowledgeable about country music) and we were singing it, to Julian's obvious discomfort.

Three months later I was sitting on the porch of a country inn in North Carolina with Sharyn, Dorothy, Charlotte MacLeod (a.k.a. Alisa Craig), Margaret Maron, Sandy Graham, and Barbara Mertz (a.k.a. Barbara Michaels and/ or Elizabeth Peters). "But *Mistletoe in Maggody* is not a great title," I whined as we sipped tea and nibbled crumpets. Brilliant suggestions ensued, but Barbara receives full credit for that which graces the jacket.

During the months of execution (I did have to fill in the prose), Margaret Maron and Kristen Whitbread provided tidbits of original country music lyrics. Terry Jones, Ray Guzman, and Terry Kirkpatrick fielded legal questions, while Sarah McBee and Dave Edmiston did the same with medical ones. Linda Nickle attended a country music symposium on my behalf, and Martha McNair shared her knowledge of literature. Ronna Luper of Crossbrooks Graphics graciously provided information regarding the contents of the souvenir shoppe. Amy Abbott saved me numerous hours at the post office and smiled despite it all. The Fayetteville Police Department told me about a dog named Larry. Ellen Nehr provided astute editorial insights, as did Michaela Hamilton, my official editor; Danielle Perez, her adjutant; and Dominick Abel, my literary agent. Last of all, I would like to thank the Keebler elves, who kept me company while I worked into the wee hours of the night.

Chapter One

"You're a detour on the highway to heaven," sang Ruby Bee Hanks as she ran the dust mop across the minute dance floor of Ruby Bee's Bar & Grill. Her voice wasn't bad for a woman of modest years, she thought with a smile that lit up her chubby, well-powdered face. It weren't nothing like Matt Montana's, not by a long shot, but she carried the tune faithfully. That wasn't surprising since the song came on the jukebox every five minutes from noon till midnight.

There wasn't any question Matt Montana could sing, but nobody'd ever claimed he made the best scalloped potatoes west of the Mississippi. She'd bet her last dollar he'd never won blue ribbons at the county fair for his canned tomatoes and watermelon pickles. This last thought reminded her that she needed to check the apple pies bubbling in the oven, so she took the dust mop and went into the kitchen to get ready for the noon rush. Presuming there was one, for a change.

★

"I am lost on the back roads of sin," warbled the checkout girl at Jim Bob's SuperSaver Buy 4 Less. The proprietor, Jim Bob Buchanon, who also happened to be the mayor of Maggody among his other sins, gave her a dark look, then went out the door to the mostly empty parking lot. Beneath his noticeably simian forehead, his eyes were yellowish. Those were the two dominant physical traits that proclaimed his lineage in the Buchanon clan, although a geneticist would be quick to point out they were both recessive. There were about as many Buchanons in

Stump County as there were varmints up on Cotter's Ridge. Some Buchanons were more intelligent (and less ornery) than these same varmints, but they were few and far between—and living elsewhere. Most of the rest regarded family reunions in the same fashion young executives did singles bars.

Jim Bob leaned against the concrete block wall and watched a lone pickup truck rumble out of view. Business was bad; there was no getting around it. The cash registers weren't pinging, and his bank balance was dwindling to a worrisome level. He shaded his eyes and looked across the highway at Ruby Bee's Bar & Grill, which didn't appear to be faring any better. Down the road, no one was filling up with gas at the self-service pumps, nor was anybody waddling into the Suds of Fun Launderette with a basket of dirty clothes. There weren't any cars or RVs parked in front of Roy Stiver's antique store, and he'd heard that Roy was threatening to close for the winter and go flop on a beach somewhere to write more of that highfalutin poetry he was so proud of. Jim Bob had written some in his day, although his had been calculated to melt comely maidens' hearts and soften their protests. Roy's stuff didn't even rhyme, and gawd help you if you tried to sing it.

Jim Bob figured he might as well be writin' poetry as standing in the parking lot looking at nothing. Like the ancient oak tree out behind his house on Finger Lane, the whole damn town of Maggody was in danger of crashing down in the next gust of wind. The best he could recollect, there were still 755 citizens living along the highway and on the unpaved back roads that led to other depressing towns or petered out up in the mountains. There were more citizens buried out behind the Methodist church, but nobody he knew of had been planted—lately, that is. More folks than usual seemed to have been murdered since Arly Hanks had skulked back home to become the chief of police (and the entirety of the department). But, Jim Bob added to himself, trying to be fair about it, it most likely wasn't her fault. She hadn't brought back a busload of muggers and rapists with her from her high-and-mighty life in Manhattan. No, she'd just brought her smart mouth and snippety way of putting her fists on her hips and staring like a goddamn water moccasin when she pretended to be listening to him. He couldn't think when he last made her blink.

"I have got to get back on the four-lane," the checker was singing as he stomped back inside.

He was about to fire her on the spot, when he realized she wasn't all that unattractive, if you were willing to ignore her stained teeth and rabbity eyes and lack of chin, and concentrate on her undeniably round breasts.

"Malva, isn't it?" he said in a right friendly voice. "Why don't you take yourself a little break in the lounge? I'll get us a couple of cans of soda and a box of cookies, and then you can sing me some more of that pretty song."

Malva wasn't fooled one bit, but she was dim-witted enough to think she might get a raise (along with the rise) out of him. "Whatever you say, Mr. Buchanon."

His fingers tingling, Jim Bob took off for the Oreos.

★

"So that I can see Mama again," sang Perkins's eldest as she maneuvered the vacuum cleaner down the hallway and deftly turned into the living room, the electrical cord whipping behind her like a skinny black sidewinder.

"I wish she'd hush up," said Mrs. Jim Bob (a.k.a. Barbara Ann Buchanon Buchanon) as she came back into the sun-room with a fresh pot of coffee. Her hair was brown and sensible, her face devoid of the devil's paint, her eyes mostly brown with only a few flecks of mustard. She wore a blue dress and freshly starched underwear in case there was some sort of untimely disaster and she found herself submitting her resumé to the Lord.

Elsie McMay gazed solemnly across the table. "Did you hear those hippies what own the hardware store are talking about closing up and moving away?"

"It'd be a blessing if they did. They're lewd and lascivious, probably all sleeping in one bed. There's a fancy French name for what they do, but I'm too good a Christian to even know what it is. I told Brother Verber to go over there and give them a word of warning about eternal damnation, and he said he would just as soon as he had the time.'' Her thin lips grew thinner as she thought this over. ''I seem to recall that was more than two years ago.''

The mention of the pastor of the Voice of the Almighty Lord Assembly Hall led to a discussion of the latest uproar in the Missionary Society (too many ballots in the box) and several cups of coffee.

After Elsie left, Mrs. Jim Bob pulled on a sweater and went out to the front porch. It was a mite crumpy for November, maybe an ominous sign of things to come. If business was as bad as Jim Bob had sworn, then they were in trouble. He'd used all their savings to open the supermarket, even getting his hands on the nice little sum she'd inherited from Great-Uncle Arbutus Buchanon, who, for the record, was a Buchanon from her side of the family rather than Jim Bob's.

As befitting the mayor's wife, she had the finest house in all of Maggody, a two-story red brick structure on the top of a hill where everybody in town could see it, and a driveway that wound down to a gate with the letters J and B formed out of bricks and spanned by a wrought-iron arch. But if the store went broke, they'd be lucky to have a rusty mobile home at the Pot o' Gold.

Mrs. Jim Bob was shivering as she went back inside to rinse out the coffee pot and have a stern word with Perkins's eldest about the baseboards.

★

''When Mama lay a-dyin' on the flatbed,'' sang Estelle Oppers, although the words were muffled on account of the bobby pins wobbling between her lips. More were scattered across the counter among bottles of shampoo and conditioner, combs, hair nets, plastic and foam rollers, hair dryers, curling irons, and other accoutrements of the profession she ran out of her living room.

Eilene Buchanon frowned at her reflection in the mirror as Estelle caught a wisp of brown hair and pinned it back in place. ''Can you make it less fluffier on top? My niece —the one on the drill team over in Farberville—she says it makes me look like a French poodle.''

Estelle gave Eilene a hand mirror and swiveled the chair around. "I think this looks real sweet, Eilene. These teenaged girls today all think they have to wear their hair so it looks like they were lined up to be the next bride of Frankenstein." She glanced in the mirror at her own fiery red beehive, today festooned with a row of spitcurls across her forehead. Yesterday she'd tried a two-tiered effect, but this was undeniably more becoming. "Amateurs don't know about the artistry of cosmetology. Just the other day I offered to fix Arly's hair—not that she's a teenager by a good fifteen years—but she ducked her head and said her schoolmarm bun was dictated by the police manual. If that wasn't a platter of barbecued Spam, I don't know what is!"

"She still moping around the police department?" Eilene asked as she handed back the mirror and stood up, wondering in the back of her mind if she didn't look just a tiny bit like a dog that answered to Gigi.

"Moping like a wet mop. I can't tell you how many times Ruby Bee and I have tried to talk some sense in her. We might as well be arguing with a box of rocks. Arly says she's perfectly happy to spend her days at the police department and her nights in that shabby one-room apartment, except when she's wolfing down biscuits and gravy at Ruby Bee's or slurping cherry limeades from the Dairee Dee-Lishus. The most exciting thing that's happened to her in the last month was stopping a silver Mercedes for speeding out by the remains of Purtle's Esso station and finding out the guy was a state senator."

"She give him a ticket?"

"In a Noow Yark minute, and still giggling about it."

Eilene paid Estelle and booked her next appointment. "Kind of sad, isn't it? Arly ain't bad looking, but she isn't going to find herself a man in this town. At the rate things are going, this may be a ghost town afore too long. Earl keeps busy repairing burst pipes and unstopping toilets, but he hasn't had a subcontracting job in months. He heard Ira Pickerell down at the body shop had to fire his own first cousin Jimson on account of business being so poor. I guess folks can't afford to get their dents fixed when they have to worry about rent and groceries. Christmas is gonna be real bleak this year, if you ask me.''

Estelle went out to the front walk and stood watching as Eilene backed her car onto County 102 and drove away. As if she didn't know business was poor these days. All she had scheduled for tomorrow was a trim for Joyce Lambertino's little niece after school let out. She'd heard about the hippies leaving, and she wasn't all that surprised about Ira having to get rid of Jimson. More times than not, Ruby Bee's Bar & Grill was half-empty at noon, and happy hour was downright gloomy these days. The poultry plant in Starley City had cut back the night shift. The used-car lot was nothing but a field of weeds. Everybody was hurting.

Out by the ditch, the sign that read ESTELLE'S HAIR FANTASIES creaked in the bone-chillin' wind. What paint that hadn't flaked off was nearly illegible, and one corner of the sign drooped where a screw had fallen out. With a sigh, Estelle went back inside, switched on the television to her favorite soap, and settled back for an hour of somebody else's misery.

★

''She warned me not to truck with girls like you,'' sang Dahlia (nee O'Neill) Buchanon. She had a sweet voice, but at the moment she was so depressed that the words were oozing out like molasses on a winter morning. Her eyes kept overflowing with tears that ran down her chunky cheeks and leaked into the cracks between her numerous chins. She was slumped on the sofa of what her new husband kept describing as ''our little love nest,'' but anyone with a pittance of a brain could see it was nothing but the same house where she'd always lived with her granny. Her granny'd put up quite a fight when Dahlia made her move to the county old folks home; lordy, how she'd covered her ears and squawked like a chicken whenever Dahlia tried to reason with her about how nice it would be to sit with the other old ladies on the porch every day. She was still clamming up when Dahlia visited every Sunday afternoon, but she'd stop being a crybaby sooner or later.

Dahlia heaved all of her three hundred pounds to her

feet, wiped her face, and trudged into the kitchen to make supper for Kevin. Marital bliss sure wasn't the way they showed it on television. The honeymoon had been one disaster after another, and then they'd come back to find out that Kevin had lost his job at the supermarket and Ruby Bee couldn't afford the salary for one barmaid, not even part-time.

Spilling a can of beans into a saucepan, she wondered if she'd done the right thing getting married in the first place. Kevvie'd talked about a cozy cottage and going to the picture show every Friday night, but he took the first job he could find—selling fancy vacuum cleaners in Farberville—and hardly ever got home before ten o'clock at night. Just what was the new Mrs. Kevin Buchanon supposed to do all day?

She popped a couple of cookies in her mouth and imagined herself on the Grand Ole Opry stage next to Matt Montana, whose photograph she kept tacked to the wall in the living room and whose face had been known to invade their double bed on those rare nights Kevin didn't stagger through the door and fall asleep in the recliner. In her daydreams, she was always as thin as Ronna (but with Dolly's bust), with Barbara's exquisite seashell blue eyes, with Wynonna's cascading blond hair, with Katie's stark and mysterious cheekbones. She was dressed in a white sequined gown and cute little cowgirl hat, and her boots were dainty as ballet slippers.

"But I was caught in the glare of your headlights," she recommenced to singing, this time in perfect two-part harmony with Matt, "and went joyriding just for the view."

★

"Your curves made me lose my direction," sang Brother Verber as he stood in the doorway of his trailer parked beside the Voice of the Almighty Lord Assembly Hall. He dearly hoped the highway he was gazing at wasn't the one in the song, because it wasn't clogged with cars and trucks heading for the Pearly Gates. A cadaverous hound was asleep on the dotted yellow line, threatened only by an empty beer can rattling across the road.

The collection plate was getting lighter every week, which meant not only were the little heathen orphans in Africa missing out on the opportunity to be enlightened (as soon as he got their address), but also that he'd been obliged to quote a verse from the Good Book to that sassy young woman who'd called that very morning. " 'The Lord is my light and my salvation: whom shall I fear?' " he'd demanded of her. She'd suggested the rural electric cooperative.

Religion ain't immune to recession, he thought bleakly as he went to the kitchenette to pour out another tumbler of wine, and then lay down on the sofa. Why, he couldn't find the energy to change out of his pajamas and bathrobe, and it was already early afternoon. Hanging over the end of the sofa, his bare feet looked like a pair of dead fish. All in all, at the moment even he would admit he wasn't the epitome of evangelical inspiration.

Brother Verber got up long enough to turn on his television to one of those talk shows where people seemed eager to tell the whole world about how they'd lusted after their household pets or dressed up in leather underwear and performed degrading acts on the kitchen floor, or both. Brother Verber didn't approve of this kind of thing being shown on television, but he figured watching it fell into the realm of better preparing himself should a sinner come a-knockin' on the rectory door.

It occurred to him that he might could charge a small fee for eternal salvation, maybe even run some kind of special at Christmastime.

★

"But you were just one more roadside attraction," sang Kevin Buchanon as he walked up the sidewalk of a house in Farberville, "and it's been ten thousand miles since I prayed." He wore a dark suit and a tie, and despite the fact that his trouser cuffs failed to hide a good three inches of white socks, he was sure he looked like a bright young businessman. After all, his manager, Mr. Dentha, had slapped him on the back and told him that exact thing at the regular morning sales meeting at the Vacu-Pro office.

Kevin tightened his grip on the case containing the body of the vacuum cleaner and its thirty-five attachments. The proud owner of a Vacu-Pro could not only clean her carpet but also shampoo upholstery, sand wood, spray-paint walls, dust venetian blinds, strip furniture, and so many other useful things that it had taken Kevin more than a week to memorize the list. Now he could rattle 'em off in under a minute. And who wouldn't want the finest vacuum cleaner on the market, a contraption on the cutting edge of the technological revolution? Sure, a Vacu-Pro was expensive, but so was a jet airplane—and try to scale a fish with one of them!

His shoulders squared and his chin held so high that anyone in the neighborhood could see his throat rippling, Kevin pushed the doorbell.

The door opened slowly, and all of a sudden he was gulping and fighting for air as he found himself staring at a woman wearing a scarlet nightie, lace panties that hung on her shapely hips, and not another stitch. He jerked his eyes up to her face, which was wearing a bewitching grin amidst a cloud of crimpy blond hair that looked soft as cotton candy.

"Well, hello," she purred, her tongue curling along her scarlet lips. "I've been waiting all day to have my carpet shampooed. Nobody told me they were sending a handsome young man to do . . . it. I've been told there are all sorts of interesting things to do with the attachments. You did bring your attachments, didn't you, honey?"

Kevin knew he was supposed to launch into the joys of owning a Vacu-Pro, but not a single word made it out of his mouth. All he could do was gurgle as she took his arm and pulled him into the house.

★

"So he did it again," muttered Pierce Keswick as he grimaced at his younger brother. They shared a family resemblance strong enough to give Pierce ulcers. Ripley had the same hawkish nose and washed-out blue eyes, and the same sharp chin, but his hair hung to his collar in an untidy mess that begged for a comb (or, in Pierce's opinion, a weed whacker). Pierce wore silk; Ripley preferred corduroy and one hundred percent cotton. They rarely—just short of never—communicated outside of the office, which suited both of them just fine.

"I am not overwhelmed with amazement," Ripley said with only a faint smirk.

"This is the second time since Matt won the award that he's been arrested. He was scheduled for a couple of telephone interviews this morning, but I called the radio stations and made excuses. He missed two shows in Memphis last weekend, just flat out didn't show up. Harry says he and the Hellbellies are thinking about backing out on the tour and just riding out the winter here in Nashville. This latest crap gets out, no one's gonna risk opening for him and we might as well cancel the tour and kiss off the quarter of a million we've put into the album."

"I said right after he won the award that Lillian wouldn't be able to control him. The annals of country music have proven that small-town rednecks are notoriously incapable of handling fame and fortune."

"That's it!" Pierce said, hitting his desk with his fist so hard his secretary glanced up from her computer and inadvertently added a zero to some lucky devil's contract. He got up and went to stand at the wide window, smiling at the mountains faintly visible through what the Nashville chamber of commerce elected to describe as haze. "The club agents, the deejays, the fans, even the Hellbellies— they all need to be reminded that despite his newly acquired reputation as a total fuck-up, Matt's nothing but a simple country boy with treasured memories of his hometown. Tie in this Christmas thing—'tis the season, deck the halls, away in a manger. Help me here, Ripley. We need some kind of publicity about where he grew up . . . and we need it before the tour starts falling apart. Let the media see him surrounded by his kinfolk, decorating the Christmas tree, singing carols in the high school gym, and reminiscing about his beloved granny. Get him on the line and ask him where he grew up."

"I should think at the moment the poor boy's sleeping

off what must be a ferocious hangover. In interviews, he talks about Little Rock.''

''Little Rock's too big for a hometown. Come up with someplacè quaint and honest, with hard-working folks and a café where everybody has coffee on Saturday morning.''

''There's something in the file . . . I seem to think he spent at least part of his childhood in some little cesspool in the Arkansas Ozarks. Let me check his bio.'' Ripley left the room, then returned with a folder containing a few grains of truth and a lot of whimsy. ''I was right, of course. On his AFM application, he says he was born in a place called Maggody. There's a next-of-kin listed, too.''

Pierce rubbed his hands together. ''Perfect! Matt Montana's going home for the holidays.''

Chapter Two

"Matt Montana was born in Maggody?" I said. This dutiful display of incredulousness in no way delayed a forkful of mashed potatoes destined for my gullet via my gaping mouth. "I don't think I've ever heard that."

"There's a lot of stuff you ain't heard," Ruby Bee said from behind the bar, glaring as if I'd criticized the meat loaf or voiced doubts about the greasy perfection of the collard greens. I preferred to live another day.

Perched on her favorite stool at the end of the bar (elbow room and proximity to the ladies room given equal consideration), Estelle rolled her eyes beneath artfully drawn eyebrows and in a smarmy voice said, "And here I thought we were blessed by the company of Miss World Almanac."

They weren't blessed by much other company. The room was empty except for the three of us, two unemployed poultry processors drinking beer at a table, and an insensible truck driver in the last booth. For the first time in weeks, the jukebox was not blaring "You're a Detour on the Highway to Heaven," or its flip side, the less popular but loyally played "I Bit My Lip and Held My Tongue When You Walked Out the Door." It was, therefore, the first time in weeks that I'd been able to eat without feeling as if I were being aesthetically assaulted. I'm an old rock-and-roll fan, myself—something I'd hidden well in a previous life in Manhattan. It doesn't play all that much better in a backwater where the primary decor in a lot of living rooms is a depiction of The King on black velvet. And I don't mean one buried in Westminster Abbey; this one's planted by a swimming pool in Memphis.

Estelle slid a glossy magazine down the bar in my direction. "But I got to admit it's peculiar," she said, twisting a red curl around her finger and nibbling on magenta lipstick. "According to this interview, he grew up in Little Rock, and there ain't one word about Maggody. He's not but twenty-five now, and I'd like to think I'd remember someone who went on to become as famous as Matt Montana. But Patty May Partridge out at the county old folks home said that the man who called was real insistent. She ought to know, since she was the one who had to talk to him on account of Adele having one of those days."

"I'm sorry to hear that," Ruby Bee murmured. "She back to listening to aliens on her hearing aid?"

"Just like it was the six o'clock news. Anyway, Patty May said the man was going to call Adele again before too long when maybe she'd be in a more responsive state. Patty May went back to the sitting room to find out what on earth he meant, but Adele kept right on clicking her dentures and peering real grimly out the window."

Ruby Bee snatched up the magazine before I could look at it, although I may have been more interested in my stomach than in outlunging her to get my hands on the latest issue of *Country Cavalcade*. "Look at this, Estelle," she said as she jabbed at a photograph. "This is Matt when he was seven years old. Cute little fellow, with those jug ears and curly eyelashes."

"And we might assume," I said idly, "that Montana is a stage name."

Ruby Bee blinked at me. "Like an alias?"

"Don't be a ninny," Estelle said with a snort. "Lots of famous actors change their names when they go to Hollywood. Some do it because they have sissified names and others because they have peculiar foreign names with sixteen consonants and no vowels. Writers do it, too, although they're so goofy nobody cares what they do. Matt must have changed his name, but it's kind of hard to understand why he'd pick another state."

"Albert Arkansas doesn't exactly roll off the tongue like Tennessee Ernie Ford," countered Ruby Bee, no doubt insulted at the idea she wasn't fully aware of the shenani-

gans pulled by famous movie stars and impoverished writers. She tossed aside the magazine and began to wipe the
immaculate surface of the bar with a dishrag.

Eating steadily, I used my free hand to open the magazine to the page of photographs of the singer who purportedly was Maggody's most renowned hometown boy.
"I'll tell you who he looks like in a vague way," I said,
then paused to pursue a slippery green bean. Successfully,
I might add. "He looks like Adele's nephew or whatever
he was. He came to visit for a few years. The last time I
saw him was the summer after I graduated from high
school. He and some nasty little savage from the trailer park
were spying on us out by Boone Creek."

"And what were you doing out there, missy?" said
Ruby Bee.

I finished off the meat loaf and pushed my plate toward
her. "Counting lightning bugs for biology class."

"Thought you said the summer *after* you graduated?"

"Must have been a graduate project," I said coolly.
"They were snickering behind some bushes and we—"

"*We*?" said Ruby Bee.

"Yes, *we* chased them down to explain how polite
young men should behave."

"How about young women? Don't think you're fooling
me with this—"

"You didn't make much of a lasting impression on
them," Estelle said, rescuing us from what might have escalated into a full-fledged maternal diatribe concerning an
incident of no postcoital consequence. "I read in another
magazine that just last week Matt was arrested at a bar in
Nashville. He got into a fight over Katie Hawk, that mysterious black-haired singer who's supposed to be part
Indian."

"Wonder what his wife had to say about that," Ruby
Bee said under her breath as she took my plate into the
kitchen. Pots and pans clattered as she made known her
disapproval of biology projects, infidelity, and barroom
brawling, but when she rejoined us, she was back to business. In this case, business meant shaking the grapevine to
find out if Matt Montana was really Adele Wockermann's

nephew or whatever and what Adele was going to do if those Nashville folks called her again. And, when she had some spare time, searching through the boxes out in the storage room for my high school yearbooks.

I left them to their plotting and walked back to the PD to sift through flyers begging me to protect my loved ones with a wise investment in life insurance. The only loved one I had was Ruby Bee, and nothing could protect her from her sharp-eyed, sharper-tongued, meddlesome self. Picture the two of us in a boat out in the middle of a pond. A sudden breeze blows off her scarf. I get out of the boat and walk across the surface of the water to retrieve it for her. If you think she'd be impressed, think again. "What's the matter, Miss Tippy Toes?" she'd say tartly. "Forget how to swim?"

Hell, I'd probably apologize. A couple of years in Maggody and I'd regressed into childhood. The symptoms were hard to overlook. After a brief romantic fling with a state cop, I'd shrugged him off and subsequently dedicated my life to reading Sears catalogs and watching grainy black-and-white movies in which the heroine dies in her paramour's arms in time for a message from Bad Bubba at the discount furniture farm. I was bored, petulant, and, somewhere not too far in the back of my mind, usually wondering what my mother would fix me for supper.

Whose fault? I'd blamed it on my ex-husband for a while, righteously telling myself I was so scarred from his betrayal that I was incapable of anything more complex than a do-nothing job in a town where there was nothing to do. I was merely being realistic about my temporary emotional debilities. When the time was right, when I was no longer a bruised orchid but something more like an invincible kudzu vine, that's when I'd venture out into the real world. Bear in mind, when all you do all day is mark the minutes until your next meal, you can come up with some impressively eloquent metaphors for sloth.

Berating myself had become so boring that I dozed off. When the dispatcher from the sheriff's office called to invite me to a "real humdinger" of a truck wreck near Emmet, I heard myself come too damn close to bubbling over with gratitude. I hung the CLOSED sign on the door of the PD and left to go scrape bodies off the pavement. With any luck, I'd be busy trying to match arms and legs until suppertime.

★

Mrs. Jim Bob parked in front of the county old folks home. As the mayor's wife, it was only proper that she be the one who determined what all this call from Nashville was about, and why in heaven's name some man had insisted on talking about Matt Montana to doddery old Adele Wockermann.

The gloomy foyer smelled of a disinfectant pungent enough to make her eyes water. Pinching her lips, she listened to the faint squawk of a television set behind one of the closed doors and voices that drifted down the passageway beyond an uninhabited desk. She hadn't been in the building since Cousin Vinnie Buchanon had been placed there temporarily while his daughter dealt with his mail-order bride from the Philippines. He'd been in the wing to her left. The ladies resided in the one to her right. The common rooms were clumped in the middle, and somewhere there was a nursing ward. The memory of it made her uneasy. Good Christians knew it was their duty to visit the sick and dying, but she figured that Brother Verber's seminary training had better prepared him to offer a dose of bedside solace.

After a terse mental lecture about the gravity of her visit, she went by the desk and tracked down the voices to a pair of aides in a staff lounge. Both wore drab green smocks and white stockings. One of them, a chubby young woman with tortoiseshell glasses and a ponytail, had taken off her shoe to massage her foot. The other, made up like a tart, was filing her nails and nattering.

"Is one of you Patty May?" asked Mrs. Jim Bob.

"Oops, a room buzzer," said the tart. She didn't exactly run out of the room, but she didn't dawdle either.

The remaining one squinted nervously from behind thick lenses. "I'm Patty May," she admitted.

Mrs. Jim Bob decided there wasn't any reason to beat

around the bush, especially when it looked like it was missing a few leaves. "I'm going to visit with Adele Wockermann, but first I'd like to hear exactly what that Nashville man said."

"Are you a relative?"

"I am the wife of the mayor of Maggody. I suggest you stop asking questions and worry about answering them."

"I got to fix the medicine cups. Maybe you ought to talk to Miz Twayblade. She's the day supervisor, and—"

"I don't believe I've seen you around town," Mrs. Jim Bob said, "and I'm sure I've never once seen you attending services at the Voice of the Almighty Lord Assembly Hall. You are a good Christian, aren't you?"

Patty May gaped as she tried to figure out if she'd just been accused of being a heathen. She decided she had and, in a huffy voice, said, "Of course I am, ma'am. I've been a member of the Mount Zion Baptist Church in Hasty since the day I was born. I'm in the choir and—"

"Very commendable, I'm sure. Now stop flapping your lips like you're eating soup and tell me about this telephone call from Nashville, Tennessee."

Patty May obliged.

Once she was armed with the scanty details, Mrs. Jim Bob sent the girl about her business and went down the hall. She was beginning to wonder if she was supposed to go out the door marked EMERGENCY EXIT and look for some sort of annex when she saw her quarry's name on a hand-printed card. She opened the door of the room that Adele Wockermann seemingly shared with a hairless cocoon under a thin gray blanket. "Afternoon, Adele. How are you today?"

Adele was seated on the edge of her bed, dressed in a thin cotton robe and shapeless slippers. She was deflated with age, her fingers swollen as they plucked at a snarly mess of yarn, her back bent, her skin as translucent as tissue paper. It was a shock to Mrs. Jim Bob, who could remember when Adele had been tall and strong, her head so high she always looked down her nose at you, often brusque, never one to hunt for a tactful word or spare a smile.

Adele shot her a spiteful look. "I'm fine and dandy,

excepting that Miz Twayblade went and canceled the finals of the volleyball tournament." Cackling, she pointed at her roommate. "Iva and me were the favorites for the gold medal."

"Have you been taking your medication, Adele?" Mrs. Jim Bob retorted, unamused.

"I hide them horse pills under my pillow, and then slip 'em to Iva. The last thing I need in my dying days is a roommate who blathers like a goat. Got no time for visitors who do the same. State your business, Barbara Ann Buchanon Buchanon, and then be on your way."

At least she was lucid, Mrs. Jim Bob thought as she twisted her gloves. The only chair in the room was piled high with soiled towels; she wasn't about to touch them, much less move them. Iva most likely wouldn't have minded if she sat on the bed—or even on her head—but it didn't seem polite. She stayed where she was. "I happened to hear that a man from Nashville called to speak to you yesterday, but you—"

"Never been there. Mr. Wockermann and I went on the train to New Orleans for our honeymoon. I didn't know what to make of all those dark-skinned faces and wild music and dancing in the streets. Still don't, come to think of it."

"Matt Montana is the name of a person, a real popular country music singer. Just last month he won a prize for writing the best original song of the year. Why would this man from Nashville say he was born here and you'd know about it?"

"The man from Nashville was born here? Seems to me he'd be the man from Maggody." Adele put aside the yarn and lifted her hand to the hearing aid in her left ear. "It's time for you to go, Barbara Ann Buchanon Buchanon. There's trouble brewing in places you'll never see, and I aim to tune in for the latest bulletin."

Mrs. Jim Bob sprang forward and caught Adele's wrist. Abject supplication wasn't among her most predominant talents, but she did her best. "Please give me one more minute, Adele. One more teeny, tiny minute. Maggody's in a bad way. If this Matt Montana fellow is a hometown boy, he can save us.''

''Never heard of him.''

''That's his professional name. You would have known him as Matt something else or maybe Matthew. Could he have been one of Mr. Wockermann's kinfolk?''

Adele stopped struggling and gave Mrs. Jim Bob a sly smile. ''If I was to recall, what's in it for me?''

''What do you want?''

Adele wanted a number of things. Telling herself this was no time to worry about what Adele planned to do with swim fins and an electric can opener, Mrs. Jim Bob dutifully made a list, tucked it in her purse, and promised to return the next morning, Adele having made it clear she was tuning out until she had her spoils.

Patty May hovered on the porch, swinging her arms to keep herself warm. ''Did she tell you anything?'' she demanded eagerly. ''I'd about die if it turns out Matt Montana's Miz Wockermann's kin.''

''No, but I'll be by in the morning to see if she's remembered anything. Listen real carefully, Patty May. If that Nashville man calls again, I want you to give him my name and my telephone number. Tell him I'm acting as Adele's agent in all matters concerning Matt Montana. Furthermore, I don't want Adele disturbed by anyone else—especially Ruby Bee Hanks and Estelle Oppers. They're nothing but a pair of magpies who'll yammer away until they exhaust the dear old thing.'' She thought for a minute, then waggled her finger at the aide. ''This needs to be our secret. If you do what I say, I'll make sure you'll be the very first person in all of Maggody to meet Matt Montana and get his autograph. Can I count on you?''

Patty May nodded, but after Mrs. Jim Bob was gone, she went to find Tansy to see what she thought.

★

Lillian Figg paused in the doorway of the bedroom, debating the merits of adopting a celibate life-style. She was a solid woman, broad-shouldered, taller than most of the men with whom she did business, and able to both shout them down and drink them under the table when negotiations demanded it. Her income as an agent and manager depended on her image, and at forty-two, it was taking more and more time each morning to fine-tune it. She did so religiously and effectively.

Matt was spread across the bed, his face submersed in a pillow, his hands dangling on either side. He was still dressed and his boots were in the corner where she'd set them; as far as she could tell, he hadn't moved in the last six hours. Although it would probably take something along the lines of a sonic boom to disturb him, she moved quietly to the bathroom, which smelled worse than the drunk tank from which she'd fetched him those same six hours ago.

She went back through the bedroom to the kitchen, gathered up cleaning supplies, and returned to the bathroom. Struggling not to gag as the stench enveloped her, she mopped up the splattered mess, wiped ceramic surfaces, and finally flushed away the evidence of the night's debacle.

"You driving a bulldozer in there?" Matt said groggily.

"Welcome back to the land of the living—or the land in which some of us, present company included, have to earn a living."

"Will ya fix me some coffee, Lillian? God, I feel like I ate a pillow and what feathers aren't stuck down in my throat are rammed up my ass."

Lillian considered offering to make it a reality, but instead went into the kitchen and started the coffee maker. Pipes gurgled in the wall as Matt turned on the shower, and by the time he reappeared, barefoot but dressed in a bathrobe, she'd rescued what she could from a loaf of moldy bread and made toast.

"You got any aspirin?" he said as he took a gulp of coffee, shuddered, and put down the cup with a shaky hand. Blood oozed from a nick on his jaw, and a dollop of shaving cream clung to one earlobe like a lopsided pearl earring.

She regarded him without enthusiasm. This was not the Matt Montana who sent girls into frenzied giggles and warmed the jaded hearts of credit card–wielding housewives. That one had a freckled face, a wide mouth with generous lips that lapsed easily into an endearing aw-shucks grin, slightly crooked but very white teeth, and wide-set eyes ringed with long lashes. Floppy auburn hair with golden highlights. A crinkly squint. A voice that was boyish, rough enough to sound sincere, and lilting enough to wrench a few tears from his audience.

At the moment, Lillian figured he looked more like what she'd mopped up in the bathroom. "I assume you haven't forgotten about this evening," she said as she lit a cigarette.

"This evening?" He spat out a mouthful of coffee. "Oh, shit, it's that party at the Opryland Hotel, isn't it? Get me out of it, Lillian."

He gave her such a piteous look that she went over to him and let him lean his head between her breasts. Gently brushing his hair off his forehead, she smiled down at her husband.

And hated herself once again.

★

"You'd better mind your manners, Patty May Partridge," Ruby Bee snapped, then banged down the receiver of the pay telephone and stalked behind the bar, fuming so fiercely that steam should have been curling out of her nostrils while she pawed the dirt. "That young woman has no business telling me that I can't speak to Adele on account of how I might upset her. I'd like to think I'm not the sort to go around upsetting old ladies. I've half a mind to call her boss and report this impertinence!"

Estelle waited until it seemed safe to speak. "When I saw Millicent at the gas pump, she mentioned that she'd been out to visit her uncle at the old folks home earlier this afternoon. Guess whose car she noticed?"

"How should I know? Millicent wouldn't notice she was hungry till after she starved to death."

"Well, she noticed Mrs. Jim Bob's car parked right in front of the steps. She's liable to be behind this."

"Mrs. Jim Bob'd like to think she hung the moon," Ruby Bee said with a snort. "Just because she's the mayor's wife and the president of the Missionary Society doesn't give her any right to—''

''If Patty May won't cooperate, we'll just have to come up with something else. I suppose we could go to the county courthouse and look up all the birth certificates for that year.'' Estelle leaned forward to add in a whisper, ''In fact, according to the interview, Matt was born on Valentine's Day. How many baby boys could have been born on that day?''

''Why are you whispering?'' Ruby Bee asked curiously.

Estelle glanced pointedly at the trucker in the last booth. ''He could be a spy. How'd you like to arrive at the courthouse and find out Mrs. Jim Bob had gotten there first and warned 'em you were coming?''

''That ain't James Bond. That's Gilly Jacana and he passed out more than an hour ago.''

''Unless he's playing possum.''

''Gilly Jacana ain't got the wits to play mumblety-peg. I could go over there and holler in his ear, and he wouldn't catch one word of what I said. If you don't believe me, then you just watch—''

''Okay, okay,'' Estelle conceded in her regular voice, ''but it can't hurt to be careful. ''I don't have any appointments tomorrow, and I was thinking about going into Farberville anyway to pick up a few things at the K-Mart. We could shop early, be at the courthouse the minute it opens, and be back in time for you to get ready for lunch.''

Ruby Bee took her time considering the plan. Since it wasn't her own, she figured there had to be some holes in it somewhere. ''What if the clerks in the office won't let us look through the birth certificates?''

''Why wouldn't they? They're public records.''

''Maybe so, but bureaucrats can be slick as lizards when it comes to finding ways to protect their precious records. We could waste all morning arguing with them and still not get one peek at the record book. Anyways, I was thinking about coming in early to clean the pantry shelves. It sure does get dusty in there.''

''Suit yourself, Penelope Pine Sol.'' Estelle slid off the

stool and strode across the dance floor, her heels making more noise than spilt marbles.

Ruby Bee held back a smug grin and said, "What if his first name is made up, too? What if his ma named him Fred and he changed it when he went to Nashville? You aiming to write down the name of every single baby born that day?"

Estelle kept going. "I might."

"There could be a hundred names."

"There could be a million names."

"He probably wasn't even born on Valentine's Day," Ruby Bee called as the door swung open to admit a stripe of sunlight. "How do you know he didn't make that up on account of how romantic it sounds?"

"I don't," Estelle said by way of farewell.

Ruby Bee thought of a lot of other things she should have said, but decided there wasn't any point in wasting any brilliant comebacks on Gilly Jacana. She settled for a righteous "Humph!" before she went into the kitchen and threw open the door of the pantry.

As she knew darn well, the interior was spotless.

★

"Mr. Ripley!" the secretary called as she chased him down the hall and finally caught up with him as he pushed the elevator button. "I've been trying to find you all day. Can you stop by the legal department before you leave? Geoffry wants to talk to you about some company down in Chattanooga that's using Matt's picture on billboards for a radio station."

"Had I but known," Ripley said in a stricken voice, grasping Amy's shoulders and staring at her as if she'd announced a death in the family. "I was in Chattanooga all morning, although I traveled both ways by car rather than choo-choo. I went to see a man about a divorce."

"You're not married, Mr. Ripley."

He released her and leaned his head against the elevator door. "Alas, I am not. You've withstood my amorous advances, which is why I live at the PO."

Amy didn't bother to ask what that meant, because for

one thing he lived in a real nice house up in the hills, and for another, he was always saying crazy things. It was hard to tell if he was making fun of her or just entertaining himself, but she had more important things to worry about. "Geoffry says he has to talk to you before you leave so he can file a suit in the morning. And Mr. Pierce says to be at the hotel by four to make sure everything's ready."

"Ready? Oh, my yes, everything will be ready." Ripley straightened up just as the elevator doors slid open. He stepped forward without another word.

"What about Geoffry?" asked Amy. He bared his teeth as the doors closed. She watched the lights above the door flash as the elevator descended, then went back to her desk just as Geoffry barreled into the office.

"Did you ever find Ripley?" he asked.

"He spent the morning in Chattanooga discussing a divorce," she said, taking out her compact to see if the encounter with Ripley had had any deleterious effects on her complexion.

"He's not married."

"That's why he lives at the post office." Amy replaced her compact in her purse. "He may be headed there now. Dial the zip code and see what happens."

Geoffry had liked her better when she'd been in the typing pool.

Chapter Three

Katie Hawk looked up with the wariness of a child being offered a tantalizingly shiny piece of candy from a stranger. The analogy was apt. She was not yet twenty-one, petite and solemn-eyed, her black hair long and straight, her face gaunt. She had allowed Pierce to coax her down one of the shadowy corridors of the Opryland Hotel, and he was everything her mama back in West Virginia had warned her about—right down to his gold fillings. "Yeah?" she said skeptically. "I'll cut an album next fall?"

"As soon as you get back from this little trip, we'll start looking for material. You can even do some of those syrupy ballads you're so fond of."

"You've talked out of both sides of your mouth before. How do I know you're not just making all these promises just to save your investment in Matt's new album?"

"Katie," Pierce said in a stricken voice, his eyebrows plunging together, "your contract with Country Connections is a symbol of mutual trust. Trust and cooperation, of course. The only way we'll get Matt to agree to this hometown visit is if you go, too. You do this little favor for us, and I swear on my granny's grave that you can cut an album within a year. Then again, if we have to cancel the tour, it's gonna put a real hole in our corporate resources. You'll be lucky to cut a single."

"This is blackmail, ain't it?"

"I would never stoop to that, honey. This is simple bribery. Let's go back to the party and I'll make the announcement."

They started toward the ballroom, Katie asking about

the details of the trip and Pierce doing his best to describe an idyllic town in which the adults flossed daily and all the children went on to college.

"Lemme ask you something," he said as they hesitated at an unmarked intersection. "Matt's a good-looking guy, rumored to be quite the stallion. He bathes on a regular basis, and as far as I know, he isn't into drugs or beating up on women. Gawd knows he's got money to spend on a lady friend, and he might stay out of barroom brawls if you'd be a little friendlier. How come you don't . . . ?"

" 'Cause three months later he'd be sitting outside some new girl's front door, singing songs and swearing undyin' love because she won't let him between her sheets. Matt's not famous for his attention span, you know."

Pierce couldn't argue with that.

★

"If he's the one you're talking about, I reckon he was born here," Adele said uncertainly. "His mother was my sister's gal. Belinda started raising cain the day she came into the world and everybody knew she'd been to Memphis by the time she was thirteen. She turned up sprung during high school, so my sister sent her to me." She picked up the swim fins. "What size are these?"

"They're the only ones I could find. Bear in mind this is November, Adele, and stores don't carry much in the way of summer items."

"November already? No wonder Miz Twayblade canceled the volleyball tournament."

"I don't recall a niece staying with you," Mrs. Jim Bob said suspiciously. "An unmarried pregnant girl would have raised a few eyebrows right here in Maggody, too."

"Which is why Belinda wasn't allowed to set foot out of the house except to go down by the creek in the evenings. When her time came, she had a baby boy just as pretty as a new-laid egg."

"So he was born in your old house out on County 102?"

"Are you saying we should have made her go out in the barn? Belinda weren't no Virgin Mary."

Mrs. Jim Bob had no doubts about that. "So then what happened?"

"Belinda and the baby stayed with us for another three months or so, then she found a job in Starley City and we lost track of her for a long while. Six, maybe seven years later, she showed up at her parents' house with another bun in the warmer and a bad case of some fancy medical condition that took her and the unborn baby, too."

"I'm sure she regretted all that fornication when she found herself stoking Satan's furnace for all eternity. What about the baby's father?"

"Belinda told me he was killed in a car wreck, and his parents said she was nothing but a tramp and anyone on the football team could have been the baby's father. She had to admit there was some truth to that, and she couldn't rule out the basketball team, neither."

"What happened to the little boy?"

"My sister and her husband had no choice but to take him in and raise him. They took to shipping him to me for the summers, and I went along with it even after Mr. Wockermann passed away. But that boy was as wild as his mother'd been, and I finally told my sister I wasn't gonna put up with him no longer. I swear, if he wasn't trying to steal candy at the gas station or peek up girls' skirts at Sunday school, he was pawing through junk in the attic. Mr. Wockermann used to pick up all kinds of trunks and cartons of diaries and old letters at church rummage sales. When someone moved away, he was quick to see what old papers they'd discarded. I told him time and again that he was wasting money, but he always said that one day he wanted to write a book about all the folks who'd ever lived in Maggody. Why would anybody read a book about a bunch of simple country folk, most of 'em too stupid to spit downwind? Belinda's little boy must have been the last one to even open some of those filthy old trunks. I can't count the times I caught him hiding up there and had to tan his backside with a belt."

"Sometimes you have to beat the sinfulness out of children what come from bad seed. When's the last time you saw the boy?"

"I don't rightly recollect, Barbara Ann Buchanon Buchanon. I get confused sometimes, especially when . . ." Her hand moved toward her hearing aid.

"You promised!" Mrs. Jim Bob said a mite more shrilly than she'd intended.

Adele grudgingly lowered her hand. "It must have been a good ten years ago. After three days, I put him on the next bus home, and that was the end of him. Unless you count when he came two years, I guess."

"Matt Montana came to town two years ago?"

"I thought we were talking about little Moses Germander. He's what came and sat right there and visited for most of the afternoon. He was all growed up and filled out. He brought me some real pretty flowers and a box of candy. I had to give the candy to Iva on account of the pecans. Pecans have always given me gas. Everything gives her gas, so I figured it didn't matter either way."

"What did he want?"

"He didn't want nothing except to see how I was getting along. I'm old, you know. I've got my plot out by Mr. Wockermann and a paid-up burial policy that cost me three dollars a month for seventeen years."

Mrs. Jim Bob was not about to be distracted by Adele's approaching demise. She took a magazine from her purse and opened it to a photograph of a handsome young man in a rhinestone-studded suit. "Is this the boy?"

Adele frowned for a long time, sliding her tongue over her dentures and scratching her chin, letting the suspense build just to get even with her visitor. "Iva's better at faces than I am, but I don't think you should wake her. She's been asleep like that since last Thursday or Friday. She ain't dead, though. She grunts every time I poke her."

"Is this the boy who came in the summers?"

"This cain't be him. He wore ratty jeans and shirts with the sleeves chopped off. He was skinny as a rail, with red blistery pimples all over his face and back, and he wore his hair down to his shoulders like a girl. If Mr. Wockermann had been alive, he'd have dragged that boy down to the barber shop and held him in the chair while ol' Grubbins shaved his head."

"Is this who came two years ago to visit you?"

"I reckon it is."

Mrs. Jim Bob thought she heard a muffled noise from out in the hallway, but she didn't hear anything else and she finally dismissed it as a manifestation of Iva's problem. When she looked back at Adele, she realized that her hearing aid had been turned on and the only responses from then on would concern the high jinx taking place on the far side of the moon.

Not that she cared. She had the story just as she'd promised Mr. Ripley Keswick in Nashville, Tennessee, and she had time to call him back and relate every word of it before she got dressed for prayer meeting.

★

The "real humdinger" of a wreck had made for a lively day, but the next day was less exciting than one of Brother Verber's hell-and-damnation sermons. I ran a speed trap at the north end of town until I finished my book, and then followed the school bus to the county line, watching the children behind the dusty windows stick their little pink tongues at me. The older ones, and we're talking ten or eleven, preferred a more traditional hand gesture to express their contempt for the law. I figured we could discuss it in a year or so, when I caught them drinking beer, smoking pot, or drag racing out on the back roads. Maggody doesn't offer its youth much in the way of wholesome entertainment. Count the condoms and the whiskey bottles out by Boone Creek if you don't believe me.

It was close enough to dusk to call it a day, although not much of one. I drove back through town slowly, not sure if I wanted to go back to my one-room efficiency over Roy Stiver's antique store and drown my sorrows in chicken noodle soup, or suffer through the whiny songs on the jukebox in order to get a decent meal.

Chicken soup it would be, I decided as I pulled into the parking lot in front of the redbrick PD and went inside. My latest gift from the town council sat on the desk, blinking angrily at me. The town councilmen—there'll be a councilwoman right after the local ducks start quacking in

French—don't give me things in order to express their deep and abiding respect for my dedication to duty. They're just too damn cheap to pay a salary for a deputy.

The red eye was menacing, the blinking nearly hypnotic. I eased past it and went into the back room to put my radar gun away in the metal cabinet that also held my gun and a box with my last three bullets. If the Four Horsemen were to come thundering into town, I'd shoot Famine first and then start drawing straws.

The front door opened and someone shuffled into the room. The accompanying odor swept through the office like a tidal wave, swelling into corners and butting against the ceiling. If it had color, it would have been bilious green. I recognized it as the unlovely emanation of Raz Buchanon, the local moonshiner. Tourists find him quaint. I find him a royal pain in the ass.

"We're closed, Raz," I said as I glumly regarded his filthy overalls, stringy gray hair, bloated belly, food-encrusted whiskers, and the ominous bulge of his cheek. "No crimes allowed after five o'clock. And do your spitting outside, please."

I would have had equal luck communicating with a tree stump. "Now, Arly," he sniveled, "I got some right important bizness with you. Somebody dun went and broke the law, and you being the police, you're the one what ought to do something."

"Did Perkins steal another of your dogs?"

"If that sumbitch so much as looks cross-eyed at any of my dawgs, I'm gonna blow his goddamn head off." Raz sat down and began to scratch aimlessly. He comes from a particularly thorny branch of the Buchanon clan, one renowned for mindless retribution and infrequent displays of animal cunning. I doubted he'd ever been to a wedding or a funeral in which shotguns failed to outnumber guests. None of them differentiates among uncles, aunts, siblings, cousins, and parents. The consanguinity's too complex.

I sat down behind my desk and reminded myself to breathe through my mouth. "Okay, Raz, let's hear it."

"Well, the thing is, I was a-drivin' into town from over

by Hasty, and out of the blue, Marjorie gits a funny look on her face like there's a flea in her ear.''

"There probably was a flea in her ear, Raz," I said, not pointing out the obvious source of said flea.

"This ain't the time for jokes, Arly. Anyways, Marjorie's been acting odd lately, but this time she's acting so dadburned odd that I stop my truck, turn around, and go driving back to the low-water bridge, looking real careful like for whatever was puzzlin' her. Then I seen it, and I liked to run clean off the bridge.''

I have to admit I was getting interested. "And?"

"Some low-down sumbitch moved the sign.''

Here I'd been hoping to hear about aliens emerging from a silver saucer, or Mrs. Jim Bob and Brother Verber capering indiscreetly in a cornfield. "What sign?" I asked.

"The town limit sign." He creaked to his feet and stomped over to the front door to spit in the parking lot. To my regret, he stomped back and sat down. "That sign used to be right past Estelle's. Now any fool can see it's by the bridge. What are you gonna do about it?''

I stared at him. "Have you and Marjorie been lapping up too much moonshine?''

"I don't know nuthin' about any moonshine. Don't take to bein' accused, neither.''

"Jesus H, Raz, every last person in town knows you have a still on Cotter's Ridge. I've been trying to find it for three years. Cut the crap about not knowing 'nuthin' about any moonshine,' okay?''

"I don't know nuthin'," he muttered into his whiskers. "So what are you aimin' to do about the sign? Nobody kin just up and move a sign like that.''

"If the sign has been moved, what earthly difference does it make to you? You live out the opposite direction.''

"It just ain't right," he said, then again creaked to his feet and went to the door to spit. "You better have a look fer yourself," he said over his shoulder, scratched his butt, and ambled through the doorway. "And check your messages.''

I did, but they were all from Ruby Bee and centered on how displeased she was to have to speak to an answering machine. It was getting dark and I was getting hungry, but I was curious enough to take a flashlight out of a drawer, hang the CLOSED sign on the door, and drive toward County 102. The obvious explanation was that Raz was confused, I thought, more than a little confused myself. He was sly enough to hide his still from the long arm of the law, but he was a Buchanon, after all. I would have had no problem if he reported the sign was shot full of holes or embellished with an obscene word. Vandalizing property is a popular hobby for young and old. But to move a sign fifty feet?

Estelle's house was on the right, and farther down the road, the Wockermann house loomed on the left. It was dark and deserted, just as it'd been since the last tenants moved away. The house had been in disrepair then; surely by now it deserved to be condemned.

I continued past the chicken houses, one charred and the other merely ramshackle, and parked by the low-water bridge, which, for the uninformed, is a concrete swath that allows water to flow across it. After a hard rain, it can make for an exciting minute or two. The sign was where Raz had claimed it was. It was pockmarked and rusted to the edge of indecipherability, but after a couple of years in Maggody, most everything and everybody is.

I'd never paid attention to its location, however, and I felt pretty damn foolish standing in the dark and shining my flashlight at it. It finally occurred to me to direct the beam at the ground. The earth was fresh. Frowning, I walked along the road until I came to spot where I found a depression, the earth also freshly disturbed.

And to think I keep griping that nothing ever happens in Maggody. Tsk, tsk.

★

"No luck at the courthouse?" Ruby Bee asked solicitously. "You look as worn out as a cow's tail on a humid day. Let me get you a glass of sherry."

Estelle considered marching out the door, but reconsidered and perched on her stool. "I spent all morning looking through the birth certificates for the whole year, but all of 'em had home addresses that weren't in Maggody. There was one rural route that got me stirred up. Then the clerk got out a county map and we tracked it down to a road out by Hamilton.''

"All that work for nothing." Ruby Bee set down the glass of sherry and made sure the pretzel basket was filled. "I'm sorry I wasn't there to help you, but some of us had better things to do all day than to flip through dusty old books." She took a dishrag and began to wipe the bar, her expression perfectly innocent except for a bare trace of a smile. Just in case Estelle missed the message, she started humming Matt Montana's best-known song.

"I suppose I could call Patty May Partridge and ask her if she's heard anything new,'' Estelle said with a sigh.

"She got off work at noon today."

"Then maybe I'll call her tomorrow, although it probably ain't worth the effort."

Edging closer, Ruby Bee hummed louder and made sure she wiped in time with the music.

Estelle remained oblivious. "I saw a real pretty sweater at the K-Mart, and nearly bought it, but then I couldn't think what I'd wear it with, so I put it back. It was pink, with brown flowers and seed pearls."

Ruby Bee's eyes were bulging and her lips beginning to ache. She quit the humming and said, "Did I mention that Patty May got off work at noon?"

"I seem to recollect that you did." Estelle inspected a pretzel and stuck it in her mouth. After a moment of thoughtful mastication, she said, "These are a mite stale. You ought to throw 'em out tomorrow and open a fresh bag. I know they ain't the reason business is so bad, but you don't want to let your standards slip."

"Aren't you gonna ask why I happen to know the precise time that Patty May got off work?"

"I think I'll go home and heat up the lasagna I fixed last night." She slid off the stool and acted like she was leaving, although she wasn't about to until she heard whatever it was that was setting Ruby Bee to twitching like she had her finger in a light socket and her foot in a bucket of water. "Don't forget that we're going to that flea market on Saturday morning. On the way, we may just have to run by the K-Mart so I can take another look at that sweater.''

"Because she came here to tell me her big news,"
Ruby Bee blurted out in desperation. She snatched up a
piece of paper and flapped it. "I wrote down the details so
I wouldn't forget anything."

"How'd you find time to do that during your busy
day?"

"Do you want to know or not?"

It could have escalated into a fine Mexican standoff,
but Estelle swallowed her pride (for the moment, anyway)
and climbed back up on her stool.

★

"I don't know what's wrong with Kevvie," Dahlia
wailed, rocking back and forth so wildly that Eilene was
worried about the future of the swing, the porch, and even
the second story of the house. "I ask him what's wrong,
but he won't tell me. You're his ma. You got to make him
tell me what's wrong!"

Eilene looked down at the moist mountain of misery.
"All newlyweds have problems getting adjusted to married
life," she said as warmly as she could, considering she'd
said it—or other similar platitudes—for the best part of an
hour. On the other hand, Dahlia hadn't offered much in the
way of variations and it was beginning to wear thin.

"Tell her to turn it down out there," Earl called from
the living room, where he was leaning so close to the television screen that his nose hairs tingled with static electricity. "The ball game's in the last quarter. I can't hardly
hear the announcer over all that racket she's making."

"He's changed," Dahlia continued. "Yesterday there
was a woman doctor on Sally Jessy, talking about how to
save your marriage. I listened to every word she said. Last
night when Kevvie walked through the door, I was wearing
a naughty black nightie. I'd pinned my hair up on top of
my head, put on makeup, and splashed half a bottle of
cologne behind my ears. He went right by me to the bedroom like I was invisible."

Eilene fought back a grimace as she imagined the scene.

"He was tired, honey. Going to all those houses, lugging that heavy suitcase—it's wearing him out."

"Something's wrong with Kevvie," she recommenced to wailing, making so much noise that dogs across town were howling and most of the neighbors on Finger Lane had come out on their porches to listen.

★

"Are folks going to remember you?" Ripley asked as he studied his notes.

Matt grinned. "It was a good ten years ago and I was just a runty kid trying to keep himself amused. If the same hick's running the pool hall, he'll remember kicking me out on my ass for stealing field whiskey from his stash in the back room. Used to be an antique store across from that, and if it's still there, the old guy might tell the reporters about the time I tried to set fire to his cat. The preacher might remember how close I came to screwing his daughter in the basement of the church while the choir sang 'Come Unto the Bosom of Jesus' ten feet above us."

"What about your great-aunt?"

"She's the one what caught us in the basement."

Ripley sighed as he imagined the reporters' collective glee (and ensuing articles) if they were privy to Matt's attempts to amuse himself. The tour would collapse, as would the opportunity to sell Country Connections, Inc. Pierce and Lillian refused to even meet with Whitey Breed, but Ripley'd had several clandestine conversations and had gone so far as to offer rosy financial projections based on the success of Matt's new album.

Damn.

Chapter Four

Mrs. Jim Bob settled her gloves in her lap, smoothed her skirt over her knees, and said, "Now, Brother Verber, I know you think it's sinful for a woman to work outside the home. You quoted a passage from the Bible about how women are supposed to glean and reap in their husband's field. At the time, you said anything to the contrary was sinful and an abhorrence unto the Lord." She gave him a look of such unfathomable intensity that it sent a trickle of sweat down his back. "Do you still hold with that?"

"Has Jim Bob taken up farming?" he asked cagily.

"No, he hasn't taken up farming. Just how sinful is it for a woman to work outside the home?"

Brother Verber slithered to his knees and clasped his hands on the back of the pew. "Let us pray for help on this, Sister Barbara. Let us beseech the Lord to tell us if He's changed His mind in recent years. It ain't up to a lowly preacher like myself to speak on behalf of Our Father who art in heaven, hallowed be Thy name."

"I don't have time to sit here while you beg the Lord for an update on His opinion of feminist propaganda. Just this morning I had another call from Ripley Keswick. He wanted to know if the same folks still own the pool hall and the antique store from ten years ago and if you were the preacher back then."

"What'd you say?"

She struggled to keep a civil tongue. "That the pool hall changed hands last year, that Roy Stivers left last week for Florida, and that you came eight years ago. He seemed relieved, for some strange reason. Then he said for the benefit concert we're supposed to come up with someone to be benefited. What he wants is a little child in need of an organ transplant, but I couldn't think of a soul. Can you?''

"Can't think of anyone off the top of my head," he admitted. "We can hope for the best, but if no child starts ailing, we might have to settle for a family in dire straits. We've got a town full of them these days."

"Well, we're gonna have a town full of media folks and fans driving in from all across the country to have a look at the birthplace of Matt Montana. Thousands of people visit Graceland every year, and Elvis has been dead for years."

Brother Verber whistled under his breath. "Paying to tour the house, eating in restaurants . . ."

"And more than likely eager to see the church where baby Matt was baptized."

"Where would that be, Sister Barbara?"

She began to tug on her gloves. "Adele attended the Assembly Hall three times a week for seventy years before she had to go into the old folks home. I can't see her lugging a baby down the road to the Methodist church."

"But according to your story, Adele didn't want anyone to know that her niece had given birth to a bushcolt, so she wouldn't have announced it to everyone in town by having a public baptism, would she?"

"Mr. Keswick doesn't want any mention of Matt's illegitimacy. I told him I'd speak to Adele about remembering how the girl's husband was killed early on, maybe in a war. If she'd been married, then the baby wouldn't have been a bastard. Therefore, this is where he'd have been baptized, isn't it?"

"I suppose so," he said, bewildered by her logic but willing to go along with it if she was.

"And if there was a brass plaque in the vestibule that said as much, nobody'd dare argue. It's in everybody's best interest to give those tourists places to see so they feel like they're getting their money's worth. You know what those tourists are going to need? A map showing all the important places. I'll call the shop in Farberville and see what kind of deal they'll give me.''

''What shop might that be, Sister Barbara?'' Brother Verber asked meekly, embarrassed by a growing sense of his own ignorance in such matters as Matt's baptism and maps of Maggody and whatever else she had in mind.

''The shop that's doing the T-shirts, coffee mugs, place mats, coasters, and other high-class items. Didn't I already explain I've taken a lease on the hardware store and am aiming to open a souvenir shoppe? I've always known I have a keen head for business and was just waiting for the perfect moment to share my God-given talent with the less fortunate. You get to work on that plaque, Brother Verber, and consider some sort of table with an offering plate and a little sign requesting contributions to maintain the church. You can put it next to the postcard racks I ordered for you.''

''Twenty-five years ago Brother Hucklebee was baptizing folks in Boone Creek,'' he felt obliged to say. ''Up until four years ago, so was I. 'Member how everybody agreed to chip in on an indoors facility after the water moccasins chased the choir half a mile downstream? I still can see Eula Lemoy, her robe hitched up to her waist, skedaddling across the gravel bar. I laughed so hard I liked to split my britches.''

''Then what we'll have to do is find the place alongside the creek and put out some sort of historical marker. I'll just add it to the map.'' She took out a pad and wrote a note to herself to stock snakebite kits in the store. ''I've got to track down Merle Hardcock and finalize the lease agreement. You get busy on what we've discussed, and do try to think of some child in need of a new liver.''

Brother Verber sat for a few minutes, lost in thought not of a bilious child but of bushy-tailed tourists lined up outside the Voice of the Almighty Lord Assembly Hall. When he finally got to his feet, it wasn't to go find a church directory and see if any of the names jogged his memory. Instead, he went back to the rectory and started making calls to learn what was involved in being able to accept all major credit cards.

★

I was sitting at the desk, the remains of a cheeseburger and onion rings sprinkled in front of me. I'd been forced to seek sustenance from the Dairee Dee-Lishus because Ruby Bee had called earlier and announced she and Estelle were heading for a flea market outside Starley City and wouldn't be back until midafternoon. Why she'd bothered to call the likes of me was the only interesting element in the story, but I'd given up musing about it and reconciled myself to lunch as described above.

The case of the transient sign was the only thing on my agenda. I could go fingerprint the pole, but then I'd have to fingerprint the entire local population (we lacked "the usual suspects") and that sounded like a lot of trouble. I could keep it under surveillance all night from the derelict chicken house. That also sounded like a lot of trouble. No motives came to mind, and Raz Buchanon was the only person in an uproar over this particularly heinous crime. Everybody else was too concerned with rent and grocery money to volunteer for a stakeout.

No, I thought as I leaned back and propped my feet on the corner of the desk, the case would remain a mystery, and somewhere down the road, perhaps it would qualify as a local legend, replete with sinister overtones. Rather than dating every event as before-or-after Hiram's barn burned, we'd use before-or-after the city limits sign came to life one dark and stormy night and went for a stalk down County 102.

The door banged open, interrupting my pleasantly spooky reverie. I opened my eyes and confronted Dahlia O'Neill Buchanon's puckery scowl. Her cheeks were puffing like a bullfrog's and her hands were clinched into massive fists. Every ounce of her quivered with fury, which meant there was a lot of quivering in the room.

"I got to talk to you," she said in lieu of salutations.

"If the road signs have taken to hiking in front of your

house, it's not my jurisdiction. Call the highway department.''

This disconcerted her, as intended, and a few of the quivers subsided. "Road signs don't go hiking, Arly."

"Don't be too sure of it," I said as I gestured at the uncomfortable chair I keep to discourage visitors. I was mildly curious to see if it could withstand her bulk, and mildly disappointed when it did. Just mildly, mind you. I am not a mean-spirited person, and to prove it, I asked a seemingly innocuous, neighborly sort of question. "How's married life?"

"It's just plain awful! I keep asking myself if I went and made a terrible mistake when I married Kevvie. It ain't to say that I don't love him, because I do, but I don't know if I can stand it any longer." She buried her face in her hands and began to sob, her shoulders convulsing and her feet stamping so violently that I glanced at the plastered ceiling.

"Dahlia," I said loudly to compete with her ululations of despair, "I'm not a marriage counselor. I'm not the right person for you to talk to. Listen to me, please."

I carried on in that vein until she finally calmed down, took a tissue from a pocket in the cavernous floral tent dress, and blew her nose in a manner reminiscent of a car's backfiring.

"I know you ain't a marriage counselor," she said between hiccups. "You being a cop, I figure you're trained to investigate like those private eye fellows on television. They're mostly in the reruns these days, of course. You know who I mean?"

I didn't, but I wasn't about to contradict her and I sure as hell wasn't going to ask any more "innocuous" questions. "My expertise is geared more toward radar guns and paperwork."

"But you know how to investigate crimes, doncha? Every time somebody goes and gets murdered in Maggody, you're the one who solves the case. You snoop around and find little clues and question people just like that nice Perry Mason, except he asks his questions in the courtroom. At least that's where he did it until he had the accident and had to get hisself a wheelchair. I always felt real bad about that.''

''What are we talking about, Dahlia?''

''I want you to follow Kevin and find out what he's doing.''

''He's selling vacuum cleaners in Farberville. If you want to know the ins and outs of it, why don't you ask for a demonstration in your living room?''

''He already practiced on me so much that the carpet's worn through and I have nightmares about some of the attachments,'' she said in a voice that hinted of an impending eruption of some sort. ''He's up to no good, and I have to know. Our vows said through sickness and health, and richer and poorer, but I didn't swear to sleep alone every night. His mother says he's just tuckered out from carrying that case every day, but when he was a stockboy at Jim Bob's supermarket and stacking heavy cases, he wasn't ever too tired to make the bed springs squeal, and even when we were trapped all night in that outhouse, he—''

''Have you asked him what's wrong?'' I said hastily.

''I've asked him a hunnert times what's wrong, but he just shakes his head and goes to sleep in the recliner. Last week I got so plum fed up that I dragged him right into the bedroom, yanked off his clothes, and told him in no uncertain terms that I expected him to act like a husband. He wasn't up to it, if you get what I mean, and afterward, he cried himself to sleep out on the sofa. Now he won't even set foot in the bedroom except to get dressed in the morning. He rushes out the door without a bite of breakfast, and this morning, he forgot to take the sack lunch I fixed for him. I cried so hard I could barely choke it down.''

''I don't see what I can do, Dahlia. I'm not a private investigator. I'm the one and only cop in Maggody and I need to hang around town on the off chance someone takes it into his or her head to break the law. Isn't it likely that Eilene is right and Kevin's simply tired?''

''There can be only one reason why he's acting this way.'' She paused with an impressively gothic expression, then turned her palms upward and said, ''He's having an affair with another woman. It ain't necessarily his fault. He's not as glamorous as Matt Montana, but ever since his voice dropped and he grew a little hair on his chest, he's been irresistible to most every woman he meets. Some desperate, sex-starved slut from Farberville sunk her fangs in him and is draining him of his precious fluids."

Let's hit the pause button for a minute here. Kevin is one of the scrawniest, dopiest, most hopelessly inept people I've ever known. He may well be responsible for the introduction of the word *huh*? into the English language. He and Dahlia have managed to intrude into my investigations every now and then and, with their bumbling and stumbling, caused me numerous headaches and nearly brought on their own unnatural and untimely demises. I could imagine him in a lot of roles, but a mesmeric Casanova was not among them. Now hit play.

"An affair?" I said weakly.

"Which is why I want you to follow him and get me the name and address of the woman who's trying to steal my beloved and destroy our marriage. Then I'll march up to her door and tell her how the cow ate the cabbage, and if she doesn't swear to give him up, I'll knock her upside the head or shoot her through the heart or—"

"Wait a minute! You don't know for sure that he's seeing another woman, so let's not get all excited about exterminating her just yet." I glanced out the window in hopes I might see a white-coated attendant approaching the PD, an extra-large butterfly net over his shoulder for her, or even a medium one for me. Reminding myself that I was the one responsible for the basic parameters of the situation (I hadn't packed my bags and flagged down a Greyhound bus several years ago), I looked back at her smoldering eyes, ham-sized arms, and bloodless fists. A calm, soothing voice seemed called for. "Now, Dahlia, I am not going to tail Kevin on his appointed rounds. I realize that you're unhappy, and maybe you have a good reason for worrying. If your talk with Eilene wasn't helpful, why don't you find someone else who can give you advice?"

She rose as if she were a thundercloud appearing over

the ridge, and I could definitely feel the barometric pressure plummeting. "I reckon I can think of someone else who can give me advice. I'm gonna have a nice talk with the man at the pawn shop in Hasty, and let him give me advice about which gun to buy and how many bullets it takes to kill a man-eatin' harlot!"

I was still gaping as she swept out the door and continued down the road. Most of the time, folks in Maggody mind their own business (and their neighbors') in a mundane fashion, but at other times, everybody turns downright queer.

This appeared to be one of 'em.

Dahlia was without a car, and I decided to call Eilene and warn her not to loan hers to her homicidal daughter-in-law. I looked up the number and was reaching for the telephone when it rang. I reacted as if it'd hissed at me, but I finally took a deep breath, picked up the receiver, and admitted the caller had reached the Maggody PD.

"This is Patty May Partridge," whispered a voice.

"This is Arly Hanks," I whispered back.

"We got a terrible problem out here at the county old folks home," she continued in the same insubstantial voice, "and Miz Twayblade'll skin me alive if she finds out that I called you. She's awful worried about losing our license, but I think when you lose a resident, that's a lot worse."

"So who'd you lose?"

"Adele Wockermann. Every day after lunch, all the residents are supposed to take a nice little nap so Tansy and me can clear the tables and help the cook clean up the kitchen. Well, today the dishwasher was leaking all over the floor, so Miz Twayblade had to mop right alongside us until the plumber could get here and do something. Usually she sits out at the desk and keeps an eye on things, but what with the flood in the kitchen and all, there wasn't nobody to notice Miz Wockermann was gone until I went in at two to fetch her roommate's tray."

"What does her roommate say?"

After a pause, Patty May said, "She didn't say anything about it. Miz Twayblade sent Tansy and me to search outside. We went all the way to the edge of the woods without catching sight of anybody, and then we got in our cars and drove both ways down the road for miles.''

I rubbed my face and tried to calculate how far an octogenarian, or perhaps a nonagenarian, could get in a maximum of two hours. ''Stop whispering, okay? This is quite a bit more serious than a license, which Miz Twayblade will lose in an *ex officio* minute if anything's happened to Mrs. Wockermann. I'm going to notify the sheriff's department. What's she wearing?''

''I don't know,'' Patty May said, sniffling but speaking in a more normal fashion. ''She wadded up her robe and gown and pulled the blanket over 'em so no one would notice she'd left. Her dark brown coat isn't hanging on a hook inside the closet. Her spending money, just a couple of dollars, is gone from her drawer. I can't tell what else is missing—except for Miz Wockermann, of course.''

''Is there any vital medication she needs?''

''Not really. We give her vitamin supplements and calcium pills. Missing them shouldn't cause her any harm. Actually, she's one of our feistiest patients, all the time complaining and getting into arguments about which television show should be on in the lounge. Two times last week she started food fights in the dining room. Last spring she crept around in the middle of the night and switched all the dentures. You can't imagine what a time we had trying to match the sets to the mouths!''

''And I don't want to.'' I badgered Patty May until I had a decent description of the prodigal prankster, swore not to reveal my source to her supervisor, and then hung up on her and started calling area law enforcement agencies. In the middle of one call, it did occur to me that Ruby Bee and Estelle had also disappeared, and I'll admit I stuttered until I convinced myself it was just a coincidence.

Once everybody'd agreed to cruise for Adele Wockermann, I grabbed my purse and went out to my car. The sun was shining, but there was a bite to the wind and the forecast had mentioned a chance of rain. Even if Adele Wockermann was mentally competent, she could hardly fare well once the sun went down. First the county home, I decided, and then some cruising of my own.

★

"Katie," Matt whimpered through the locked door, "why won't you let me in? I'm so lovesick I'm gonna die out here in the hallway."

The door opened as far as the chain permitted. "You're making a fool of yourself. Go away."

"Katie, you know how much I love you. I gotta come in where at least I can see you."

"You've seen me before, and I haven't changed. I haven't changed my mind, either. I told you that I'm not going to mess with a married man. The way my pa carried on with every whore in the county liked to kill my mama, and I ain't gonna be the source of another woman's grief."

He sank down to the floor, and if he'd had a tail, it would have been wagging pathetically. "Lillian understands. She's seventeen years older than me."

"Then go home and cry in her lap." Katie tried to close the door, but Matt had managed to slip his boot into the crack in the midst of his eloquent entreaty.

"I've begged her to divorce me," he continued, bravely ignoring the pain in his toes, which in all reality was a sight sharper than the one in his heart, "but she wants to think about it a little longer. I don't want to hurt her, so I have to give her time to get used to the idea."

"I'm closing the door. If you don't aim to hobble through life without your toes, I suggest you move 'em."

He did, and the door banged shut. He would have stayed if the elevator doors hadn't opened and a woman with a bag of groceries hadn't stopped in her tracks and gasped his name. He rose, gave her a shot of the aw-shucks, autographed her grocery list, and went down the stairs to avoid fans in the elevator. The tinted windows of his car protected him from further adulation, and after a few minutes of gazing at Katie's window, he drove toward the Dazzle Club to see if the boys in his band might be in the mood for a couple of beers and a game or two of eight ball.

★

Lillian drove past the Dazzle Club and headed for her office. Matt wasn't likely to get into too much trouble at this time of day. He'd been inside Katie's apartment building for almost an hour, moping outside her door and making a fool of himself as he'd done the other times when she'd crept up the stairwell and watched him through the cracked window.

Unbeknownst to him, he was her fourth husband. She wasn't trying to set a record; the first three just hadn't worked out well. She'd been fond of them, but she'd known from the minute she saw Matt that she needed him in ways that frightened her. She was so tangled up in lust and tenderness and fierce protectiveness that his announcement that he wanted a divorce had left her shivering like a hound dog in a blizzard. But she hadn't let it show; she wanted him, not his pity. All she could do was keep searching for ways to hold on to him until his infatuation faded and he could see how foolish he'd been.

But now Charlie was back.

Chapter Five

When I returned to the PD, the red rat's eye was not blinking on the answering machine. I went ahead and called LaBelle, the day dispatcher at the sheriff's department, to make sure they hadn't forgotten to call with the information that they'd found Adele Wockermann and were offering her coffee and cookies in the lounge. They hadn't, so they weren't. LaBelle assured me that the sheriff himself, a sly ol' boy named Harve Dorfer who took pride in playing the stereotypic southern lawman right down to the splintery cigar butt between his teeth and a beer belly that shielded his feet from the sun, was out checking logging trails in his own four-wheel drive. Every deputy was doing the same. We may not venerate the elderly in the outlands, but we do try to keep track of them.

"You know," LaBelle continued, "I read just the other day about some senile old fool who wandered away from a nursing home over in Blytheville and was found three days later in the woods, stiff as a board. Animals had gnawed off most of his face but didn't touch his feet."

"Thank you for sharing that with me," I muttered, then called the police department in Farberville to see how long it'd take to get a dog. A minimum of two hours, I was told, which would be about the time it began to grow dark . . . and the temperature dropped.

I called the county home and asked for Mrs. Twayblade. "No, no one's spotted her," I said in response to her question (which answered mine), "and we'll have a dog to try to find a trail in a couple of hours. If you hear anything, call the sheriff's department and have them get hold of me immediately."

I was too anxious to waste time making further futile calls. I could think of nothing else to do but continue driving down the same back roads looking for a white-haired scarecrow in a dark coat, and I was halfway to the door when it flew open in my face.

"What's this I hear about Adele Wockermann?" shrieked Mrs. Jim Bob, her face screwed up as tightly as I'd ever seen it and her hair as mussed. Her hat hung over one ear. Her fingers were blotched with anger and rigidly splayed as if she intended to throttle yours truly. The over-all effect was that of a Queen Elizabeth impersonator on steroids.

"I don't know what you heard," I said truthfully, "but as much as I'd like to stay and find out, I've got more important things to do just now. Come back later and we'll chat, okay?"

"I'll say you've got more important things to do, Miss Chief of Police! The idea of that poor doddery thing wandering around in the woods! What if she was to trip over a log and break her hip? What kind of a chief of police would loiter in the office when someone is writhing in pain and being eaten by a bear?" She stopped short of shrieking "off with her head!" but it would have made a fitting finale.

"Not a very dedicated one," I said, bemused by this display of irrational yet sincere compassion. Mizzoner was notorious for rattling on about the depth and breadth of her Christian charity, but she'd never actually displayed any of it, as far as I could recall. "I'd love to hang around and discuss this flibbertigibbet of a police chief, but I need to go search for Adele Wockermann."

"Why haven't you organized a search party? Helicopters? Why don't we have helicopters flying over the woods? How many helicopters can it take to find one old woman?" Suddenly her hands stopped rotating and fell to her sides. She went past me and sank down on the chair, now downcast and demoralized. I wouldn't have characterized her behavior as manic-depressive, but she certainly wasn't squandering time on the transitions.

"I cannot believe it," she groaned. "I cannot believe this is happening just when I . . ."

I was becoming more and more suspicious with each of her utterances. "Just when you what, Mrs. Jim Bob? Do you know something about Mrs. Wockermann's disappearance?"

"Of course not! This is a dreadful thing, and if I had even the tiniest inkling where she might be, I'd be over fetching her instead of putting up with your impertinence. You owe your job to the town council, missy, and you'd best remember who's got the ear of the mayor of Maggody."

She was back to *lèse-majesté*, and I hadn't learned anything that might help me. "You'd better give it back," I said as I started for the door.

Once again it flew open in my face, this time propelled by Ruby Bee and Estelle. The former grabbed my arm and began to shake it. "Where's Adele? The minute we got back to town we heard how she dropped out of sight earlier in the afternoon and nobody's seen her since."

Estelle latched onto my other arm. "Adele's nigh onto eighty, and there ain't no way she'll survive out in the woods all night!"

I jerked free before each of them ended up with a detached appendage, took refuge behind my desk, and said, "We have the makings of a fine search party. Why don't the three of you draw straws to determine who gets to be the patrol leader and start combing the woods within a two-mile radius of the county home?"

It was such a preposterous suggestion that all three of them stopped gabbling at me and locked eyes (we're talking five here; as I've said in the past, one of Estelle's wanders). The unspoken communication flying back and forth was hard to miss, but harder to tap than a politician's telephone line.

"I would dearly appreciate knowing what the hell's going on here," I continued, and rather nicely, considering. "If you all are so damned worried about Adele Wockermann, you might try to help me find her. For starters, let's discuss this sudden interest in Adele's well-being. Why don't you go first, Mrs. Jim Bob?''

She looked down as she considered her response, which probably meant it wouldn't be worth the expenditure of carbon dioxide. ''Adele is Matt Montana's great-aunt, and as you know, he's coming to Maggody in a few weeks. He'll be real disappointed if she's not here to welcome him home.''

''That's right,'' said Ruby Bee. ''He'd be heartbroken. You can tell from his photographs that he's sensitive.''

Estelle ran a finger under her eye. ''Imagine coming home for Christmas and finding out something terrible had happened to your beloved great-aunt . . . That'd sure take the twinkle off the tinsel.''

''In a flash,'' Ruby Bee contributed sadly.

I waited in case the other two wanted to offer another shovelload of manure. ''Then you all are motivated strictly by concern for Matt's emotional well-being? You don't have any self-serving motives?''

They were into denial. I listened to them bristle and sputter for a minute, then stomped out to my trusty police car and squealed out of the parking lot, all the while cussing up a storm and vowing to find a way to arrest the three of them so they could continue their mendacious little games under the supervision of a burly matron with an overabundance of body hair.

Halfway back to the county home, I realized I'd forgotten about the Wockermann house. It was a good five miles from the county home, and it didn't seem likely that Adele could have made it that far on her own. Then again, there wasn't much else to do until the dog and its handler arrived from Farberville.

I parked in the rutted driveway and unenthusiastically walked through knee-high weeds to the porch. The front door was locked, and there was no indication anyone had entered through a window. I went around the side of the house. The windows were too high to be entered by an elderly lady, no matter how feisty she was purported to be. In back, the cracked flagstones of the patio were ringed by yellow crabgrass and sow thistles. Beyond that was a screened-in porch, although the screens had pretty much disintegrated with rust and the door lay out in the yard.

I stepped over more broken glass and tried the back door. It opened with a shudder. It was just a big, vacant house, I told myself, and I was more likely to encounter roaches and rodents than characters from a Stephen King plot.

The kitchen was a holy mess, the floor thick with mud and garbage, the dinette set and appliances victims of brutality. The beer cans scattered about and piled in the sink let off a sourness that seemed to settle in my stomach. Everything was stale, dusty, in some stage of decay. No doubt Matt Montana would have bit his lip and held his tongue as he walked through the room. All I could do was grit my teeth.

The hallway led to a sitting room, where vandals had been equally successful in their impact on the interior decorating. I peeked in the other rooms on the first floor, then tested each step as I went to the second floor and regarded several closed doors.

The musty air was beginning to clog my sinuses, and the odd creaks to induce the stirrings of anxiety. I checked the bedrooms in rapid succession. The iron bed frames were broken. Mice had chewed the mattresses and left dribbles of stuffing on the floor. Cigarette burns marred the surfaces of dressers and bureaus, none of which had knobs. Initials had been carved in the drab wallpaper, and light bulbs methodically broken, the fragile glass mingled with the sturdier shards from mirrors.

The porcelain fixtures in the bathroom had fared no better. A single sodden towel was so mildewed that its color was indistinguishable—not, of course, that I meant to hang it in my bathroom if it fit the decor. Relieved at not encountering any embodiments of my worst nightmares, I was about to go downstairs when I noticed a narrow door at the far end of the hall. Self-congratulations on this display of acuity were out of the question, but so was sneaking away without making absolutely certain Adele was nowhere in the house.

I went up the narrow steps to the attic. The only light

came from long windows at the far ends of the three narrow
corridors made all the more claustrophobic by trunks,
stacks of boxes, and wardrobes with splintered panels. The
shadowy rafters looked like a dandy place for bats. I explored one of the corridors, peering as best I could over
and around the junk. The window offered a view of the
road and the field across the street. I retraced my path and
tried the center corridor, which led to an uninspired view
of the chicken houses and the ribbon of sludge called
Boone Creek. The last window was on the back side of the
house. The yard looked no better from my lofty perspective,
nor did the scrubby growth beyond it and the denser tangle
of stunted trees and masses of thorns. Late afternoon sun
glinted on the broken glass on the patio, reminding me that
I needed to stop worrying about rabid bat attacks and find
Adele Wockermann. She wasn't hiding behind any of the
trunks, and if she was hiding in one . . . well, I hoped she
was in a nice one.

A piece of white fabric on the floor caught my attention.
I picked it up and went down to the second floor, where
the light was better. It was a handkerchief, trimmed with
frayed lace and darned in several places. The initials A.W.
had been embroidered in blue thread on one corner.

I took it out to my car and sat down on the hood, staring
at the handkerchief as if it were a map of Adele's escape
route to her current hideout. It was not remarkable to find
an item initialed A.W. in the house. There well might be
towels, sheets, and pillowcases with similar markings in
one of the trunks. The "hers" of the towel sets would be
initialed A.W. The reason that I was so baffled by the handkerchief was that it was clean, crisply ironed, and smelled
faintly of lavender.

The radio in the car worked, although it crackled and
popped periodically. LaBelle acknowledged my request for
backup with a cheery "you betcha" rather than a trite combination of numbers, and ten minutes later, Les pulled into
the driveway.

It was dark outside when we closed the last trunk. As
he got into his car, Les gave me the strained smile of someone who did not suffer fools gladly, especially ones who

ruined his chances for a pitcher of beer before he had to go home for supper.

For the record, we found no towels or sheets monogrammed with A.W. Or the body of an old woman. I wiped my hands on a napkin from the floor of my car, put the handkerchief in the glove compartment, and began to compose a written report that would make a helluva dull screenplay. Coming soon to a theater near you: *The Handkerchief from Hell.*

★

Matt stood behind Lillian and kneaded her shoulders, then bent down and let his lips tickle her ear as he said, "After we get divorced, you'll still be my agent and manager and get to see me all the time, and we can still make love whenever you want. Hey, we can do it right now on the sofa if it'll help you change your mind. I got a few minutes till I go to the studio."

She pushed him away, wondering what on earth was wrong with herself. Something obscurely ingrained and riddled with ghastly Freudian complexities, she supposed, although her family had been as healthy as the Cleavers. "I'd take you up on your charming offer, Matt, but I need to make calls. No matter what happens, I will indeed remain your agent and manager for at least four more years because you signed a contract. Right now I take ten percent of the gross as your agent and twenty percent as your manager, leaving you seventy percent to pay court fines. If you file for divorce against my wishes, I'll come back like a starving polecat and end up with alimony equal to half your net income. Seventy divided by two doesn't leave you much, Matt, especially when Uncle Sam's relying on you to help reduce the deficit. Katie's under contract to my agency, too, and I can make sure she never does anything more than two-bit county fairs and mall openings until she hits bottom within a year or two. Hillbilly singers seem to biodegrade pretty quickly in this town. Are you and Katie going to live on love?"

Matt snatched up his guitar case and stormed out of Lillian's private office and into her secretary's room, where

he promptly stumbled over the outstretched legs of a shab-
bily dressed man with a beard.

"Hey," the man said, "aren't you . . . ?"

Matt got to his feet and jammed his hat back on his
head. "It don't matter who I am."

"You're Matt Montana," he continued, beaming. "My
name's Charlie, and we've got something in common, you
know."

"The only thing we got in common, Charlie, is that we
both fucked your sister."

Lillian's secretary gripped the armrests of her chair and
said, "Have yourself a nice day, Mr. Montana."

Matt did not reply, nor did he follow her suggestion.
By the time he reached the sleaziest redneck bar in the
county, he'd received one ticket for reckless driving and
avoided another one only because the police officer was an
unpublished songwriter and just happened to have a copy
of "Nightcrawler Woman" in his glove compartment.

★

Mrs. Twayblade tilted her head like a chicken within
pecking proximity of a worm, her sharp nose and piercing
eyes reinforcing the image, as did the clipboard clutched
under her arm like a wing. "Adele Wockermann did not
wander away in a daze. She made a cunning effort to keep
us from realizing she'd slipped away."

I sighed. "What if her friends on the far side of the
moon suggested the plan and told her to wait for them down
by the creek? The banks are slippery and the water's icy."

"Her ridiculous stories served her well. They gave her
an excuse to avoid civilized interaction with the other residents and cut short unwanted visits. Whenever her hearing
aid was supposedly tuned in to this extraterrestrial radio
station, she refused to join in a game of canasta or even
participate in the little crafts projects that Patty May arranged. Adele was the only resident who did not spend a
pleasant afternoon making turkeys out of pinecones and
construction paper for our Thanksgiving table decorations."

"Hard to believe she'd skip that," I said, "but we still have to find her."

Her pinfeathers bristled. "No, Chief Hanks, you still have to find her. I have to start filling out paperwork for the Department of Human Services. As far as I'm concerned, we have an unfilled bed."

A woman with wisps of yellow hair came to the doorway. "There's a cop car out front. They finally coming to take you away, Mrs. Twayblade?"

I went out to the porch. The officer opened the passenger door to let out a German shepherd of indeterminate rank, and they came up the steps.

"Thanks for coming," I said, squinting at her name tag. "Hope this isn't interrupting your dinner, Officer McNair. Yours and . . . ?"

"Larry's. No, he's always ready to go for a drive, and he knows we'll stop for a sundae on the way back if he does a good job."

McNair was brisk but not brusque. She asked a few questions, tugged Larry's leash, and we went down the corridor to the end room. Doors along the way popped open, and comments, some delighted and some apprehensive, wafted in our wake. I opened the closet door and gestured at the clothes. "These belong to Mrs. Wockermann."

McNair encouraged Larry to take the scent. The dog galloped out the door, his feet skidding and his toenails clicking on the vinyl floor. After a few circles, however, he sprawled on his haunches and looked expectantly at McNair, who looked at me and said, "He can't pick out the most recent trail."

"Let's try the exit," I said, holding open the metal door.

Larry seemed to think this was a splendid idea. Rumbling in his throat, he bounded into the parking lot, hesitated only a moment, and then took off like a canine backhoe. McNair and I smiled at each other as we followed along for fifteen feet. We frowned at each other as Larry tried a few different directions, stopped rumbling and wagging his tail, and sat down with an air of certainty that foreboded ill.

McNair shrugged. ''She must have gotten in a vehicle. Let's be thankful she didn't leave a trail that led us to the woods. She wouldn't have survived long.''

I thanked both of them, then went inside to find Mrs. Twayblade, who was attempting to put down a rebellion of sorts in the corridor. Once she persuaded all the women to close their doors, she led me to the lounge.

''Did that slobbering animal find anything?'' she demanded.

I suppose I should have defended Larry's maligned salivary glands, but I let it go. ''Mrs. Wockermann seems to have gone out the emergency exit and gotten into a car. Did you notice anyone parked out there between noon and two o'clock?''

''I was busy in the dining room, and once the meal was finished, I came out to the desk to do some paperwork. I can't see anything on that side of the house. Neither can any of the residents in that wing.''

''What about Patty May and the other aide?''

''Their shift ended at four. Since we now know that Adele did not stagger off to drown herself in a pond, I see no reason to continue this investigation tonight. You may speak to the girls tomorrow morning. Shall we say ten o'clock, Chief Hanks?''

I could think of a lot of other things to say, but I needed her cooperation and she did have a valid point. I said, ''Good night.''

Chapter Six

Mrs. Jim Bob came out to the porch of what had been the hardware store and inspected her husband's handiwork. "It's crooked. First it was tilted to the left, and now it's tilted to the right. I really don't have time to stand out here all afternoon while you play with the sign like it was a teeter-totter."

Jim Bob sat on the top of the ladder, slapping the hammer against the palm of his hand and doing his level best to keep his temper, even though he knew he looked like a damn turkey buzzard perched on a rickety roost. For one thing, it never did one bit of good to argue with her when she was hell-bent on some fool thing. For another, he had hopes that her venture would succeed so that he could hire an assistant manager at the SuperSaver and get in some serious deer hunting.

"Lookin' mighty fine, Sister Barbara!" boomed Brother Verber from the edge of the road. He wore a pale blue suit, a pink-and-blue plaid shirt with silver-rimmed snaps, and high-heeled boots that the salesman had assured him looked exactly like real leather. His cowboy hat was adorned with medallions on the band and a spray of small feathers. It was all he could do not to preen in his fine new clothes, but he reminded himself of his Christian commitment to humility. "Mighty fine, indeed! The tourists are gonna be thrilled at the chance to come browse in 'The Official Matt Montana Souvenir Shoppe.' Why, it's all I can do to bide my time until the grand opening!"

She nodded at Brother Verber, wondering why he was dressed up like the host of a cable cartoon show. "I trust

you'll be on hand to offer the benediction," she called.
"I'll take comfort in knowing the Good Lord has seen fit
to bless my little shoppe and to guide me through the pit-
falls of the retail business. I'll make sure to express my
gratitude in the offering plate."

"Praise the Lord!" replied Brother Verber, still boom-
ing away on this crisp and crackly November morning.
"Everybody in town should be following your upstanding
Christian example. Don't you agree, Brother Jim Bob?
Wouldn't the world be a kinder and gentler place if we all
followed Sister Barbara's example?"

Jim Bob suspected the world would be a damn sight
quieter place if he bounced the hammer off the preacher's
forehead, but he figured he was in enough hot water as it
was. "Listen, Mrs. Jim Bob, I can't tell from up here if the
sign's straight or not. Why doncha move out that way and
tell me when I got it right?"

"I'd have to move to Oklahoma before you got anything right," she muttered loudly enough for him to hear
as she went out to the gravel parking lot, crossed her
arms, and squinted up at the sign. "The right side needs
to go up . . . up, I said . . . no, that's too far. No, that's
too far the other way. I swear, I'd climb up on that ladder
and do it myself if I didn't have more important things to
do."

Jim Bob didn't point out that he had more important
things to do hisself, one of them involving an hour at Malva's trailer on account of her husband being out of town.
He was getting real fond of her rabbity little eyes, those
and other parts of her anatomy. In the aftermath of lustful
abandon, he'd promised to promote her to assistant manager, but of course he wouldn't because she was a woman.
This wasn't to say some woman didn't have a head for
figures. Mrs. Jim Bob could say down to the last cent what
the coffee mugs cost wholesale and how much sales tax to
tack onto the dish towels featuring a sanitized depiction of
the Wockermann homestead. She'd badgered the delivery
company into cutting her a cheaper rate and talked the
printer into doing the sing-along songbooks in record time.

She'd scheduled half the high school girls in town into part-time jobs to avoid workman's comp and payroll taxes.

And now she was bitching at him. He wiggled the sign up and down until she jabbed her finger and told him not to let it move so much as an inch while he nailed it firm.

"Did you hear about Adele?" Brother Verber asked her.

"Yes, but from what I heard yesterday evening, she just got in somebody's car and left. My best guess is that some distant cousin popped up out of the blue and took Adele home for a cozy little visit before Christmas. Since she's not dead, I don't see why Arly can't have her back in plenty of time."

Brother Verber was relieved to learn everything was under control. "Me neither," he said emphatically.

She went back up to the porch and looked up at Jim Bob, grimly thinking to herself that she'd never once looked up *to* him and couldn't imagine doing so in the foreseeable future. "Put the ladder away and come inside to start on the shelves. I need to poke Perkins's eldest into getting off her lazy rear to help me assemble and dress the mannequin that's going in the front window. Tourists will be standing in line to pay five dollars and have their photographs taken with—"

The door closed on whatever else she said. Jim Bob crawled down the ladder, tossed the hammer in his toolbox, and assessed his chances of just sort of fading away to his truck, where he had a nice bottle of bourbon under the seat and a heart-shaped box of candy in the glove compartment. His wife was safely out of sight, but for some fool reason Brother Verber was still standing by the road, twiddling his thumbs and grinning mindlessly at the facade of the souvenir shoppe. "How's it going?" Jim Bob said as he dropped the toolbox into the bed of the truck.

"Just fine, Brother Jim Bob. Sister Barbara has ordered the postcards and racks for the vestibule in exchange for a percentage of the profits, and she's working on a little booklet that explains the history of the church and has a letter from Brother Hucklebee telling all about the sunny

Sabbath morning when he baptized baby Matt Montana. Well, it would have been from Brother Hucklebee if he hadn't upped and died a few years back.'' He wiped away a tear as he gazed reverently at the perfectly aligned sign above the door of the shoppe. "We all owe Sister Barbara our undyin' gratitude for what she's done for Maggody."

"Okay with me," Jim Bob said as he eased into the front seat of the truck and closed the door as quietly as he could, his lips aching as he imagined Malva's kisses.

Brother Verber loomed in the window. "Our undyin' gratitude, like I said. I may just put that on a portable sign in front of the Assembly Hall. The week the tourists start coming, I thought I'd put up something along the lines of 'This Is It! Your First Stop on the Highway to Heaven.' Then I got to thinking about it and I wasn't so sure." He stuck his head into the truck, warming Jim Bob's face with exhalations of peppermint. "I don't want people to think they'll die because they visit the Assembly Hall and purchase mementos of the occasion. Whatta you think, Brother Jim Bob?"

"I think you should pray over it," Jim Bob replied piously, "and it's not a minute too soon to start. I'm sure the Good Lord has advertising executives on retainer. Maybe not sitting on that heavenly throne in the sky, but there's gotta be at least one somewhere this side of the fiery furnaces of hell."

Brother Verber indignantly withdrew his head. "That's edging toward blasphemy, and blasphemy's the first step down the path of wickedness." Despite his brand-new trousers, he fell to his knees in the dusty gravel and clasped his hands tightly. " 'Ye have heard the blasphemy: what think ye? And they all condemned him to be guilty of death.' Guilty of death! Is that what you want, Brother Jim Bob?"

Actually, Jim Bob wanted to drive away, so he did.

★

Things weren't so lighthearted at the old house out on County 102. Ruby Bee had cobwebs in her hair, black crescents under her fingernails, new blisters on top of old blisters, and a nagging pain in her lower back that even a hot soak in the tub wouldn't ease. "I don't see why," she said as she loaded a sack with beer cans from the sink, "Mrs. Jim Bob's unpacking souvenirs and dressing up the mannequin while you and I are out here in this dump like a couple of cleaning women."

Estelle finished sweeping glass into the dustpan and dumped it into a box already overflowing with trash. "Because we're on the executive committee, and somehow or other you ended up volunteering to see to the house. Mind you, I don't recall that I ever volunteered to lift one finger, so I guess that means someone else volunteered my services on a day when I planned to give myself a henna rinse and a manicure." She examined her fingernails. "Looks like I went after them with a chain saw, thanks to Miz Happy Homemaker."

"We're all in this together," Ruby Bee said, catching her breath as a small black critter scuttled down the drain. "You didn't seem reluctant to be on the Matt Montana Homecoming Committee, if I recollect. You were about as twittery as a pom-pom girl." She dropped the last beer can into the sack, carried it to the back porch, and then went through the house and out to the front porch to see how the work was coming along.

Nicely, she thought. There were new panes in the windows, and the shutters had been retrieved and repaired. Now the facade was white, the shutters forest green, and the ceiling of the porch as blue as the sky. A porch swing squeaked in the wind. Paint was dribbled on the porch and there were some bare streaks, but the high school boys recruited to do the work had done well enough. She could hear them talking as they painted around the corner.

More boys were on their way to the dump with the furniture, while others were hacking away at the weeds or dragging branches to the field for a bonfire. Their girlfriends were inside, washing windows, sweeping spiderwebs off the ceilings, wiping down walls, and waxing the pitted wooden floors. They were an industrious lot, considering they were making less than minimum wage, but Mrs. Jim Bob had laid it out plain and simple at a high school assembly. She'd started with a plea for civic pride, pointed out there would be money to be made from the influx of tourists, assured them that they would all have a chance to meet Matt in person *and* get his autograph *and* sit in the front row at the concert, and then ended with a few remarks about the possibility of a town meeting in which their parents would learn from the mayor hisself about the prevalence of drugs, liquor, and fornication—should no one sign up to work for the Homecoming Committee.

It had been a potent mixture, Ruby Bee thought as she looked across the road at the freshly painted sign in front of Estelle's house. She wasn't sure Matt Montana had hair fantasies, but she supposed he could. Estelle's new rates implied she was harboring some pretty wild ones of her own.

She shaded her eyes as Earl and Eilene Buchanon pulled into the driveway. In the back of Earl's truck was a mountain of furniture secured by crisscrossed ropes and black rubber snakes. Ruby Bee thought Eilene looked a mite peevish, so she wasn't real surprised when Eilene jumped out of the truck the minute it stopped and slammed the door hard enough to bust Earl's eardrums.

"Any word on Adele?" Eilene demanded as she came up to the porch without so much as looking back to see if Earl was in pain. "There was a hard freeze last night. I could hardly sleep worrying about her."

"She's fine. She went off to visit a cousin, but she'll be back in a matter of days. How'd you do at the junk store?"

"We got most of the big pieces. The old crow gave me twenty percent off because we bought so much, but I still went over the budget by forty dollars. We're shy end tables, floor lamps, family pictures for the hall, a couple of braided rugs, and a quilt. I made a list."

Ruby Bee shrugged. "I reckon we can borrow some oddments from Roy's antique store, and if worse comes to worse, we can use some of our own furniture. Let me check how the girls are doing inside. If they're done with the floors, the boys can help Earl unload the truck."

"He can do it by himself." Eilene sat down on the porch swing and sighed.

Ruby Bee felt obliged to sit down next to her and pat her knee. The last thing the Homecoming Committee needed was more discord. At the meeting the fussing and fighting had gone on past midnight, what with everybody voicing opinions about what they should do and what they could do and how in heaven's name to pay for it. Now they were operating under a very uneasy truce of sorts that divided the territory and certain profits. The fees for touring the Wockermann house, for instance, would go into the committee coffers, along with what they charged tourists to go down to Boone Creek. The parking lot next to the ruins of the branch bank was deemed community property, since it belonged to folks who lived elsewhere and wouldn't know the difference. Joyce Lambertino had wondered out loud if that wasn't cheating the bankers, but she'd been hushed up real fast by her husband. There'd been a good hour of squabbling about the skeletal remains of Purtle's Esso station out at the edge of town, with half the room saying it could be fixed up as Matt's favorite hangout and the other half arguing that it'd take a miracle to fix it up in two weeks. Joyce and Larry Joe were on opposite sides of the room on that one, too. Now it looked like Eilene and Earl were bumping heads over something, Ruby Bee thought as she glanced from Earl's snarly face to Eilene's teary one.

"You two have a spat?" she asked Eilene in a low voice so Earl wouldn't hear.

"You could call it that. While we were driving back from the store, I said we ought to consider setting up a campground in the field behind our house. Earl snickered and said it wasn't exactly convenient, as if I'd forgotten where we live. I said we could charge a lower fee and then haul the tourists over here. Earl started braying like a jackass. It was all I could do not to slap the smirk off his face."

"How would you haul them?" asked Ruby Bee, mindful of the cow pasture behind the Flamingo Motel. It didn't belong to her, but there was no way Obiwan Buchanon would find out as long as he stayed in Florida trying to earn money for the hormone therapy and operation.

Eilene perked up. "There was an old wagon at the flea market that could look right pretty with a coat of paint. We could hook it up to that little tractor Earl uses to mow the yard, and Kevin could be the driver. I was thinking we could call it the Maggody-Matt-Mobile."

"Eilene," gasped Ruby Bee, so overcome with awe that she sank back into the swing and fanned herself with her hand, "that is absolutely brilliant. I can see Kevin in a white jacket and cowboy hat just like what Matt wears, hauling those tourists down the road and maybe even leading them in songs as they roll along. You can charge a fortune for a ride in the Maggody-Matt-Mobile."

"And do something to help Kevin and Dahlia. I guess you've heard the nonsense Dahlia's been spouting all over town. I couldn't talk any sense into her, so I told Kevin to come over before church so he and I could have a private talk. He insisted he was just working his butt off selling those fancy vacuum cleaners and was exhausted by the time he dragged home. That's what he said, anyway. Being his mother, I know when he's avoiding the truth and I have to admit there may be something fishy going on."

Earl was still out by the truck untying the furniture, but Ruby Bee dropped her voice even lower and said, "You mean Kevin really is having an affair with another woman?"

"I don't know what to think, Ruby Bee. I do know that if Earl catches wind of this supposed affair, he'll march right into their living room with a hickory stick. Earl has his faults—it'd take me a month of Sundays to list 'em—but he won't tolerate that sort of thing."

Ruby Bee clucked sympathetically, but she couldn't say anything because Earl was struggling up the steps with a sofa balanced on his back. He didn't look like he was in the mood to debate the likelihood of infidelity.

★

I'd planned to be at the county home at ten o'clock sharp, but Harve had called and I'd related everything that

happened the previous evening. I didn't argue when he said
he was pulling his deputies off the case, since there didn't
seem to be much point in their tromping through the woods.
Before he hung up, we agreed that Larry was a real dumb
name for a dog.

When I got to the home, Mrs. Twayblade was seated at
the desk in the foyer, her watch set next to her clipboard.
Even upside down, I could read the time: half past late.

"I'd better have a look at Mrs. Wockermann's files
while I'm here," I began pleasantly.

"That's out of the question. The files are sacrosanct.
They contain confidential medical records, as well as financial information of a very delicate nature. We do have a
budget, so we monitor the Social Security and Medicaid
benefits. Some of our residents have savings accounts and
pensions, too, not to mention relatives who're obliged to
contribute to their upkeep."

"Relatives are what I'm after. If I knew the name of
Adele's next of kin, I might get a lead on her whereabouts.
Otherwise, after I talk to the aides, I'm going to have to
question all the residents. This is an official investigation.
If I have to, I'll get a warrant and come back with several
deputies. We may even need the dog again." I curled my
lips to expose my canine teeth.

"Are you threatening me, Chief Hanks?"

"Of course not. I'm trying to avoid any further disrup-
tion of the schedule."

We glared at each other. An old woman clutching an
aluminum walker thumped past the desk, talking to herself
in a querulous voice. Seconds later two white-haired men
passed by, talking to each other in querulous voices. A girl
in an institutional green smock intervened and led them
away. From within the lounge at the front of the building,
a game show contestant shrieked. Pans clattered in an unseen kitchen.

"Oh, all right," muttered Mrs. Twayblade. "You wait
here while I have a quick look at Adele's file." She went
into a room at the back of her office and slammed the
door.

Smells escaped from the kitchen somewhere in the back of the building. Although I couldn't identify them with any accuracy, there was nothing on the menu that appealed. Matt Montana's Hometown Bar & Grill was closed for the day while its proprietress toiled at the Wockermann house. Unless I settled for a burrito from the SuperSaver deli, this would be the second day in a row I would be forced to swing by the Dairee Dee-Lishus and choose between a Montana Burger (adorned with "Matt's Special Secret Sauce") or a Matt's Combo (a chilidog, fries, and a small drink). Both had prices comparable to a Manhattan bistro. Over at Matt's Billiard Parlor and Family Entertainment Center, they were charging two bucks for the long-necked bottles of beer, and the big jars of pickled eggs and red-hot sausages had been replaced with sterile packages of chips. At the rate things were going, Raz was going to be selling his moonshine in six-packs.

The smells grew stronger, cabbage competing with fish and scorched milk, and I became aware of the strains of "The Little Drummer Boy" being played from behind a closed door. I was contemplating how best to smuggle in arms to the residents when the girl in the smock came back. "You're Arly Hanks, right?" she asked, watching the hallway behind me. "I'm Tansy. Have you found Miz Wockermann?"

"Not yet, but I'm still looking. Did you see any unfamiliar cars parked out on the east side yesterday, say, late morning onward?"

She widened her eyes, but the effect was minimalized by the heavy caking of mascara and midnight blue eyeliner. "Was she kidnapped?"

"Right now I'm assuming she walked out the emergency exit at the end of the hall and got into a car. Did you see anything or anybody out there that was the slightest bit out of the ordinary?"

"I wish I had, but I didn't. Miz Twayblade thinks it's real important to get all the residents in a festive mood for the holidays so they won't be too lonesome for their families. Earlier in the week we taped up stuff out here and sprayed snowflake stencils on the windows, and yesterday we were in the lounge all morning, decorating the Christmas tree. Patty May had everybody gluing red-and-green paper chains and singing 'Jingle Bells' till we went to the dining room to set the tables.''

For the first time I noticed the halls had been decked. ''Was Mrs. Wockermann in a festive mood?''

''She did come to the lounge and stuff her pockets full of divinity, but I don't remember how long she stayed. I wasn't paying much attention to anybody in particular. The ladder's wobbly, and folks kept bumping into it while they griped at me about the lights and the tinsel. They were drifting in and out the way they do. Sorry.''

''I understand.''

Tansy was not ready for absolution. ''Golly, I feel really bad. Miz Wockermann's sharper than a lot of folks give her credit, but I can't stop worrying about her.'' She shook her head sadly, then looked up with a much brighter expression. ''Besides, if she really is Matt Montana's great-aunt, then it's likely that he'd come here to visit her again. I'll faint if I come around a corner and see him standing here. He's so incredibly good-looking.''

''Matt Montana was here?'' I asked, surprised. Ruby Bee and Estelle had pored over every bit of printed matter concerning Matt and related it to me in mind-drubbing detail, as in ''then when he was in eighth grade, he played the trombone and . . .'' This isn't to say that I'd made an effort to retain the information for one second longer than it took to flow in one ear and out the other, but I probably would have at least chewed briefly on this. ''He came to Maggody to visit Mrs. Wockermann?''

''Two years ago, according to what Miz Wockermann told Miz Jim Bob. Patty May and me happened to overhear the other day.''

''I need to talk to her, too. Where is she?''

''Gone,'' Tansy said nervously. ''Deirdre's coming in on a temporary basis until Miz Twayblade can find someone.''

''Gone where?'' I demanded, not sure if she meant

"gone to the store" or "gone to live with the angels." Or "gone off her rocker," which is what I was afraid I was about to do.

"Gone to work in Farberville. She called this morning and told Miz Twayblade that she was quitting and wouldn't be in anymore. She found a super job taking care of a crippled gentleman in one of those big old houses by the park. She's making almost twice as much as she did here. She said that last night she got a call from an agency over there wanting her to start right away. Miz Twayblade was mad about not getting proper notice, but—"

"I notice," Mrs. Twayblade said from behind me, "that it's time to set the tables for lunch, Tansy. Do you think you could do that instead of engaging in gossip?"

"Yes, ma'am." Tansy fled.

Mrs. Twayblade smiled thinly. "I studied Adele's file carefully. She has no living relatives. Her sister's name has been crossed out with a notation that she passed away several years ago, as did a niece. They were the last two. In the event of Adele's death, her house is to be sold and the proceeds turned over to her church. There's a small policy to handle the funeral expenses. Is there anything else, Chief Hanks?"

"I guess not, except for Patty May's address and telephone number."

Amid comments about ingratitude and irresponsibility, Mrs. Twayblade found the information in a folder, copied it on a slip of paper, and thrust it at me. "Now, if you'll excuse me, I have to see to lunch."

I went back to my car and sat for a few minutes, idly watching squirrels scampering around in a last-ditch effort to hoard enough acorns for the winter. Three cars were parked in the lot, and in that there seemed to be at least three employees (Twayblade, Tansy, and the unseen Deirdre, for those who've lost their scorecards), they did not merit consideration. A pickup truck at the back of the building was likely to belong to the cook. But someone must have waited near the emergency exit until Adele slipped outside and then driven her somewhere. Had she taken advantage of the plumbing crisis in the kitchen—or somehow

caused it? In the former case, she must have made a telephone call. In the latter, she'd arranged the assignation in
advance. But with whom?

I decided to break for lunch, then come back and snoop
around some more. Adele had left in the middle of the day,
and not via alien space shuttle. There were houses along
the road inhabited by the sort of people who stood behind
the curtains and watched for their neighbors to do something worthy of excommunication from the church. The
county home was not as busy as LaGuardia, but it wasn't
hopelessly remote and isolated. A bookmobile pulled into
the lot to confirm my supposition.

Vowing to return, I headed for the Dairee Dee-Lishus
and another bout of indigestion brought on by Matt's Special Secret Sauce.

★

"I got the Maggody blues," Matt sang, putting every
ounce of his soul into it in case Katie had her ear pressed
against the other side of her front door. He paused to take
the last mouthful of whiskey from the pint bottle and started
off again like a lovesick coyote on a mountaintop, or at
least how he imagined a lovesick coyote would sound, having eschewed the hazardous badlands. "I got the raggedy
. . . jaggedy . . . Maggody blues."

Rather than glued to the front door, Katie was in her
bedroom, under the covers and with a pillow wrapped
around her head. He'd been sitting in her hall for the better
part of an hour, and she was as effectively trapped as a coal
miner when the shaft collapsed. Lillian had warned her to
stay away from him, and Pierce had ordered her to keep
him happy till the tour started. Only Ripley knew what he
himself preferred. She couldn't call her mama. Folks were
a sight more mannersome back home, and her mama'd
probably take the next bus to Nashville to straighten out
her daughter's suitor. Her representative at the Figg Agency
had resigned the week before to become an undertaker.
She'd been fighting to build her career too hard to get to
know much of anybody else.

Out in the hallway, Matt was working on the second verse. "I went to my gray-haired mama, I went to my bald-headed pa, I begged 'em both to show me the road to get out of Arkansas . . . 'cause I got the Maggody blues."

Chapter Seven

Ripley Keswick drove by The Official Matt Montana Souvenir Shoppe. Seconds later, he passed Matt's Billiard Parlor and Family Entertainment Center. He'd already been greeted at the edge of town by a sign welcoming him to the Birthplace of Matt Montana, noted Matt's Parking Lot: $2.00 Hourly; $12.00 If-U-Stay-All-Day, and had braked to read the billboard with an arrow pointing down a county road to Matt Montana's Birthplace & Boyhood Home (Guided Tours 9:00–5:00; Discounts for Children Under Twelve and Senior Citizens; Buses Welcome). A colossal depiction of bungled plastic surgery looked down at him, but after he'd squinted at it, Ripley realized it was meant to be Matt.

He turned the opposite way, but there was no reprieve. At the high school, a droopy paper banner proclaimed that the Maggody Marauders welcomed Matt Montana. Across from it was a drive-in, and although he couldn't make out the small lettering on the hand-painted menu, he had a fairly reasonable guess as to *les spécialités du maison*. Back on the main road, he continued past Matt Montana's Christmas Craft Boutique and a funny-looking metal building called the Voice of the Almighty Lord Assembly Hall. He was wondering why its name hadn't been changed to Matt's Chapel when he saw the portable sign on the lawn. The Good Lord apparently had endorsed this rest stop on the highway to heaven. Ripley wouldn't have been surprised to see Matt Montana's Eternal Garden out back, dotted with headstones from Matt's Discount Marble Mart (Personalized While U Wait).

Surely, he thought as he drove by Aunt Adele's Launderette and pulled into the parking lot of Matt Montana's Hometown Bar & Grill, which existed in conjunction with Matt's Motel (NO V CAN Y, alas), the town had established diplomatic ties with Hannibal, Missouri. There was only one thing they'd overlooked, but he was not going to be the hark-the-herald of bad tidings. Geoffry would see to that when the time came.

He opened the barroom door and went in warily. Strings of twinkly Christmas lights looped across the ceiling and along the walls; the room looked as if it were under siege by lightning bugs. The jukebox was blaring, and the SRO crowd was belting out the chorus of the hometown boy's number one hit.

He made his way around the dance floor, where couples two-stepped enthusiastically on each other's toes, and took a stool at the end of the bar. He would have to identify himself eventually, but he was reluctant to do so at the top of his lungs, which would be the only way to make himself heard over this welter of aboriginal sounds and smells. Oh, to be in Oxford—Oxford, Mississippi, that is—drinking bourbon and deconstructing tales of streetcars named Desire and counties named Yoknapatawpha. If Faulkner were to write about Stump County, it wouldn't be stream of consciousness. This was miles downstream from any discernible consciousness.

"What'll it be?"

Ripley smiled at the grandmotherly bartender. "A Manhattan, please."

"I went up there once, and you better believe me when I say nobody'd name a drink after that place. If they did, it'd have scum on the surface and stink like bus fumes. How 'bout a Matt Montana Moonshine Special? It's beer, on account of that's mostly all I sell in the way of spirits, but it comes in a quart jar just like the real stuff. I ordered 'em from the same place Raz gets his." She noticed his puzzlement and explained, "Raz Buchanon's our local moonshiner. I don't allow him in here because he's forever chewing tobacco, spitting, scratching his privates, and dragging along his pedigreed sow. Her name's Marjorie."

"Buchanon?" Ripley said, startled. It was the last name

of his local contact, but she certainly hadn't sounded like the wife of a moonshiner who moonlighted as a mayor.

"I suppose it could be her last name," said Ruby Bee, finding this man more than a little bit peculiar. He was a customer, however, so she gave him an encouraging look and said, "So, how 'bout that Moonshine Special?"

A woman with implausibly red hair swooped in and claimed the stool next to his. "Afternoon," she said to Ripley with a neighborly nod, clutched the edge of the bar and said, "You ain't gonna believe what I just saw, Ruby Bee. I'm almost afraid to tell you, but if I don't, somebody else will sure as God made little green apples."

"Estelle, what on earth are you carrying on about? I got a roomful of customers, and it's all I can do to handle them until Joyce gets here to help me out. If you got something to say, spit it out."

They both gave Ripley suspicious looks, as if he were dressed in a trenchcoat and sunglasses. He held up his hand and said, "Please don't think I'd stoop so low as to eavesdrop, my dear ladies."

"Then see that you don't," Ruby Bee said sternly before turning back to Estelle. "Well?"

"I was driving out Finger Lane to look for the last of the little yellow bur marigolds to make an arrangement for the table by the door where I keep my appointment book." She smiled at Ripley. "It's a maple drop leaf that I inherited from my second cousin. He died of a broken heart after his wife ran off with a preacher with a wooden leg. I guess you could say she ran off and he hobbled off."

"He doesn't care where you got the table," Ruby Bee said in her snippiest voice.

"I was just being polite by including the gentleman in the conversation," countered the accused, momentarily nonplussed when the gentleman winked at her. "So I drove by Earl and Eilene's place, racking my brain as to where I'd seen the marigolds last year, when I happened to glance at the brick pillars at the bottom of you-know-whose driveway. There's a new sign. I wouldn't be surprised if the paint's still tacky."

"There are new signs all over town. Some of 'em are real tacky."

"How many of them announce the opening of the Mayor's Mansion Bed and Breakfast?"

"You better tell me right this minute that you made this up on account of my forthright remarks about Matt Montana's Hair Fantasies."

"The sign's stuck right there on the J. The one on the B says the rates include a full country breakfast and reservations are required. Remember the meeting when we made our proposals and voted on 'em? Who objected to Joyce wanting to paint portraits of Matt on black velvet to sell out of the back of her station wagon? I myself thought it was a real clever idea."

"She's also the one who fought tooth and nail to keep Elsie and Eula from setting up their craft shop across from the pool hall. At least she didn't get her way on that one." Ruby Bee realized the peculiar man was hanging on their every word like he was paralyzed except for the tic in his eyelid and the quiver of his chin. "When we learned that the famous country singer Matt Montana is coming to town, we formed a little group to make sure he feels welcome," she explained curtly to him. There wasn't any call for tourists to concern themselves with the town's private affairs. She stomped back down the bar, snatched a jar from a customer's hand, and held it under the tap until foamy beer streamed over her fingers and down her arms to her elbows.

Ripley shrugged in apology. "I did notice all the signs about Matt Montana. He was born here?"

"You bet your bow tie he was, out on County 102 just past my house. It's been fixed up real nice, and tomorrow is the grand opening with a parade featuring the high school band and local dignitaries. After that, it'll be open to the public every day till dark, with trained guides to talk about the history of the house and point out the bedroom where Matt Montana was born. You can visit the exact place where Matt was baptized in Boone Creek, and when you get tuckered out, you can ride around the town in the Maggody-Matt-Mobile. It's like an old-fashioned hayride except for the loudspeakers."

"Are any of Matt's relatives still living here?"

Estelle ran her tongue over her lips (Tangerine Twist to complement her new sweater) while she considered how to phrase her response. "Well, he has a great-aunt who had to go into the county old folks home a while back, but she distinctly remembers the night Matt was born and in which bedroom. All this has been so exciting for her that it's like she's living in a different world these days." She felt real proud of how she hadn't told a single lie, except for maybe fudging about the bedroom. They'd chosen the one in the best condition and sealed off the rest of them. After all, tourists wouldn't pay to see where Mr. Wockermann had passed away in his sleep.

"And did I see something about a benefit concert starring Matt Montana in person?"

"We're beside ourselves. There's not one soul in town that ever believed Matt Montana would be singing in person on the stage at our very own high school. Tickets go on sale to the public in one week, so you'd better snap one up immediately if you want to be there for the Hometown Christmas Concert. You can buy 'em at most of the shops in town, including Matt Montana's Hair Fantasies." She patted her hair in case he needed a nudge to figure it out. "It's almost directly across from the birthplace."

"I'll watch for it," he said as he slid off the stool and gave her the melancholy smile of an anemic southern dilettante. "You've been so kind to share this with me, ma'am. I've always depended on the kindness of strangers."

Estelle blinked at his back as he vanished into the dark mass of bodies surrounding the dance floor. "Your mama sure raised some rum ones, didn't she?" she said to nobody in particular as she reached for the pretzels.

★

"You found that old woman yet?" Sheriff Dorfer asked genially from his office in Farberville. "It's been my experience that if you don't find someone in the first twenty-four hours, you might as well run an ad in the lost and founds and go fishing. It's been more than a week."

"I haven't given up yet," I said. "Yesterday I questioned the last of the people who live in that area. The only unfamiliar vehicle turned out to belong to the gas company. A wholesale grocery truck made a delivery late in the morning, and the driver was sure there was no one waiting in a car on the east side of the building. Same thing with a laundry service from Starley City. The cook went outside to smoke a cigarette while everyone was having dessert, and she swears she would have noticed if anyone was parked in the lot or by the road."

"Sounds like you've run into a dead end."

"It feels like it, too. The only person I haven't spoken to is one of the aides. She has a new job and her mother doesn't have the telephone number yet. I left a message for her to call me, but from what I've gathered about the morning's activities, she couldn't have seen anything either." Brakes squealed and horns blared out front. I held my breath and waited to hear a crash, but whatever tragedy was at hand was diverted. "The most popular theory is that Adele left to visit a cousin and forgot to mention it to Mrs. Twayblade. The cousin will get tired of her before too long and dump her out in front of the county home in time for Matt Montana's arrival."

"And all you have to do is hunt up this cousin and make sure Adele has her pajamas and toothbrush. It ain't an unworkable premise, Arly. Old ladies forget things all the time."

I gazed gloomily at my notes. "Problem is, she's not supposed to have any living relatives, with the exception of Matt Montana. I can't overlook the possibility that she was coerced into leaving. Maybe somebody thinks Matt Montana will pay a bundle to get his great-aunt back. I suppose I ought to call him and ask if he's putting together a collection of small, unmarked bills. Think he's listed in the phone book, Harve, or should I try the atlas?"

"I'd hold off for a few more days if I were you."

I dropped my notebook in a bottom drawer. "Mrs. Jim Bob has a telephone number for whoever's coordinating this from Nashville. I'll try it eventually. It's not like I don't have anything else to do these days."

Harve found this highly amusing. Once he'd stopped laughing, he said, "I hear the tourists over in Montanaville are thicker than fleas on a potlicker."

I would have hung up on him if I had the energy, but that would require me to first offer some cleverly scathing retort, and I was clevered out. "Some are camped out in the field behind Eilene and Earl Buchanon's house, and the Pot o' Gold Mobile Home Park's at full capacity for the first time since Buford Buchanon took to streaking every evening at sunset. I've dealt with a couple of fender benders, some heated words at the self-service pumps, and a kid who was left behind at the SuperSaver. The state police flagged down the parents three counties away, and after some dickering, they came back. Perkins threatened some picnickers who climbed his fence, but he was careful to aim well over their heads." I yawned so wide my jaws popped and my eyes watered. "I'm getting ready to quit and go take a long, hot bath."

"You want some backup for this parade tomorrow?" he said between puffs on what I knew was a vile cigar. He was in a good mood, but he usually was when he was giving me a hard time; I reciprocated when the compass needle swung my way. "I can send over Les and maybe Tinker, if he's recovered. I'm short on account of the epidemic of stomach flu that goes around every year during deer season. If I wasn't such a trusting soul, I'd almost wonder if it was something more than a coincidence."

"Yeah, send over whoever shows up. This parade is strictly small-time, from what I can gather from yet another memo from the Homecoming Committee." I found the pertinent missive under one ordering me to enforce the no-parking regulations alongside the county roads; I suspected it had more to do with filling the parking lot than pedestrian safety.

"Hard to think it'll rival that parade they showed on television Thanksgiving morning. Two deputies ought to do it, one at each end of town to stop traffic."

I yawned again, this time nearly dislocating my jaw. "Parade's at one, Harve. Tell Les and Tinker I'll meet 'em at the PD at noon."

I had turned off the coffee pot and switched off the light in the back room when an unfamiliar man came into the PD. I'd learned by now that Matt Montana fans came in all shapes and sizes, but he was a combination I hadn't yet encountered: tall, clad in corduroy, bare-headed, and with a glimmer of intelligence in his pale blue eyes.

"Can I help you?" I asked wearily.

"May I presume this is the Matt Montana Police Department and Souvenir Shoppe?"

"Probably will be by tomorrow. I'm Arly Hanks, designated upholder of the law. And you're . . . ?"

"Ripley Keswick." He sat down, crossed his legs, entwined his fingers around one knee, and gave me a twinkly smile.

My smile was less twinkly as I sat down behind my desk. "What can I do for you, Mr. Keswick?"

"I'm the executive vice-president of Country Connections, Inc."

"So you're the man from Nashville," I acknowledged with a sigh. "I've heard about you."

"Nothing slanderous, I hope. I'm only in town for a brief time to assess the progress for Matt's upcoming visit. It was not easy to overlook the profusion of signs relating to it."

I put my afflicted feet on my desk and leaned so far back in the chair that my head bumped the wall. The water stain on the ceiling was beginning to develop oversized ears and a shit-eating grin. "I hear they're painting Matt's face on the sides of all the cows tomorrow, and there's been some discussion about chipping his profile on a bluff up on Cotter's Ridge."

"You seem a bit grumpy about all this, Arly—if I may call you that?"

"You can call me Mathilda Montana if you want," I said with all the grumpiness I could muster. "I realize this is a boon to the local economy, and it's been hurting since the carpetbaggers went back home. But this town's gone berserk. Yesterday morning it was . . . well, if not normal, at least predictable. This morning signs had sprouted like toadstools after a rain and a full-grown industry was in place. I just don't know what that will mean when this Matt mania fades and we're left with a bunch of shoppes filled with dusty souvenirs.''

"Graceland does a steady business."

"So it does, Mr. Keswick."

He studied me with a dispassionate expression. "A pragmatist," he said suddenly and delightedly. "You're a rarity in the rural South, my dear. We Southerners pride ourselves on the depth and irrationality of our emotionalism, although of course we're trained from birth to disguise it under a demeanor of the utmost civility right up until the moment we've no choice but to knock someone upside the head with a pool cue.''

"I had a lot of moments like that today, Mr. Keswick," I said, hoping he'd take the hint.

"Please, you must call me Ripley. I apologize for lapsing into a philosophical flight of fancy. I wanted to let you know that we'll do everything we can to cooperate with you. Fans can be difficult, even destructive, and I want to apologize in advance for any undue burden we'll place on you." He paused in case I wanted to express gratitude for either the apology or the burden, then proceeded with a list of those descending by bus on Maggody and an assurance that the concert would be a low-key production without pyrotechnics or elaborate sound equipment. I pretended to take notes.

He finally unlocked his fingers and unfolded his legs. "My motel is in Farberville. I'll be back tomorrow to finalize a few details.''

"By the way, Ripley, have you or anyone else in Nashville had any communiqués regarding Adele Wockermann?" I asked delicately. "Phone calls from her, or maybe a message about her future welfare?" I figured I didn't need to alarm him by spelling it out in letters clipped from a newspaper.

"All of our dealings with her are through a woman who I now understand to be the wife of the local moonshiner. Should we anticipate a call from a local lawyer? Frankly, we didn't budget for the use of her house in the publicity shots, but I suppose something can be worked out." He took his wallet from his pocket and put a business card on my desk. "Have him get in touch with me."

He left before I could ask about his weird assumption that Mrs. Jim Bob was a moonshiner's wife, but I finally dismissed it as a typical city slicker's paranoia. He'd probably expected to see a washing machine on the porch of the PD and hens scratching behind my desk.

Either Matt was keeping Keswick in the dark while negotiating with the kidnappers, Keswick was lying, or my theory was a washout. I had to admit it had sounded pretty lame to begin with and had not improved. Mrs. Twayblade had stressed that the residents were free to come and go as they pleased. Adele had been pleased to go (and I couldn't blame her).

I sat in the gloom and tried to figure out how she had managed to disappear and where the devil she could be . . . and what Ripley Keswick would do when he learned about it the next day. From the moonshiner's wife, no less. Marjorie would be livid with jealousy when she found out.

I locked the door and went home.

★

Dahlia had borrowed Eilene's car through deceit, having said she needed a yard more fabric for her vest and another foot of fringe for her skirt. To minimize the sin, she'd gone by the fabric store in Farberville and picked up a packet of sequins, then stopped at a grocery store for provisions before parking in the driveway of a vacant house half a block away from the Vacu-Pro office.

Belching mournfully, she swallowed the last of the orange soda pop and tossed the can into the back seat with the cellophane wrappers and empty onion dip carton. It was already getting dark, and before too long, she wouldn't be able to spot Kevvie if he showed up. Spot him and what? She'd already asked herself that question about once a minute since she'd arrived, and she hadn't come up with much of an answer.

It wasn't at all like the television shows, where the suspect appeared before the commercial. She'd been sitting there for more than two hours, and the only person who'd entered the Vacu-Pro office was an old guy with silver hair, most likely Kevin's boss, Mr. Dentha, coming by to pick up the profits. He hadn't come out yet.

She was scrabbling for the crumbs in the bottom of the potato chip bag when the office door opened. A skinny little woman as frumpy as Elsie McMay paused to put on a scarf and button her coat, said something over her shoulder, and then marched down the sidewalk. When she reached the corner, however, she spun around and stared right through the darkness as if she could see the car and every pore of its driver's face.

Dahlia's hands shook so hard she could barely turn the ignition key. She fumbled with the lights, backed out of the driveway, cringed as the fender grazed the rock wall, and raced away in the opposite direction. What she hadn't seen, and had come within inches of running down in her panic, was the silver-haired figure who'd emerged from an alley and was in the midst of writing down her license plate number when the car barreled toward him. She hadn't seen him leap sideways into a crackly bush either.

Once Mr. Dentha'd extricated himself, he was forced to sit down on the curb and wait until his heart stopped jumping inside his chest. When he got back to the office, he poured himself a shot of scotch and sank back on the sofa, his lips still bluish and his eyes watery. If only he'd gotten a glimpse of the driver. Could it have been a process server lying in wait for him? An irate husband? A goon sent by the bookie? A disgruntled ex-employee? A spy from the regional office? The possibilities, if not limitless, were abundant—and uniformly alarming.

Dentha finished his drink, grateful for the warmth that eased the iciness of his hands and feet. After another, a devious idea came to him. He went into his secretary's office and sat down by the old-fashioned typewriter. "Miss Vetchling," he pecked carefully, "the car we noticed belongs to a very pleasant real estate saleswoman, so we needn't worry further about it. Earlier this afternoon I thought I recognized an old army buddy at a stoplight, but the light changed before I got a good look at his face. He's the gunner whose life I saved when our plane went down in the Pacific. Please call the vehicle registration office in Little Rock and ask them to help a nearsighted old WWII vet by finding out who owns the car with the following license plate.''

He took a paper from his pocket, smoothed it out, and searched for the appropriate keys. He was initialing the note when the telephone rang. The office was ostensibly closed, but he worked late most evenings and every now and then one of the boys would call to cinch a sale with a plea for a ''special discount just this one time because of the regional sales contest.''

''Vacu-Pro Systems,'' he said into the receiver.

''This is—huh, this is Arly Hanks, and I—huh—I want to see about having one of your vacuum cleaner salesmen come by because—because my husband said just this morning that I could have a fancy new vacuum cleaner if I let a salesman show me how it works first. Tonight—he has to show me tonight!''

''There's no need to be nervous, Mrs. Hanks. We'd be delighted to demonstrate the Vacu-Pro System. One of our salesmen will arrive within an hour to shampoo the carpet of your choice at absolutely no cost to you so that you can see the actual germs that lurk in the pile and pose a deadly threat to your children and family pets. Your address and telephone number, Mrs. Hanks?''

''I'm at a pay phone.''

''That won't do us much good, will it? I need your address and your *home* telephone number so that Solomon can call if he has trouble finding your house.''

''Solomon?''

''Solomon is our very finest Vacu-Pro System salesman. He's been with us longer than anyone else, and—''

''I don't like the sound of this Solomon fellow. I want somebody who's still fresh in his mind about the attachments.'' There was a wheezy lull, replete with gurgles and a muffled belch. ''I got it. A friend of mine said this real nice young man came to her house a while back, just as mannersome as a body could be and sharp as a tack when it came to rattling off all the amazing uses for the attachments. She said his name was Kevin . . . Kevin Buchanon, I seem to think. He's the one I want.''

He dropped the pen and closed the book. "You're out of luck, Mrs. Hanks, because the young man left the Vacu-Pro sales team two weeks ago. If we're talking about the same salesman, that is, and I have my doubts.''

He might have recounted them, and indeed they were numerous, but he would have been doing so to a dial tone.

Chapter Eight

Over the next few days, my optimism dwindled and I began to worry that Adele's biological clock (in the purest sense) might have slowed down or even stopped ticking. Hospitals, bus stations, homeless shelters, and county morgues had been notified to be on the lookout for her, but Arkansas is not as densely populated as, say, Manhattan, and there are vast mountainous areas in which a body can remain undiscovered for months. Conventional channels were useless: Adele had never had a driver's license, credit cards, department store charge cards, or a long-distance calling card. I doubted she'd ever had a library card.

None of the homeowners in the vicinity of the county home had called me back to say they'd remembered seeing an unfamiliar car. The only one I'd heard from was a widow who reported Papists were training in the woods behind her house. I suggested she contact Larry at the Farberville PD.

The only person left to question was Patty May Partridge. She'd purportedly called home twice and her mother had passed along my messages—a good half dozen of 'em thus far.

If I'd had so much as a thread of a lead, a stone left to be unturned, an assurance that there was a needle somewhere in the damn haystack, I wouldn't have bothered with Patty May. If she'd seen anything, she'd have told me at the time or made an effort to call me back. As it was, I drove over to Hasty and rang the doorbell of a nondescript brick house.

A tired-looking woman in an apron came to the door,

a hot pad in her hand. The toasty air smelled of cinnamon and ginger, and in the background, falsetto voices belted out a Christmas carol.

"Yes?" she said.

"I'm Arly Hanks, Mrs. Partridge, and—"

"I already told you I don't have a telephone number for Patty May. She says the agency has a rule that caretakers can't receive personal calls, even if it's an emergency. This is a good-paying job and she doesn't want to lose it. She'll call you when she has time."

I almost pointed out I'd had better luck getting lawyers to return my calls, but I smiled deferentially and said, "I understand that, Mrs. Partridge. The thing is, this is a police investigation, and Patty May could be a witness. Her agency may not be happy if I show up at the doorstep with a warrant."

"I already told you she never mentioned the name of this agency, either. I got baking to do, Chief Hanks, on account of family coming down from Springfield tomorrow. I'll remind Patty May how nigh onto hysterical you are to talk to her, and she'll give you a call."

"When do you intend to do that?" I asked, not pleased by her offhanded aspersion. I was eager, but hardly hysterical. I'd had a town full of Montanamaniacs for more than a week. I was barely breathing.

The woman ran a flour-streaked hand through her hair. "I'll be sure and tell her tomorrow evening when she— when she calls. I've got your number right by the telephone in the kitchen." She shut the door.

I headed back for Maggody. Since my regular car radio was broken, I didn't have to listen to Christmas music or a single rendition of "You're a Detour on the Highway to Heaven," which in my mind made the entire trip worthwhile. As I slowed down at the low-water bridge, I noticed the sign was back to its original position across from Estelle's driveway. I'd pretty much forgotten about its trip (now a round one), and apparently Raz and Marjorie had, too. I didn't know what he'd been doing lately—beyond peddling moonshine to the tourists out of his truck—but Marjorie'd nearly chewed the leg off one of Perkins's goats, and bitter threats had been exchanged in front of Aunt Adele's Launderette.

The Maggody-Matt-Mobile was chugging toward me as I approached the sacred site of its namesake's birth. Dahlia looked grim, her hat jammed over her ears and her mouth poking in and out like a piston, but she wasn't clutching a .38 Special. In the wagon behind her, passengers with maps stared reverently at a white wooden cross in the ditch. The cross marked the spot where young Matt had found an ailing dog and carried it home to nurse it back to health. Everybody in town agreed Mrs. Jim Bob was showing more creativity than your regular Buchanon, even though the dog was called Ol' Yeller.

Traffic was getting into a snarl by the entrance to the parking lot, but I saved myself a headache by turning the other way and driving back to the PD. Once inside, I poured a cup of coffee and opened the yellow pages of the telephone directory. After a frustrating exercise in Southwestern Bell logic, I stumbled onto the pertinent heading, "Home Health Services," and started calling. No one recognized Patty May Partridge's name. A sympathetic woman at the last agency (WeCare, Inc.) said that private referrals were commonplace, if not approved by the state licensing board.

I certainly wasn't having any success unraveling the mystery of Adele's whereabouts. I went out to my car to see if I could do any better with the traffic.

★

The bus, leased for the tour and emblazoned on both sides with MATT MONTANA'S CHRISTMAS TOUR, rolled westward like a Conestoga wagon with a kitchenette. Katie sat alone near the front, studying a short but flattering interview with herself in a fanzine. She'd made it clear she wasn't feeling congenial, and even Matt had given up trying to wheedle a friendly word out of her. He was sitting at a table with three of the boys in the band, playing poker, drinking beer, and smoking cigars and pot. They were very congenial. The driver, the fourth member of the band and also the sound technician, was getting more and more con-

genial as they sped along the interstate toward Memphis.
Out of wary respect for the state cops, he kept the wine
bottle in a Burger King sack.

"Charlie came to my office," Lillian said to Ripley as
she sat on the arm rest of the seat across the aisle from
him. Despite the urge to grab him by his coat lapels and
shriek the words into his face, she kept her voice low. "The
divorce was legal, damn it, even if it was done in Tijuana.
I was broke, but I wasn't too drunk to make sure all the
paperwork was filed. You had no call to track down that
bastard and suggest otherwise to him."

Ripley put aside a slim volume of poetry. "I merely
suggested he review *el documentos*, Lillian. I would be
quite as appalled as you if the divorce turned out to be
void. That would mean that your third marriage was biga-
mous, which then casts doubts on the legality of the clause
in Rufus Figg's will wherein you inherited the agency. It
might even imply that the agency contracts are suspect. And
as for your current marriage . . ."

Lillian leaned forward until her face was inches from
his. "Did you send him to Matt?" she hissed.

"No, of course not, and I didn't send him to Pierce,
either. This is just my little way of reminding you of your
promise, Lillian. None of us wants to see Country Connections go belly-up—at least not until it belongs to someone
else. But as long as Pierce thinks he'll be showing a healthy
profit by late spring, he'll dig his heels in and hunker down
for the duration of the cold spell."

"Keep Charlie out of this, please. I just need a little
more time to let Matt get over this . . . pathetic infatuation,
and then I'll pressure Pierce to sell."

"You know that I'm simply trying to achieve what's
best for everyone in the long run—you, Pierce, Matt, Katie,
even Charlie. If by pure serendipity this coincides with my
simple desire to return to a more intellectual life, so be it.
A year from now, you'll thank me."

"A year from now I'll be watching my lawyer argue
that your death was justifiable homicide!" Lillian went into
the bedroom at the back of the bus and slammed the door.

Ripley picked up his book, but was once again interrupted as Katie sat down next to him. The problem with buses, he thought as he smiled wanly at her, was that they offered so little privacy.

"What was Lillian upset about?" she asked.

"Just a bout of pretour jitters. Everybody'll lighten up when we get to Maggody. It lies somewhere between Green Acres and God's Little Acre. Did Pierce tell you about this parade they staged while I was there?"

"He said they were gettin' all geared up for our arrival, but he didn't mention a parade."

"The participants gathered in the high school parking lot, and animosity flared up immediately. The owner of the local bar clutched her bosom and accused the mayor's wife of undermining the diligent efforts of some committee by opening a bed-and-breakfast establishment. The mayor's wife clutched her bosom and said she'd seen a sign outside the bar that claimed that official Matt Montana souvenirs were available inside. This was a violation of the fair trade agreement, also."

"Official Matt Montana souvenirs?" she said wonderingly. "Is this town on central substandard time?"

"You may think so when you see it." Ripley paused to take a sip of bourbon from a bottle in a brown bag, licked his lips, and leaned against the window, propping his slipper-clad feet on the far arm rest. "The two women did not lapse into hair pulling and scuffling in the gravel, to the disappointment of the observers, and eventually agreed to sit together on the back of a convertible borrowed from a used-car lot. Other committee members were obliged to ride in a station wagon driven by a woman with a hairdo that screams of repressed sexual frustration."

Katie self-consciously tucked her hair behind her ear. "So what happened?"

"The high school band played such a painfully atonal version of 'Detour' that a tourist was motivated to attack them with a tire iron. They prudently scattered, but the head majorette was so incensed that she beat the man senseless with her baton. The mayor's wife and the bar mistress passed by the fracas like twin icebergs in the Bering Strait. Then"—he paused to fortify himself from the brown bag

—"we got our first glimpse of the Matt-Mobile. Following that was a flatbed truck with the one and only Matt Montana. They'd dressed up some pimply kid in white, and he was lip-syncing. The tape recorder was in plain sight by his boot, but the tourists were restless and the rumor that it really was Matt swept down the sides of the road like a canebrake afire. I heard the poor chap had to be hospitalized."

Katie regarded him with a shrewd expression. "I don't understand why we're taking this risk. If this town is as manic as you've said, then it's hardly going to provide an idyllic background for Matt's fresh-scrubbed country boy image. He could really lose it, start busting up the pool hall or staggering down the street like a three-legged calf. What is Pierce thinking?"

"He's confident Matt will pick up on this nostalgia business and get real mellow. The great-aunt was away when I was there, but she'll be swaddled in a shawl and ready to reminisce when the time comes. The old house has been cleaned up and festooned with Christmas decorations. We may do a candlelight thing at the church, dress him up in a choir robe and a halo. The school auditorium can handle five, maybe six hundred people for the concert."

"Have they chosen a recipient?" she asked. If the locals were as Ripley described, she didn't want to imagine what the proceeds of the concert would go for.

"We don't have to worry about a thing," Ripley said, patting her arm reassuringly. "The preacher was scouting around for a photogenic tyke for the concert and said he'd find one shortly. We're all set, as far as I can tell." He picked up the book and opened it, and Katie drifted away to a seat to try to sleep.

"I've got the Maggody blues," Matt howled from the back room, hiccuping so that each word had lots and lots of syllables. "The raggedy, jaggedy, Maggody blues . . . !"

★

Mrs. Jim Bob banged down the receiver and came storming into the living room. "That Arly Hanks is driving me crazy! She's had the best part of three weeks to find

Adele and bring her back before the bus arrives. Is that too much to ask?''

" 'Course it ain't.'' Jim Bob pressed the clicker to raise the volume, caught his wife's icy look, and lowered it real quick. "So how's business at the shoppe?''

She took the clicker from him and turned off the television set. "Not as brisk as I'd hoped, but of course Ruby Bee went sneaking over to Farberville as soon as she heard what I was planning to do and ordered the same things. Now she won't let her customers out of the bar until they load up on T-shirts and beer mugs with Matt's face on the bottom. She put shelves all the way across the back of the room, loaded them with all kinds of tasteless, overpriced trash, and hired Joyce Lambertino to sit at a card table with a money box. I hope she's set aside some time to pray for her immortal soul.''

Jim Bob gazed longingly at the clicker, but he wasn't foolish enough to so much as mention that the game was down to less than two minutes and the Razorbacks were trailing by a basket. "Me, too,'' he said lamely.

"You can just stop vegetating on the sofa and commence to doing something useful for a change. The Mayor's Mansion needs a cozy fire for the Nashville folks, so go buy a rick of wood and stack it outside the kitchen door. After that, fix up your cot in the utility room.''

"Utility room? Jesus, Mrs. Jim Bob, it's colder than a well digger's ass out there, and so cramped I'll have to put my head in the washer and my feet in the dryer.''

"I will not tolerate blasphemy in this house! Mr. Keswick'll have your room, and Katie Hawk will sleep in the guest room. I'm hardly the one to sleep out there, am I?''

He hung his head. "I reckon not.''

"I'm going back to the store to make sure Darla Jean locked up properly, then fetch Ruby Bee and Estelle so we can see to a small chore.'' She took her coat from the hall closet, but came back into the living room in time to see Jim Bob reach for the clicker. "By the way, I was thinking about that girl who works at the SuperSaver, the one with dingy teeth.''

His hand stopped in midair. "What about her?''

"Once business picks up, I might just see if she wants to work for me. Selling souvenirs is a lot more interesting than checking groceries, wouldn't you say?"

He couldn't so much as twitch a finger, much less get his hand to cooperate. "Malva seems to enjoy getting to gossip with everybody," he said in a strangled voice.

"Gossip? Is that what you call it these days?" Mrs. Jim Bob left through the front door.

Jim Bob wasn't sure if the cold wind filling the room came from outside the house or not. He finally got hold of the clicker, but he was trembling so badly he couldn't press the right button and the television screen stayed as blank as his mind.

★

I banged down the receiver and said to no one at all, "Mizzoner is driving me crazy!" I went to the back room to pour a cup of viscous coffee, resumed my seat behind the desk, and gave serious consideration to the idea of catching the next Matt-Mobile to Missoula. "Everybody thought she was at her cousin's house," I said in Mrs. Jim Bob's self-righteous simper, "but you should have made sure of it two weeks ago. Now stop playing with your radar gun and go find her!"

She was not alone in the conspiracy to drive me crazy. Included in fine print on the list were the Homecoming Committee, the sheriff's department, Matt Montana's Special Secret Sauce, the broken dryers at the launderette, and the rowdy crowd at Matt Montana's Hometown Bar & Grill, where a person could no longer nurse a beer and ponder philosophical issues regarding meat loaf versus pot roast. Tomorrow, when the tour arrived, all hell was scheduled to break loose, and I was going to be in the middle of it, directing traffic with a pitchfork. Harve had promised me Les and Tinker part of the time, but he'd been known to promise me the moon and the stars, and then start hedging until I ended up as empty-handed as a beggar outside a Baptist church.

I dialed the number of the county home and asked for

Mrs. Twayblade. "I'll keep it short," I said before she started sputtering.

"That's not been my experience thus far, Chief Hanks, but I'll try to be charitable." She sighed, then said in a guilty voice, "I don't suppose you've heard anything from Adele, have you? We have a box of her clothes, and I'm reluctant to dispose of them. Frankly, I'd feel better if I knew she was safe. Not back here, mind you, but safe."

"I haven't given up," I said. "I'm still waiting to get in touch with Patty May. By the way, was she in the kitchen every minute of the dishwasher crisis?"

"The residents were in their rooms and I'd just sat down at the desk in the front hall when Patty May came galloping out to tell me how water was gushing all over the floor. I instructed her to call the plumber and hurried to the kitchen to see how extensive the water was. Patty May stayed out in the hall for a good fifteen minutes."

"Did you ask her what took her so long?"

"She claimed the plumber's number was busy. Are you implying she was up to no good?"

"I'm not implying anything whatsoever, Mrs. Twayblade. I just wanted an idea of what happened during the critical period when Adele slipped away." I didn't bother to add that I had the beginnings of a pretty good one. Sherlock Holmes had commented astutely on the dog that did not bark in the night. There had been no strange cars in the lot. Patty May Partridge had not struck me as capable of conspiracy, much less kidnapping, but now I wasn't sure. Adele was Matt Montana's great-aunt. The utterance of his name could drive some of us crazy, and others of us right over the brink of madness.

I drove out past the Wockermann house, but I saw no mysterious hint of light in the attic window. I turned around on the far side of the low-water bridge and drove back. No one was home at Matt's Hair Fantasies. The souvenir shoppe at the intersection was dark, and the lot beside the remains of the bank was empty. A dog began to bark, setting off a chain reaction that eventually would stretch across half the county. I wished I could put out a message to Adele so easily.

All hell tomorrow, I reminded myself as I parked at the PD, walked across the road and up the steps to my apartment, then froze as I saw a ghostly light on the living room window. Wishing I had my gun and at least one of my bullets, I flung open the door and, in a deep and menacing voice, shouted, ''What's going on?''

The small figure hunkered down in front of the portable television set turned around and gave me a beguiling grin that stretched from ear to shining ear. ''Howdy, Arly, how the fuck are ya? I dint think you'd mind if I watched this ball game till you got here.''

My prediction was wrong: all hell had already broken loose. Hammet Buchanon was back in Maggody.

★

It was getting close to midnight. Ruby Bee felt like she was part of a coven as the executive members of the Homecoming Committee silently filed into the Assembly Hall and sat down in the front pews. Beside her, Estelle was picking at a puffy blister on the palm of her hand. Eula Lemoy and Elsie McMay sat down together, and Jimson Pickerell took a seat behind them. Eilene Buchanon came in and sat at the far end of the pew, her face duller than a widow woman's ax.

Ruby Bee counted heads and determined they were all there, with the exception of Brother Verber, who was fussing around in the storage room behind the pulpit, and Mrs. Jim Bob, who'd called the emergency meeting and should have had the common decency to be on time.

They appeared from opposite directions. Brother Verber moved instinctively toward the pulpit, eliciting groans from those in the pews who'd sat through his interminable sermons, but he realized his error and plopped down on the pew next to Estelle. She was so relieved that she patted his knee.

Mrs. Jim Bob went right up next to the pulpit, clapped her hands like they were an unruly Sunday school class, and said, ''We have a crisis, and it ain't gonna do any good to pretend we don't. Our chief of police has failed to locate

Adele Wockermann, and we're running out of time. The Nashville folks arrive tomorrow.''

"What time?" Jimson asked, trying to ingratiate himself into the group by acting all businesslike. In reality, he was kinda slow when it came to telling time, never having gotten his "tills" straight on account of a personality conflict with his first-grade teacher.

"I don't know what time, Jimson! You just make sure your parking lot attendants are dressed in their T-shirts and are keeping an eye out for cars trying to sneak into the lot from the back." She clapped her hands once again, although nobody else'd said a word. "I promised Mr. Keswick that Adele would be in her rocking chair next to the Christmas tree and eager to greet her famous great-nephew as soon as the cameras were ready. I don't think an empty rocking chair will have the same effect."

Ruby Bee stood up and cleared her throat. "It ain't Arly's fault that Adele turned out to be slick as a peeled onion when it came to disappearing." She sat down and reminded herself to tell Arly about her spirited defense.

"That remains to be seen," Mrs. Jim Bob retorted, unimpressed. "After some painful negotiating, I've come up with a contingency plan."

"And I've come up with a li'l orphan for the benefit concert," said Brother Verber, who was so proud of himself that he didn't notice he was interrupting. "He doesn't need a liver, but he's living in a foster home where money's tight and he needs a warm winter coat and mittens and maybe a shiny red bicycle. I went and fetched him this evening. He was tickled pink when I told him we'd get him a cowboy suit and hat just like Matt Montana's. It liked to bring tears of joy to my eyes to see this orphan's beaming face.''

"Where is he?" asked Mrs. Jim Bob.

Brother Verber swelled up so much one of the snaps on his shirt popped open. "I dropped Hammett off at Arly's apartment. By now, they've had a warm reunion and are sharing stories over steamy cups of cocoa and toasted cheese samwiches.''

He was surprised when the committee members stiffened and stayed mute, particularly at a time when he was expecting a few words of congratulations. They didn't have to go all out and break into applause, he thought, but they could stop sitting there like they'd been dunked in ice water. He'd sacrificed most of the afternoon and a full tank of gas. Couldn't saintly Sister Barbara say anything?

"He's a real cute little fellow," he added as he took his handkerchief to blot his forehead. "The man from Nashville made it plain that he wanted a child that could pluck at the heartstrings of the audience—and this orphan's one fine plucker." He wiped the back of his neck, stuffed the handkerchief back in his pocket, and waited for one single word of admiration for his noble sacrifice.

"Meeting adjourned," said Mrs. Jim Bob.

Chapter Nine

The bus pulled to the side of the road in front of Matt Montana's Hometown Bar & Grill. I'd seen it go by the PD and was walking toward it at an admirable clip when the doors hissed open. A good-sized crowd had already gathered, and the stores were spewing out tourists right and left. Cars and pickup trucks from both directions stopped in the road. We had the makings of a crackerjack traffic jam.

I arrived at the lot as Ripley Keswick peered out the doors of the bus, no doubt assessing their chances of slipping into town without being noticed. They'd have a better chance of hearing a Maggodian mallard quack, "*Bienvenu!*" He gestured for me to come to the door, offered his hand to help me up the steps, and then told the driver to close the doors.

I'll admit I was curious to learn how the rich and famous traveled. The front section of the bus was fairly standard, with rows of seats facing forward and some turned to provide optimum seating at two tables. The last third of the bus was hidden by a partition with a door. The rich and famous traveled amidst a horrendous collection of aluminum cans, paper cups and plates, overflowing ashtrays, and crumpled sacks from fast-food joints. It reminded me of the back seat of my car.

"Arly, my dear," Ripley said, still holding my hand as if we were newlyweds, "let me introduce you. Bart here is our driver and bass player."

Bart looked neither rich nor famous, and, in fact, looked mostly drunk. We nodded at each other.

Ripley gestured at three men seated around a table.

"The other boys in the band—Beau and Brad are brothers, and Buck is their cousin, as is Bart."

They were clones from the same laboratory that had produced a couple of patchwork movie monsters. They had frizzy, carrot-colored hair pulled back in ponytails, mutton-chop sideburns, and droopy mustaches. They wore black hats and black vests over dingy T-shirts, and on their upper arms were tattoos of snakes and eagles intertwined in improbable procreative activity. I nodded. Brad blinked. Or maybe Beau . . . or Buck. I wasn't sure they could tell themselves apart, if they'd ever tried.

My ersatz groom continued, "And there in the back is Miss Katie Hawk, one of our hottest young talents."

"Nice to meet you," I said as she smiled unenthusiastically at me.

"Well, then," said Ripley, "I'm not sure how best to proceed, what with the crowd around the bus and the problem with traffic."

I wasn't ready to proceed, period. "Where's the hometown boy? You've got close to two hundred people out there who're going to tump the bus if Matt's not on it."

I may have underestimated the size of the crowd, but Maggody doesn't present many opportunities to practice the art. The parking lot was packed. Faces were pressed against the tinted windows of the bus as if it were a shrine. A chant was in its infancy, but it was gaining momentum like a Baghdad political rally.

Ripley arched one eyebrow, a particularly eloquent movement that I've not mastered after countless hours at the bathroom mirror. "Matt and Lillian are in the back. How do you suggest we handle the logistics, Arly?"

"What logistics do you have in mind?"

"Arly!" shrieked Ruby Bee, who'd wormed her way to the door and was pounding on it with her fist. "You got to let me in! They're gonna rip me limb from limb!"

Ripley told the bus driver to open the doors wide enough to admit her. As she squeezed through the opening, we got a sound bite from the frantic fans. It wasn't anything innovative, but the message was hard to miss.

"It ain't the most civilized crowd," she said between

gasps, proving herself the master of the understatement. Once she'd caught her breath, she added, "Welcome to Maggody! We're so thrilled to have you all—" She stopped and poked me in the rib cage. "Where in tarnation is he?"

"Fuckin'," contributed one of the boys.

"Or fightin'," said another.

The third inhaled deeply from a joint and shrugged.

Ripley put his hand on Ruby Bee's arm. "Matt was so excited to be coming home to Maggody that he hardly slept last night. He and his wife are in the suite at the back of the bus. But, look, there's Miss Katie Hawk in person. You can say hello to her."

"Hello," said Ruby Bee, albeit sullenly.

Katie smiled for a nanosecond. "H'lo."

I was going to repeat my question regarding logistics when I realized the bus was beginning to rock back and forth. The faces squashed against the window looked more like snarling gargoyles than adoring fans, and there was a lot of scuffling in the crowd. We were liable to have fist-fights and butts flying through the air before too long. The boys in the band were thumping on the table with each lurch of the bus and hooting obscenities at the faces on the other side of the glass. Katie screamed as a gorilla-sized hand replete with black hair flattened on the window next to her face. Ruby Bee hung onto my arm for dear life. Trash scooted across the floor. We were no longer in a bus, but in the fun house at a carnival. I'd always considered the name a misnomer.

"How do you handle a mob like this?" I shouted at Ripley.

"I haven't any idea. I do ad campaigns, not mobs."

I lost my balance as the floor tilted, and Ruby Bee and I stumbled into him. "You'd better think of something!" I shouted in his ear before we stumbled away. I turned around to order the driver to get us out of there, but he had passed out across the steering wheel. Splayed like a spider across the windshield was none other than Hammet Buchanon, waving excitedly at me. A woman with hair to rival Estelle's snapped off a windshield wiper and triumphantly held it aloft. She stopped grinning as several women charged her. Ruby Bee and I went flying back into Ripley, this time pinning him against the door. He winced as Ruby Bee's elbow caught him in the stomach.

Abruptly the bus stopped bucking. The chant faded to a few uncertain voices, then dried up. Hammet slithered out of view. Faces unglued themselves from the windows, and fans at the door of the bus drifted away.

"Are we missing the second coming of Christ?" said Ruby Bee. "Look over there at Jim Bob in the doorway of the bar. He sure looks like he's facing the wrath of God."

"More likely to be his wife," I said as I heard a disembodied voice singing reverently as if easing into a hymn, then growing stronger.

"My sweet angel Katie on the top of the tree, we'll celebrate Christmas for eternity . . ."

★

Dentha was deeply confused. The car that had been parked down the street from the office was registered to one Earl Buchanon of Maggody. He presumed this Buchanon was related to his former employee in some way, but that didn't explain much. He hadn't fired the boy. He never fired anyone, no matter how poor their sales were. His problem was recruiting new salesmen, most of whom would sell at least one or two Vacu-Pro Systems to members of their families before they became discouraged and quit. He and Miss Vetchling were the only constants in the office, and she was beginning to sniffle about the lateness of her paycheck.

He went to the door of his office. "Miss Vetchling, would you be so kind as to hunt up the personnel file on Kevin Buchanon?"

"If I can find the strength, Mr. Dentha. I had only a bowl of soup for supper last night, and a cup of tea and a cracker for breakfast. I had to empty my checking account to pay my rent on the first of the month."

"I feel dreadful that the regional office is dragging its heels, Miss Vetchling. I'll call over there as soon as I have a look at the Buchanon file." He returned to his desk, and after she'd set down the file and limped bravely back to the front room, he wasted a few minutes wondering what she'd do if she learned her check had arrived three weeks earlier. Its paltry sum had saved him from a broken kneecap, or so his bookie had sneered. The memory of the confrontation was enough to set Dentha's heart beating arrhythmically, and he slipped a pill under his tongue and closed his eyes until he felt steadier.

He opened the file. Yes, Earl Buchanon was Kevin's father and lived at the address reported by the vehicle registration office. Had Kevin borrowed his father's car, or was the father implicated? And how did this Arly Hanks woman fit into things? He turned over the application form and flinched as he saw the name printed crudely but legibly. Kevin had listed his previous employers, and between stints as a convenience store assistant manager and a bank security guard, claimed to have served as an investigator under the supervision of Chief of Police Arly Hanks of the Maggody PD. This time Dentha could barely get the cap off the vial of nitroglycerine tablets.

When he felt calmer, he went to the front office and waited impatiently until Miss Vetchling had finished her telephone pitch. "I'm going to be out of the office for the rest of the day, possibly until Monday morning. Can you look after things?"

"I'll do my best, Mr. Dentha."

"I've had a call from the home office. I can't name names, but I've been asked to investigate the possibility that someone at the regional level has been diverting funds to an account in the Cayman Islands. For obvious reasons, this requires the utmost discretion. If anyone calls, say that I'm at a sales meeting in Little Rock."

"What if there's a call from the regional office?" Miss Vetchling asked shrewdly.

"I'm confident you'll think of something." He put on his hat and coat, picked up his briefcase, and stopped to give her a look of avuncular concern. "You really should add red meat to your diet, Miss Vetchling. You look a bit anemic." He was already halfway down the sidewalk when he heard something inside the office shatter, but he was too preoccupied to go back and inquire.

★

"I am so honored to have you all as guests in my home," Mrs. Jim Bob said to Ripley as they sipped tea in the living room of The Mayor's Mansion, now officially filled to capacity. A fire crackled and snapped in the fireplace and the mingled scents of pinecones and potpourri added to the overall coziness. Every doily had been handwashed, starched, and pinned back in place on the arm rests, and every cushion plumped like a marshmallow. The spruce tree in the corner was decorated with red glass balls, red-and-white gingham bows, and little plastic candy canes; the gaily wrapped packages beneath it were empty but the effect was festive.

Mrs. Jim Bob was proud of the ambiance, but as Brother Verber often expounded from the pulpit, pride went before destruction and a haughty spirit before a fall. Having time for neither of those calamities, she lowered her eyes modestly and said, "I hope Miss Katie finds her room pleasant, and you, too. I put copies of the Bible in the top drawers of the nightstands. I want all my guests to go to bed knowing they're in an upright Christian household."

Ripley smiled. "It's charming. I hope you'll forgive Katie's haste to go to her room. She's tuckered out from the drive and needs a nap. I'm hoping to meet Mrs. Wockermann and warn her that Matt's coming to see her in the morning. If he surprises her, all that excitement might make her fly . . . off the handle."

"First, we ought to drive around town so you can see for yourself how everything's all fancied up for Christmas. I myself went all the way to Farberville to find the perfect wreath for the front door of the house. Then, why, we can have a nice visit with Brother Verber, who said a special prayer last Sunday entreating the Good Lord to watch over your bus. The church is decorated for Christmas, too, but Millicent McIlhaney saw to that, and it's overdone, if you ask me. Millicent and I don't see eye to eye about—"

"I'm sure it's fine," Ripley interrupted. He winked reassuringly at her, but rather than soothing her, it startled her tongue back into action.

"You'll want to walk down to the creek and see where Matt was baptized. The official map shows it as being upstream just a ways, but we didn't think folks wanted to walk all that—"

"A brilliant idea, Mrs. Jim Bob. Let me pop upstairs for my coat and gloves, and we'll be on our merry way."

He started to rise, but she caught his shoulder and pushed him down. In an uncharacteristically tremulous voice, she said, "Why don't I call first and let everyone know we're on our way? You just sit here and have another cup of tea. I'll be back in one tiny minute." She went into the hall, realized he could overhear her call, and hurried out to the breakfast room to use the extension.

Ripley leaned back and crossed his legs, amused by her panic. Before long, he'd be back in Oxford, this time living in a fine old antebellum house with mahogany bookcases, books with cracked leather spines, and a group of students awaiting his learned remarks. Decorum would require that he invite pasty-faced young women with thick ankles and thicker glasses, but he would also include malnourished young men in dark cotton sweaters and baggy khaki pants. The thought was enough to bring a sheen of perspiration to his forehead.

"I wanna talk to you."

Ripley opened his eyes. "You're the mayor?"

"Yeah, the mayor of the fuckin' utility room." Jim Bob sat across from him and got right down to business. "I was over at the bar and grill when your bus drove up and that kid started caterwauling out the back window. You and me got a few things to get straight, Mr. Nashville Hotshot."

Ripley put his fingers together and regarded Jim Bob as if he were one of the distaff students of his reverie who'd just made a disparaging remark about Miss Eudora. "Would you care to elaborate?"

Jim Bob, who could spot 'em a mile away and had bashed a few in his time, didn't give a shit if this fellow was the fairy princess of Opryland. When money was involved, he could be real tolerant. "I sure as hell would."

★

"About the time I was resigned to a broken back, Matt Montana came to the rescue," I said over the telephone to Harve, who was puffing away in his office in Farberville. I was in the PD, gazing wearily at the rings left on the desk by innumerable unfinished cups of coffee and at the wad of wax paper that had contained the lunch I'd gulped down. "After he gave the impromptu concert from the window of the bus, he was so gosh-darn grateful for their presence and golly-gee apologetic and all that crap that his fans practically begged him to stay inside and rest. Some of the women were crying, for chrissake, and even Hizzoner looked all choked up. He's the last one in town I'd have accused of being a softie. Anyway, everybody backed off and the driver roused himself to move the bus around the corner of the bar. I blocked off the motel parking lot with sawhorses and deputized a couple of unemployed chicken processors to fend off the tourists for the rest of the day. I armed one of the deputies with a beeper that'll keep him in touch with your dispatcher, who can call me here or at home if there's a problem."

"You didn't arm Hammet, did ya?" drawled Harve. In the background, LaBelle giggled like a serial killer.

"Heard about that, did you?" I said mildly, hoping he couldn't hear me grind my teeth.

"Ain't but a handful of folks in Stump County that haven't heard Robin Buchanon's bushcolt is back in town. Around these parts, he's a sight more famous than Matt Montana. His mouth any cleaner since his last visit?"

"No, and he's expanded his vocabulary to include a lot of obscenities I've never heard before. His foster mother lets him watch MTV."

Harve chortled until he choked. After he'd ordered LaBelle to thump him on the back, then hacked and wheezed for a while, he came back on the line. "Wait till dark, then bundle him up in a blanket and take him back to his foster home."

"You know I can't do that," I muttered, not allowing myself to entertain the possibility for more than an idyllic second or two. "Ever since he stayed with me after his mother was murdered, he's been convinced that I'm going to relent and adopt him. He watches me out of the corner of his eye for any sign of weakness. He's not a bad kid, considering he spent his formative years in a gawdawful sorry excuse for a shack up on the ridge, and he's really pretty bright. He's also unbelievably excited about being dressed up in a cowboy suit and brought onto the stage with a real live star. He kept me up all night talking about it. How am I supposed to drop him at the curb?"

"Your funeral. Did you get me and the missus tickets for the concert?"

I admitted I did, although I made it clear that the tickets were in exchange for a six-man security force outside the auditorium. Matt Montana was not in danger of an assassination attempt by a highly trained agent from a hostile country. I wasn't worried about snipers on rooftops or bombs in the auditorium. All six hundred tickets had been sold, with locals given twenty-four hours to snap them up before they were offered to the public. Rumor had it that scalpers were already commanding fifty dollars a ticket, and we still had more than forty-eight hours to go. It had overtones of a bad movie, R-rated for violence, if not sex.

". . . and they'll be there midafternoon," Harve was saying. "I'll send over some more sawhorses to set around the school parking lot to keep the gawkers at a distance. You want the bullhorn, Arly?"

I did not want the bullhorn, any more than I wanted half a dozen deputies, more sawhorses, six hundred concertgoers, or a horde of ticketless folks who'd sell their grannies into white slavery for a glimpse of Matt Montana. I did not want traffic jams on the highway, dented fenders in the parking lot, brawls outside the bar and grill, shoplifters in the souvenir shoppes, or witticisms from Harve Dorfer.

"Nope," I said and hung up, the last being the only one of the above over which I had any control. I went to the door and regarded what I could see of my jurisdiction.

It was getting dark, which meant the souvenir stores would close shortly, the tours would terminate for the day, the one streetlight would come on of its own magical accord, and I could start rolling up the sidewalk.

But I'd have to unroll it the next day, when the home-town boy emerged from the bus for two days filled with photo ops at the Wockermann house, the Assembly Hall, the high school, and whatever other sites the homecoming committee had decided he would fondly remember, given adequate forewarning. I'd tried to remember him, but all I could come up with were blurry images of bad acne. Nothing a kid did was of interest to a bona fide teenager, with the exception of said kid creeping through the moonlit scrub down by Boone Creek. All I'd seen of him then was his backside (which, possibly, was all he'd seen of me).

The faux-deputies had agreed to work all night in exchange for overtime, which I'd bill to Harve. The manager of the Pot o' Gold Mobile Home Park, as well as Earl Buchanon, could handle security in their respective campgrounds. The two potential hotspots were at best tepid. Ruby Bee kept a baseball bat behind the bar, and the guy at the pool hall had hired a bouncer who parked a chopper out back. I'd run the license plate, and his parole officer had told me she herself was making sure he stayed on his medication this time.

The Springfield splinter of the Partridge family was likely to have arrived in Hasty before dark. If I'd read Patty May's mother's quasi-slip correctly, Patty May would soon be sipping egg nog and munching cookies in the kitchen with her kin. I decided to take Hammet with me. After my surprise visit, we could drive around Farberville and look at the Christmas lights, go to a movie, get ice cream, or anything else that appealed to him as long it took place outside the town limits of Montanaville.

I'd turned him loose for the day, telling myself the townsfolk deserved no mercy for having dumped him on me in the first place. Everybody'd sworn it was Brother Verber's doing, but I figured the blame belonged to the entire committee, none of whom had best ease through a yellow light as long as I was in office. Was I vindictive? As Hammet would say, you bet your ass.

I was headed out the front door when I heard a knock on the back door. Figuring my houseguest was being pursued by a lynch mob, I sighed and went to let him inside the sanctuary. I found myself admitting Matt Montana, who touched the brim of his cowboy hat as he ducked under my arm. He wore a fleece-lined jacket and denim pants, but his photograph had been held under my nose so often that I had no problem recognizing him.

"Evening, ma'am," he said.

I regret to say I was speechless.

"Hope I'm not disturbing you," he continued as if used to dealing with the dumbstruck, which he probably was. "I was feeling cooped up like a chicken in the bus, so I thought I'd slip away and hunt up some of my old friends in Maggody." He went into the front room and sat down in the chair across from the desk. "Bet ya don't remember that night down at the creek, do ya? Lordy, your eyes was a-blazin' when you came after us. I was surprised I didn't end up with burn marks on my butt."

"The good ol' days," I murmured. I was so stunned that I had to clutch the arm rests of my chair as I sat down behind the desk. "Your memory's better than mine."

"Mebbe 'cause it was the first time I saw tits in the moonlight. Sure was a pretty sight."

I couldn't decide whether to grin back or go get my gun and shoot him in the middle of his forehead. I decided to delay the decision for the time being, although I had not unilaterally dismissed either option. "Everybody's excited about your triumphant return to Maggody. Guess you saw all the signs along the road?"

He pushed back his hat and did what he could to get comfortable in the chair. "Aw, they didn't have to go to all that trouble for me. I just came to visit with old friends and family and sing a few songs at the gym."

"Which is why press releases were sent to every newspaper and radio station within a thousand miles?"

"To tell the truth, the media folks have gotten kinda

tiresome since I won the Country Sound Award back in October for best original song. You hear about that?''

''Something to that effect.'' I could not for the life of me figure out what the hell he was doing in the PD, his boots now resting on my desk, his grin as wide and white as a crescent moon, his eyes locked on mine like we were sharing some steamy secret. ''How'd you escape all those fans milling around the parking lot at the bar?''

''Weren't nothing to it. I cut around the back of the motel and across the field, climbed a barbed-wire fence, and stayed in the shadows until I got to your back door. I was awful glad the light was still on.'' His tone implied the light in question had metaphorical implications.

''Lucky you,'' I said levelly. I forced myself to withdraw to a more analytical perspective (yeah, sure I did) in an attempt to figure out why my stomach was in knots and my tongue hanging out. He wasn't all that handsome. His mouth was too full and wide, and his eyes protruded slightly as if he had a hormone imbalance. There were crinkles at the corners of his eyes, and deeper lines from incessant, lopsided grins. He was the cherub in the Christmas pageant, sincere and unaffected, oblivious to his impact on women. And I was Beverly Sills.

''So how come you're still stuck here after all these years?'' he asked. ''Seems like you'd have gone off your rocker by now, unless you're the kind who's content to just sit in it out on the porch.''

''I moved away, went to college, got married, lived in Manhattan for a time, got divorced, and came back here to pull myself together again. It's a temporary situation.''

''How long's it been temporary?''

''Not all that long. It's an undemanding job in an undemanding town, or at least it was until a few weeks ago. Long about noon yesterday the population doubled, and tomorrow the media alone will triple it.''

He laughed at my minor display of belligerence. ''Whoa, you don't think this was my idea, do you? I spent maybe three summers here before Aunt Adele got fed up and put me on a bus. I can still see her in a cloud of black smoke, shaking her fist and shrieking, 'Good riddance!' I hardly think of this place as my hometown, but I don't call the shots. I'm nothing but a simple country boy who got lucky. I jes' do what they tell me.''

"Do you have any relatives left in Little Rock?" I asked, thinking about my missing person case. I could have told him why I asked, but I was reluctant to take him into my confidence, which would lend veracity to his implication that we were dear old friends who'd simply missed the opportunity to become lovers. He seemed to have forgotten he'd been nothing but a greasy little voyeur.

"Not a one. My grandparents died a few years back, and their only surviving daughter sold everything and became a missionary in Africa or some place like that. Her bishop wrote and said she'd died of malaria, but I'd like to think she made a tasty supper for her congregation.''

"Then Adele Wockermann is your only living relative?''

"All that I know of. We're supposed to go see her in the morning. Do you reckon I ought to take flowers and candy to perk the old girl up?''

"Like you did two years ago?''

The grin dried up faster than a raindrop in the desert. "Whatta you talking about?''

I wasn't any more inclined to explain the intricacies of the grapevine than I was to share confidences. "An aide at the home said something. You were here, weren't you?''

"Yeah, I came by to see how she was doin'. I'm surprised she remembered, that's all.''

He was back to grinning, and I was trying to read his mind (if he had one) when he glanced out the window, gasped, and jerked his boots off the desk so hurriedly that he lost his balance and fell on the floor.

"Fans out there spotted me," he said as he scuttled into the back room. "Great to see ya after all these years.'' The back door banged.

"You, too," I murmured. There were a few people wandering around outside, but none of them was paying any attention to the PD. The price of fame appeared to be paranoia. I locked up and went across the street, where Hammet sat on the landing outside my apartment.

He'd been getting bored, he explained as we got into my car, because nobody was doing anything interesting (i.e., flippin' buses) and he'd been run out of the pool hall three times. Rather than learn why, I asked him about school and we discussed the sadly outdated philosophy of the public school system all the way to Hasty and then pulled into a vacant lot across the road from the Partridge house.

Lights were shining and half a dozen cars were parked in the driveway. I decided not to crash the party. Hammet was delighted to be on a stakeout, and after I'd dissuaded him from creeping up to the living room to peek through the window, we resumed our spirited discussion.

An hour or so later, several figures came out to the front porch. Kissing and hugging ensued. Then Patty May took a foil-covered plate from her mother, got into a small car, and drove down the road in the direction of Farberville. I waited a minute before falling in behind her. Hammet felt we ought to pull alongside her and aim a gun at her head, run her off the road, or at least shoot out her back tires, but I stayed as far back as I dared until we passed the airport and traffic picked up.

"There she is!" Hammet shouted, pounding the dash-board between bouts of hanging his head out the window. "Watch out fer that truck! That sumbitch! Cut him off!" He went back out the window to wave his fist at a truck the size of Rhode Island. "Hey, fuckhead, we kin arrest you!" Before I could stop him, he was in the back seat and hollering out the opposite side at a church van. Pale faces turned in horror.

Patty May exited at an intersection ablaze with neon signs. None of them read CITY PARK. She turned into the parking lot of one of the largest motels in Farberville and drove behind a row of yellow buses.

Cursing, I cut in front of several cars and took a speed bump hard enough to momentarily lose my grip on the steering wheel. Hammet whooped gleefully and almost climbed onto the roof of the car.

I had to stop at the last school bus as a group of teen-agers emerged with suitcases, backpacks, pillows, sacks of provisions, and other vital paraphernalia. I finally eased through them and went around the corner. Parked cars lined both sides of a lot that seemed to stretch endlessly. Lights flashed and car doors slammed as families unloaded luggage and ice chests. Children dashed in front of me, clutching stuffed animals, and the balcony on the second story was as busy as a mall the day after Thanksgiving.

"Shit," said my deputy as he scratched his head.

I drove slowly down the asphalt, searching for Patty May's unprepossessing car amidst the bustle. We finally found it parked on the third side of the quadrangle, but Patty May was long gone.

"No problem," I said. "We'll ask at the desk." I made him wait in the car and went inside the lobby, found the desk, and got a clerk's attention long enough to request the manager. She was a thin woman with an expression that reminded me of Mrs. Twayblade. I showed her my badge, asked for Patty May Partridge's room number, and sat down in the shade of a plastic rubber tree.

"No one here by that name," she told me as she came out from behind the desk.

"Try Adele Wockermann."

"Anyone else while I'm looking?" she asked. "We're full, which means we have at least eight hundred guests. There's a wedding in the Razorback Room and private Christmas parties in the Ozark Room and the Clinton Room. The high school kids have taken over the indoor pool and the hot tub, and we're already getting complaints. I simply cannot hunt through the—"

"Adele Wockermann," I said, spelling the last name for her.

She returned shortly and with a strained smile said, "There's no one here registered under that name either."

Temporarily foiled but not defeated, Hammet and I went to the movies.

Chapter Ten

"I am so sorry to keep you waiting, Ripley," chirped Mrs. Jim Bob as she swung around the corner into the living room. She was momentarily startled when she saw who else was sitting there, but she was too uneasy to worry about it. "I do hope you two had a nice chat while I was on the telephone. What with one thing and another, I didn't realize how late it was getting, so we'll just have to wait until morning for our tour of the town. Jim Bob, I was thinking that our guests might enjoy a nice picnic supper. You go down to the SuperSaver deli and pick up some cold cuts and rolls, and I'll whip up a batch of potato salad. I seem to think there's most of an apple pie in the refrigerator, and it won't take any time at all to make some fresh iced tea and a pot of coffee. How does that sound?" She put her hands on her hips and defied them to offer an argument. If either had, she might well have burst into tears, a most unbecoming rejoinder from a mayor's wife.

"That sounds fine," Ripley said, nodding faintly, preoccupied with what Jim Bob had told him and not sure how best to profit from it. "I'll . . . uh, I'll go knock on Katie's door and let her know." He was considering whom to blackmail as he went upstairs, which is why he failed to see the figure glide into a bedroom and close the door.

Jim Bob waited until Ripley was out of earshot, then rubbed his hands together gleefully. "Next year come winter we can take a vacation to one of those resorts where they bring you pastel drinks while you lie by the pool."

"What in heaven's name has gotten into you?" snapped Mrs. Jim Bob. "Here we've got a houseful of paying guests, supper to be served, disaster breathin' down our necks in the morning—and you're spouting nonsense. Exactly how are you planning to pay for this so-called vacation of ours?"

It hadn't occurred to Jim Bob to take his wife along, the "we" having referred to himself and Malva, or whoever was deserving of his generosity when the time came (his manhood being significantly longer than his attention span). He pretended to consider her question, then said, "The shoppe's gonna do real well now that Matt Montana's here. Keswick was just telling me how well the souvenirs sell whenever they come to a town. Business has picked up at the SuperSaver, too, on account of all the campers."

Mrs. Jim Bob could see the evasive flickering of his eyes, and she knew perfectly well that the two men hadn't been discussing any upswing in the local economy. But she, like Ripley, was too preoccupied to do more than purse her lips at him for a moment before saying, "Come into the kitchen while I make a list. You can get a pint of coleslaw at the deli, too. I'll serve it in one of my Tupperware bowls and the Nashville folks will never know the difference. Maybe I'll see if Brother Verber would like to join us. He'd be real tickled to say the blessing in front of Miss Katie Hawk."

Jim Bob was too relieved to suggest the old fart would be more tickled at the prospect of a free meal than at the opportunity to consecrate the coleslaw. Once he had the list in his hip pocket, he went whistling out the door, climbed in his truck, and was sipping bourbon and trying to recall which islands had topless beaches before he reached the brick pillars at the bottom of the driveway, which is why he failed to see the figure crouched in the shadows.

★

Mrs. Jim Bob put the water on to boil for the potatoes, then sat down at the breakfast table and called Brother Ver-

ber to invite him for supper—and to warn him that she'd
had no choice but to initiate the contingency plan. They'd
discussed it earlier and, after a bout of ardent prayer, had
both agreed that lying to the media was an insignificant sin,
if that.

When Brother Verber answered the telephone, she com-
menced to rattling off a description of the crisis, which is
why she failed to see the figure skirt the oblong patches of
lights on the back lawn and vanish into the darkness.

★

At the front of the parking lot of Matt's Motel, the two
newly appointed deputies leaned against the sawhorses and
kept a vigilant watch for fans trying to sneak past them in
order to peek through the windows of the bus. Earlier, it'd
been kinda hairy, what with some high school girls gettin'
all sniffly, a couple of neckless farm boys with too much
beer in their bellies demanding to meet Miss Katie Hawk,
and a teary middle-aged couple who'd driven all the way
from Berryville just to get Matt's autograph because he
reminded them of their deceased son. The man offered a
twenty-dollar bill, but the deputies were aware of the perils
of disobeying the chief, who'd been so testy earlier that
one of them had made a crack about PMS. When she was
well out of range, of course.

The only person with free access was Ruby Bee. She'd
been miffed when Ripley told her not to disturb Matt and
Lillian, that the bus had linens for the double bed, towels
for the shower, and a tiny, well-stocked kitchenette. She'd
have liked to see all that for herself (imagine such things
on a bus!), but the curtains in the back were drawn together
tight as a spinster's knees. Even standing on her tiptoes way
at the front and clutching the stub of the missing windshield
wiper to keep her balance, she hadn't seen so much as a
twitch of movement inside.

The men in #4 and #5 were the sorriest things she'd
met in all her born days. They looked alike (scruffy), talked
alike (filthy), and smelled like the end product of Raz's
illicit labor (eighty-proof goat piss). At least they wouldn't

need to go looking for him any time soon; their rooms contained enough whiskey to stay drunk as a fiddler's bitch for a week. Leaving a stack of towels outside #4, she headed back to see how Joyce was holding up behind the bar.

"You boys think you could find a use for some burgers and coffee?" she asked the deputies. They granted that they sure could, and she was trying to keep it straight in her mind who wanted sweet onions and mustard and who wanted mayonnaise and cheese, which is why she and the deputies—all three of them—failed to see the figure slip out of the bus and disappear into the night.

★

Humming happily, Brother Verber went into the bathroom of the rectory and studied his reflection in the mirror, trying to see himself for the first time just like Miss Katie Hawk would do shortly. He'd read her interview in *Country Cavalcade*, where she'd talked about her childhood, and he'd been mopping his eyes and blowing his nose before he finished it. Her pa'd been a coal miner before his health failed, but then he'd taken to preaching at a little white clapboard church up in the mountains. Katie had told the interviewer how this had given her the strength to battle the wickedness that lurked on every corner of Nashville.

Wouldn't it be something if Miss Katie Hawk would deliver that same message from the pulpit of the Voice of the Almighty Lord Assembly Hall? Why, they could even charge a small admission fee to those who'd pack the pews to hear her preach. He pictured her in a white robe, her black hair straight and unadorned, her face scrubbed of makeup, her eyes boring into the souls of the sinners.

He went into the bedroom and sat down to figure out how much they could make if they charged five dollars a head. He finally resorted to a pencil and a scrap of paper, his forehead crinkled as he struggled with the multiplication (twenty-eight pews times twelve sinners . . .) and his lips moving silently (two times eight is sixteen, carry the one . . .) as his mind grew green with wondrous possibilities (plus eleven in the choir times five), which is why he failed to see the figure hurry past the rectory and cut through the pasture that paralleled County 102.

★

"Thanks for supper," Dahlia said as she crammed her cowboy hat on her head and yanked the cord so tightly it cut into her chins. "It was mighty good, but I guess my appetite ain't what it used to be."

Eilene hugged as much of her as she could. "It's gonna be all right, honey. Soon as we get the wagon and loud-speakers paid off, you can keep all the money and Kevin won't have to work so late every night. Have you told him how much you're making these days?"

"He ain't asked." Dahlia sighed clear down to the soles of her white cowboy boots, picked up her fringed shoulder bag, and trudged out the door without so much as a belch of farewell to her in-laws. There wasn't any call to hurry home to an empty love nest, she thought, as she turned the key and waited until the engine quit coughing and settled into a drone. She deftly maneuvered the wagon around and headed up Finger Lane to the highway.

Most of the time driving the Matt-Mobile made her feel important, especially when she was pulling a wagonload of tourists who were jabbery as blue jays. Now that it was cold and dark and the wagon was empty, she figured she looked pretty darn stupid. And it was all Kevin's fault for refusing to take the job just so he could spend his evenings with his Farberville floozy.

She negotiated the turn and drove past the souvenir shoppe, gazing sadly at the Matt Montana mannequin in the front window. Music was blaring inside the pool hall, but she didn't so much as turn her head as she drove on. The crafts boutique was closed, as was the antique store. She saw Perkins in the launderette, but he didn't return her desultory wave and she drove on. There was a night-light shining behind the yellow-and-white gingham curtains of the PD. She didn't even slow down. The SuperSaver was open, but the parking lot was dotted with only a few cars, one of which appeared to have two flat tires. She drove on.

Things were a sight livelier at Matt Montana's Hometown Bar & Grill—not that she or anybody else had laid eyes on Matt hisself. What was the good of having a celebrity in town if he turned out to be a recluse like Louisa Ferncliff Buchanon, who lived so far up in the hills that she had to walk backward to get to town and had been spotted only four times in the last twenty-three years?

Dahlia downshifted, turned, and drove up the hill past Raz Buchanon's shack. One of these nights she'd stop and buy a jar of hooch, tease her hair, and put on her red dress. She had plenty of old boyfriends in town. Wouldn't Kevin be sorry when he searched high and low until he found her down at the bar, seeing double and feeling single!

She nearly sideswiped a car parked halfway in the ditch as she imagined herself with Matt Montana, who walked into her daydream and held out his hand to her like she'd driven up to the castle in a pumpkin. Everybody else stepped back. A quarter tinkled in the jukebox, and slowly the strains of "You're a Detour on the Highway to Heaven" filled the room, but this time, Matt began to croon to her as if they were all alone. "I got lost in the glare of your headlights," he sang with such tenderness she had to bite her lip to keep from bawling, "and went joy-ridin' just for the view."

Operating on automatic pilot, she parked the Matt-Mobile in the side yard, put the tractor key in her shoulder bag and dug out the house key, and drifted onto the porch, her privates tingling as his voice caressed her like a bathtub filled with scented water. And realized the front door was not only unlocked, but slightly ajar.

Someone was in there.

Down the road, one of Raz's hounds bayed soulfully, and up on the ridge an owl screeched. Out back a critter rooted in crackly leaves. Barely audible were voices and car doors slamming in the parking lot of the bar and grill way down at the bottom of the hill. And from inside the house, someone let out a grunt of frustration.

She eased off the porch and took a step toward the gate, thinking she could hurry down to Raz's and persuade him to grab his shotgun and come back with her. She stopped. The idea of miserable ol' Raz Buchanon coming to her rescue was hard to swallow—especially when her lawfully wedded husband should be there to defend her.

Her imagination, well primed after the scene with Matt, shifted smoothly into overdrive. Inside the house was someone who knew that she went to bed alone every night, her arms empty, her feet as icy as a widow woman's. He was a sex fiend, a hunchbacked pervert with one rheumy red eye, slobbery lips, warts like a toad, and gnarly hands that would bruise her tender flesh while he had his wicked way with her.

But she wasn't some simpery princess in need of a fairy godmother to drag her out of the cinders and clean her up. No, ma'am, she was a respectable married woman, a dutiful granddaughter and daughter-in-law, and a Christian soldier since she was baptized in the muddy water of Boone Creek on her thirteenth birthday. That she'd lost her virginity that same night (and less than a mile upstream) had done nothing to deter her from enlisting in the rank and file of the Lord's Army. Dahlia squared her shoulders, thrust out her jaw, tightened her fists, and tiptoed into the living room of her love nest.

Somewhere in the back the floor squeaked. The pervert was in the bedroom, naturally, his hairy hands pawing through her underwear, his drool spilling onto her pillow, his prick rigid and ready to attack her. Her lip curled in disgust, she went into the kitchen, took a skillet off the stove, and made her way cautiously across the living room. Her breathing was ragged, but all she could do was hope that he couldn't hear it—or if he did, that he was so blinded by lechery that he'd misinterpret it.

The skillet poised above her head, she opened the bedroom door. Her white-clad body filled the space; the fringe on her vest twittered and twirled, and countless swirls of sequins shimmered in the weak light from the utility pole out back. The pervert spun around from the dresser, his hands thrown high, his face distorted with surprise as he confronted the ghost of Nashville past or present. For him, there was no future. "Aaarugulaaaa," he gurgled as he lunged forward.

She beaned him neatly and he crumpled to the floor.

Dropping the skillet beside him, Dahlia went into the living room and switched on the light, then continued into the kitchen, took a beer from the refrigerator, and downed it in one celebratory gulp. After a burp of pride that might have originated from the distant past when an ancestor had brought down a woolly mammoth with a swing of a club, she took another beer and sat down on the sofa to wait until her breathing eased and her heart stopped racing. Wouldn't Kevin Fitzgerald Buchanon's expression be priceless when he came home and found the one-eyed, hunchbacked pervert sprawled in the bedroom!

This might not happen for a long while, she realized as she squinted at the clock her second cousin Velda had brought all the way back from Memphis as a wedding present. According to Elvis's outstretched arms, it was not yet nine o'clock. Kevin hadn't made it home before midnight in more than a week. In the meantime, what was she supposed to do if the pervert woke up and made another attempt to ravish her? She set the beer on the end table and went into the bedroom to truss him up like a rodeo calf and set him out on the porch so Kevin would trip over him.

She stepped over an outstretched arm and took a belt and handful of scarves from her closet, stepped back over it to fetch adhesive tape from the medicine cabinet in the bathroom and scissors from a drawer in the kitchen, and returned to the bedroom. Only then did she turn on the overhead light to take a look at her trophy.

The scarves, belt, tape, and scissors fell out of her limp hands. He had not one eye but two, and they were plain brown. His hair was silver and combed back in a pompadour like a televangelist's, and his gray jacket matched his trousers—and his socks. A blue silk handkerchief had fallen out of his pocket. If there'd been a hump, it'd deflated like a punctured balloon. His complexion was clear and smooth, but decidedly more bluish than when she'd seen him go into the Vacu-Pro office.

She dropped to her knees and grasped his shoulders. "I'm real sorry I thought you were a sex fiend, Mr. Dentha. If I'd known it was you, you can bet the farm I wouldn't have hit you with the skillet." She shook him so roughly that his head flopped against the floor. The sound was disturbingly hollow. "Wouldn't you like to rest in the recliner until you feel up to snuff, Mr. Dentha? How about an ice bag for that lump on your head?"

The brown eyes remained blank and her offers of hospitality went unheeded.

Dahlia scooted away from him and leaned against the dresser, praying for one little blink, one twitch of a finger, one wheeze of breath. If anything, his face was as round and bland as a blueberry. And she, Dahlia (nee O'Neill) Buchanon had murdered him in her own home. The weapon lay beside him. It had come right out of her kitchen. Hers were the only fingerprints on it.

Why had Mr. Dentha come to the house? There wasn't much use asking him, she thought as she let her head fall back against a drawer and squeezed her eyes closed so she wouldn't have to look at his face. The answer was obvious. He'd come to beg Kevin to take back his job. Why'd he done that? Because she'd taken it upon herself to call the office and request a demonstration by their best vacuum cleaner salesman. She'd made it clear none of the others was half as good as Kevin, and Mr. Dentha had realized it.

She sniffled as she imagined Arly standing in the doorway, scowling down at the scene and barking out questions. Had he threatened her? Had he attempted to tie her to the bedposts with his fancy silk handkerchief? Had he laid so much as his pinkie on her? Or had she beaned him without giving him a chance to explain who he was and why he was there? Beaned him hard enough to kill him?

Her sparse knowledge of women's prisons came from black-and-white movies, but she figured even in this Technicolor day and age they weren't any less brutal than sleep-over church camps. But what else could she expect after killing Mr. Dentha in cold blood? Her throat seized up and she shuddered in horror at the idea of chain gangs and blazing cotton fields and being chased through the swamps by bloodhounds and sadistic guards with whips.

"Mr. Dentha," she wailed, "I sure am sorry I murdered you. Now I'm even sorrier about what I got no choice but to do."

Chapter Eleven

"**C**ock-a-doodle-doo!" crowed the rooster on the fence post behind Raz's shack. Onomatopoeically speaking, the sound was more like that of a balky outboard motor than the traditional storybook simplification of easily pronounceable phonemes, but it had been one helluva night in Maggody and nobody was in the mood to be picky. As familiar as the sound was (the sun came up on a daily basis in Maggody), it went over real poorly that morning.

★

Grumbling, Raz burrowed under the limp gray pillow like a wood pussy going after a grub. He and Marjorie had been busy most of the night. A dad-burned queer business it had proved to be, mebbe as queer as the time his uncle Melki Buchanon had shanghaied a wagonful of folks from a traveling freak show and locked 'em in his barn. Raz still got choked up ever' time he remembered the bearded lady.

Now the scrawny excuse for a rooster was carryin' on like he'd discovered the sun. On a pallet in the corner, Marjorie snuffled uneasily and her legs twitched as she dreamed of shady, sylvan trails that led to caches of tasty acorns. To Raz's relief, she quieted down; she was in a real ornery mood these days and needed her rest.

★

Dahlia yanked the blankets over her head and tried to go back to sleep. She'd been tormented by gawdawful nightmares ever since she got home and fell into bed just as Elvis pointed both arms at the twelve. She sat up partway and looked groggily through the doorway. Kevvie was sleeping like a baby on the recliner, but why shouldn't he? He hadn't murdered anybody in cold blood.

★

Ruby Bee wiggled around until the plastic curler stopped cutting into her ear. She'd been so tired she couldn't see straight after she shooed out the last customers, and she'd wasted no time getting ready for bed. Once her face was covered with moisturizer and her blistered hands dotted with medicine and tucked into cotton gloves, she'd fluffed her pillow, folded the bedspread at the foot of the bed, and checked to make sure the alarm clock was set. This was the exact moment when the boys in the units across the lot started up a raucous jam session that lasted long past the time when the moon dropped behind the ridge. If she owned a shotgun, they'd have been able to piss in sixteen different directions at the same time.

★

Brother Verber opened one eye and peered at the clock, then scooted toward the foot of the bed until only the top of his head was visible. One of the perks of his job was that hardly ever did a sinner come a-knockin' at his door before noon. This was only fitting since he toiled on Sundays and all your major holidays. Didn't he lead a prayer service every Fourth of July, with the choir holding sparklers as they sang "The Battle Hymn of the Republic" and the entire congregation sharing a spiritual climax when he shot off roman candles from the pulpit?

And he didn't punch a time clock at five o'clock, either. He was on duty in the evenings, like the previous one when he'd put on his best bib and tucker and gone to Sister Barbara's house. What a disaster it had turned into when Sister Barbara went upstairs to fetch the Nashville folks. In less than a minute she stormed back into the room, so sputtery with distress that Jim Bob had made her take a sip of cooking sherry. It seemed Ripley Keswick was flat-out gone, and to add to the insult (it was her grandmother's recipe for potato salad), Katie Hawk was singing inside the guest room—but she refused to unlock the door!

Sister Barbara blamed it on him and Jim Bob in a roundabout way that was a mite hard to follow. Eventually, Brother Verber had been allowed to slink away like a whipped puppy, his stomach sour and rumbly on account of its emptiness. Back at the rectory, he'd had no choice but to slap together a peanut butter and jelly sandwich—a poor substitute for the promised picnic feast—and take to the sofa with it and a bottle of sacramental wine to soothe his wounded soul. Now it was his head that was wounded.

★

Heather Riley bolted upright, rubbed her gritty eyes, and snatched up the clock. She had exactly two hours and forty-seven minutes until her personal interview with Matt Montana. As the student editor of the *Marauder Battle Cry*, she'd naturally assigned herself to do the interview, even after Traci had called her a selfish bitch.

She dashed into the bathroom to make sure her face hadn't broken out during the night, turned on the hot water in the shower, and went back to her bedroom to reconsider what to wear. At midnight she'd settled on a black miniskirt and a mostly transparent blouse, but she took another look at her brand-new jeans (so tight she had to lie on her back to wiggle into 'em).

With two hours and thirty-seven minutes left, Heather grabbed her robe and returned to the bathroom. The door was locked, and from inside she could hear her geeky brother singing.

"You git your butt out of there this minute!" she yelled through the keyhole.

"If you ever get out of the fast lane," sang Byron "The Ripper" Riley, the coolest dude in the whole eighth grade, "and get back on that highway above, I'll be waitin' for you at the tollbooth, in that land where all roads lead to looooove."

Heather rattled the doorknob, then started pounding with both fists. "You little asshole!"

The Ripper put his heart into a version of the chorus that he'd written in her honor. "My sister's got the morals of a hooker, she's screwing in the back seat of sin, she's got to get rid of his hard-on, and that big hairy wart on her chiiiiiin." The Ripper bowed modestly as the audience broke into uproarious laughter and applause.

"Ma . . . !" Heather howled as she ran downstairs.

★

Eilene sat at the breakfast table with a cup of coffee grown cold, her eyelids puffy from bouts of tears, her mouth drawn down in a frown that alternated between irritation and puzzlement.

An hour or so after Dahlia'd left the night before, Eilene called to make sure she'd gotten home safe and sound. The telephone rang twenty times. An hour later, she'd listened in growing dread as it rang twice that many times. Earl, who was as useless as a one-horned cow, said Dahlia was asleep and then went upstairs and was snoring before his head hit the pillow.

After a third futile call, Eilene pulled her coat over her robe, took the keys to Earl's truck (it was blocking her car), and drove past their house. The Matt-Mobile was parked beside the house, and Kevin's car sat in the driveway. The light above the kitchen sink was on, but Dahlia usually left it on in case she felt the need of a midnight snack.

It was way too late for a visit, even one motivated by nothing less pure than genuine maternal concern. Eilene had no choice but to drive home and force herself to go to bed, closing her ears to the glottal eruptions from her spouse but not her eyes, which searched the ceiling until a gray light invaded the room.

Now it was too early to call. In an hour, she told herself as she poured a fresh cup of coffee and went to the living room to stare at the empty road. She'd make up some excuse, maybe invite them for Sunday dinner or ask when Kevin had time to help his pa clean the gutters before they had another storm. She returned to the kitchen and paused in front of the window. What was it folks always said? Red sky in the morning, sailors take warning. Over toward Boone Creek, the clouds were crimson.

★

On the opposite side of Finger Lane, Mrs. Jim Bob went into the utility room and rapped sharply on the dryer. "You need to get up," she said, "and get showered and shaved before our guests need to use the bathroom. Make sure you go easy on the hot water, too. Then you need to run down to the SuperSaver for a can of Crisco and a jar of orange marmalade. Get the imported kind."

Jim Bob willed his teeth to stop chattering long enough to say, "What time is it?"

"Time to get up and be about your business. The Mayor's Mansion guarantees a full breakfast, and I can't start the biscuits until I have Crisco."

"All night long I could feel the wind whistling in through the hole for the dryer vent," he whimpered, trying to cover his numb feet with the moth-eaten army blanket. "The window might as well not be there. Look at it for yourself—it's covered with ice on the inside."

"I don't have time to look at windows. I don't know what time our guests plan to come down for breakfast, but Matt and Miss Hawk have interviews at nine o'clock. If no one is down by seven-thirty, I'm going to knock on their doors and make it clear that I am not a short-order cook." She left him whining and scratching and went back to the kitchen.

The schedule was on the table. Mrs. Jim Bob put on the teakettle, took the necessary paraphernalia from a cabinet, and then sat down to reread the day's activities. At nine o'clock, Matt Montana and Miss Katie Hawk would be at the high school for interviews with the press. No problem there. At ten o'clock sharp, Dahlia would arrive with the Maggody-Matt-Mobile, and Matt and Katie would be carted down County 102 to the Boyhood Home. Tourists would be allowed to line the road and take photographs to their hearts' content and then come into the yard to photograph Matt posing on the porch or playing his guitar while he sat on the swing.

Mrs. Jim Bob poured boiling water into her cup while she tried to think of a way to charge the tourists for the opportunity to take Matt's picture, since they'd lose the afternoon's revenue from the guided tours.

In any case, at eleven o'clock the crowd would have to move off the property, and the Nashville folks would get down to the serious business of taking publicity shots. This was when they wanted Adele in her rocking chair by the fireplace, bright-eyed children to trim the tree, boxes to be wrapped in the shiny paper, and gingerbread cookies to be decorated at the battered white kitchen table (which had graced Eula Lemoy's kitchen for twenty-seven years). Most of it was already in place. The ten-foot tree was positioned in front of one of the living room windows, and mistletoe drooped above every doorway. The mantel was festooned with fresh pine branches and sprigs of holly. Everybody on the committee had dragged out their Christmas cartons, and each tabletop in the Wockermann house had been assigned a chubby ceramic Santa, red and green candles, a wooden crèche scene, or other hastily appropriated family treasures. In one of the unused rooms upstairs, they'd stored rolls of foil wrapping paper, tape and scissors, ribbons and bows, strings of lights, and a stack of boxes filled with fragile Christmas ornaments.

Adele Wockermann was the one thing not in place, or in any place they knew of. It couldn't be helped, especially so late in the game. There was no doubt in Mrs. Jim Bob's mind that they were taking a big risk and that her neck was stretched out the farthest on the chopping block, but she'd never allowed indecisiveness to influence her actions.

" 'No man, having put his hand to the plow, and looking back, is fit for the Kingdom of God,' " she said firmly as she went upstairs and paused outside the bathroom door.

Intermingled with the gush of water in the shower, she heard Jim Bob singing cheerfully. His words were muffled, but she could make out most of it. "You're jest my sweet angel"—gurgle, gurgle—"on the top of my tree, we'll"—gurgle, gurgle—"Christmas for eternity."

She opened the door and stuck her head into the steam. "Stop wasting all the hot water," she said, then closed the door and went slowly downstairs to the kitchen, wondering what had gotten into him. Jim Bob wasn't one to pay much attention to Christmas. For the last eleven years, he'd given her a box of candy, a gallon bottle of scented bath oil, and a card announcing that he'd renewed her subscription to *Reader's Digest*.

★

Nobody else of any importance was disturbed by the rooster. The boys in the motel rooms, two still in their boots and vests, one in stained long johns, and the last as naked as the day he was born, remained steadfastly unconscious. Their collective presence would not be required until after supper, when they were supposed to go to the gym and test the sound equipment. Like most musicians, they were not what you'd call morning people.

Estelle's house was too far away, as was the county rest home. No one at the Pot o' Gold Mobile Home Park heard a peep, nor did campers in the field behind Earl and Eilene's house or Eula Lemoy, who was up anyway, sewing sequins on a stocking for the boutique. Heather Riley's mother, as implied previously, was in the kitchen fixing breakfast.

Elsie McMay slept with earplugs. Lottie Estes, the pianist at the Assembly Hall since 1977, had been up for an hour, trying to decide what to wear when the Nashville folks came to take photographs. Jimson Pickerell stirred, reached blindly for his wife's rump, and was elbowed in the face for his trouble.

As for the rest of the Nashville folks, the curtains on the windows at the back of the bus were drawn tightly; there's no point in speculating on what was going on inside. The two guest bedrooms at The Mayor's Mansion were locked, and even though Mrs. Jim Bob had pressed her ear to the doors, she couldn't hear anything.

★

At eight o'clock, I polished off a cup of coffee and the last bite of a doughnut, brushed the crumbs off my uniform, and drove to the high school to do what I could to get everybody through the day without undue bloodshed. The schedule had not been distributed to the tourists, but at least one enterprising high school boy had been selling photocopies at the pool hall—excuse me, Matt's Billiard Parlor and Family Entertainment Center—and I'd heard the clerks at the souvenir shoppe had some under the counter. Maggody's first black market, so to speak.

I parked next to a truck that most likely belonged to Larry Joe Lambertino, who taught shop and augmented his salary by moonlighting as the janitor, and went inside to do a spot of reconnoitering before the media descended.

Larry Joe was pushing a broom between the music stands in the band room. It was not too far from the gym and was equipped with two small soundproofed practice rooms that were designated to serve as dressing rooms for the stars. Brown paper squares with hand-drawn stars were taped across the viewing windows to provide privacy.

"Morning, Larry Joe. You ready for the big concert?" I asked from the doorway.

His shoulders slumped, and the broom looked as if it were the only thing holding him up. "Yeah, the gym's as clean as it's gonna get after last night's game. The signs say no food or drinks, but the little pissants sneak 'em in anyway. The floor underneath the bleachers is so sticky that it almost pulls your shoes off when you walk on it."

He agreed to make sure all the entrances except the main one were locked so I could monitor the influx of reporters and interviewers with cameras and recorders and then to stand guard outside the gym in case some wily fan slid through a window or crawled up a duct.

I wandered around until I located most of my old classrooms, flipped through magazines in the library, and at eight-thirty checked my lipstick in a rest room and took my position at the main entrance. Vans emblazoned with the logos of area television stations were pulling up in the lot, and a couple of men struggled to disengage elaborate recording equipment from a station wagon. I recognized a reporter from the *Starley City Examiner* and another from the *Farberville Times*. An elderly man with the oversized teeth and chubby cheeks of a groundhog produced credentials from the *Arkansas Democrat-Gazette* in Little Rock. Heather Riley bounced up the steps and managed to stutter that she represented the high school paper. I wasn't sure whether she was in the throes of excitement or unable to breathe because of her skin-tight jeans. I checked each name on my media list and gave directions to the gym.

Fans gathered out on the road, dressed in Matt T-shirts, Matt sweatshirts, and Matt caps, adoration on their faces and video cameras on their shoulders. At exactly nine o'clock, Matt and Katie arrived in the back seat of Mrs. Jim Bob's car. Ripley Keswick, who'd been riding shotgun, nodded at me as he gave his stars a moment to wave at the crowd, then hustled them through the doorway. Mrs. Jim Bob scowled at their backs and then at me before she drove away.

A few minutes later, the Maggody-Matt-Mobile came rolling down the road and turned into the parking lot. Dahlia cut off the engine, pushed her cowboy hat back, and gave me a look that seemed oddly fearful. Me, for pity's sake.

Smiling brightly, I said, "Everybody's still inside, but they're scheduled to be out here in about forty-five minutes. Do you have enough gas in that contraption to haul them all the way out County 102?"

She recoiled as though I'd spat at her. "Why wouldn't I? It ain't but half a mile, you know. Did somebody call you this morning?"

"Ruby Bee called to make sure I was awake, as did Estelle; they're holding down the fort at the Boyhood Home. Sheriff Dorfer called to assure me that I'd have additional security at the concert tomorrow night. Hammet's foster mother called to say she wouldn't mind if he stayed with me until after Christmas. A woman named Bethann called to tell me that I could protect my home with aluminum siding at a special low price. I'm sure other people tried to get through, but the line was busy until I left to come here."

"Is that all?" she demanded. "Nobody else from, say, Farberville?"

I shook my head. "Anybody in particular who you

think should be calling me?'' She looked away, but not before I saw her eyes brim with tears and her face redden. Getting more baffled by the minute, I said, ''Does this have anything to do with Kevin's purported dalliance? Did you hire a private detective, Dahlia?''

''Dint hire nobody,'' she said sullenly.

Mrs. Jim Bob's car squealed around the corner. Fans scattered as she plowed through the crowd, floored it across the parking lot, and narrowly avoided the Matt-Mobile. Ignoring Dahlia's squeal of terror, she rolled down the window and said, ''Someone broke into the souvenir shoppe! The lock on the back door is busted.''

''Did you go inside?'' I asked, just as though I didn't already know the answer.

''I took the tire iron from my trunk and marched right in to show this burglar a thing or two, but he was gone. I don't leave any money in the cash register overnight. Darla Jean and I looked over the merchandise, and neither one of us is sure that anything is missing. Darla Jean thinks maybe one of the ashtrays was taken, but we had a big crowd yesterday afternoon, and some of those children behaved like thievin' gypsies—even with their parents standing two feet away.''

''As soon as the celebrities have moved on to the next item on the agenda, I'll come have a look at the lock. I don't suppose your burglar left footprints, did he?''

''I told Darla Jean to mop the floor so we'd be ready to open at ten sharp,'' Mrs. Jim Bob said with a flicker of guilt. ''Not that you could have learned much, anyway. Maybe I should have telephoned the sheriff's department and had him send over some trained investigators. Can't hurt to call him.'' She rolled the window back up and drove away at a more decorous speed.

Dahlia pulled her hat down and refused to answer any more of my questions, although I could tell she was disturbed by something. The fans shifted nervously, and I spent the next half hour attempting to look intimidating despite the fact that I'd forgotten to bring a bullet.

Ripley came out first, surveyed the crowd, and put his hand on my shoulder. ''You've done an admirable job keeping the carnivores at a civilized distance. Matt's just about finished, and Katie stopped to powder her nose. Matt is looking forward to seeing Auntie Adele after all these years. I hope she's enjoying good health.''

"Me, too," I said. Whatever was to take place at the Boyhood Home was between him and the Homecoming Committee, and I wasn't about to be drawn into it.

The door opened and Matt Montana came out to the top step. "Sure was fun to meet all those folks and talk about the good ol' days here in Maggody," he called to his fans. "I'd about forgotten about the summer I tried to catch this granddaddy of a catfish down in the creek. That fish outsmarted me, and to this day, whenever my head starts getting swelled up, I remind myself I ain't the wiliest of God's creatures."

"How perceptive," Ripley murmured. "Where's Katie?"

Matt continued to address the crowd. "Miss Katie Hawk's looking forward to saying howdy to all you loyal fans, but you know how wimmen can be when it comes to fixin' their hair and making sure their petticoats don't peek out below their skirts. My ma used to tell me how she was late to her own wedding because she was upstairs painting her toenails pink! Finally the preacher had to go beg her to come on down the aisle before the flowers wilted and the organist got worn out and went home."

This was received with thunderous laughter, and the cameras were clicking like a plague of locusts. Even Dahlia was beaming at him as if he were the reincarnation of Will Rogers, which I can assure you he was not. Katie Hawk came out and joined him. Her wave was less enthusiastic, as was her smile, but the two of them were presenting exactly what the crowd wanted: Ken and Barbie in cowboy drag.

The media people came out and hurried to their vehicles. Matt held out his hand to Katie and chivalrously helped her into the back of the Matt-Mobile, then tipped his hat to his fans and bounded in beside her. I told Dahlia to follow my car, then suggested to Ripley that he ride with me.

We moved slowly out of the lot and down the road to the highway. I was embarrassed by the waves of screaming fans, but all I could do was clench the steering wheel and focus on getting us there in one piece. Moving at the speed of lame turtles, we turned onto the highway and almost immediately onto County 102. The bodies were packed every inch of the way, their eyes too wide for my taste, their vocal cords suffering mightily.

"There's the house," I said with a heartfelt sigh. "The high school kids are guarding the driveway. I'll park on the grass so Dahlia can stay on the gravel and everyone will have a wonderful view of Matt as he takes his first step onto the lawn of his official Boyhood Home. The first astronaut on the moon should have gotten this amount of coverage." A roar of confusion from the crowd caught my attention, and I twisted around to stare out the back window.

The Matt-Mobile chugged past the driveway. Matt and Katie were frowning at each other, clearly bewildered at this sudden change in the itinerary. Dahlia, however, looked like she was ferrying passengers across the river Styx as she drove on toward the low-water bridge.

Chapter Twelve

"Is she kidnapping them in broad daylight and in front of several hundred witnesses?" Ripley asked as we watched waves of fans fall in behind the wagon. "Or is this some sort of Pied Piper routine to lure all these people to certain death in that muddy little creek?"

It was not the time to explain that Dahlia's motives were rarely discernible. "If I had the foggiest idea, you'd be the first to hear it, Ripley," I muttered.

"What on earth is going on?" Ruby Bee shouted from the porch. She was wearing her best beige dress and, for the first time since Dahlia and Kevin's wedding, a hat.

"This ain't on the schedule!" added Estelle, also gussied up and with a hairdo that could have served for a centerpiece at a luncheon. A half-dozen little kids jostled behind one of the living room windows, and an equal number of teenagers in jeans and official guide T-shirts took off across the yard. The media people were trotting down the road in pursuit of whatever melodramatic turn of events was unfolding. One woman with a microphone tersely described "the hostage situation," while her assistant stumbled backward and kept the camera aimed at her face.

"I don't know!" I said as I headed across the pasture in an attempt to cut them off by the old chicken houses before they reached the bridge. Metallic gray clouds were moving into the valley; the filtered light gave the landscape an eerie, one-dimensional appearance. All we needed was for Rod Serling to pop out from a woodchuck burrow to capture the scene in his mildly apocalyptic voice: "Picture, if you will . . ."

I battled through the branches of a scruffy pine and lost

my balance as I encountered a well-concealed irrigation ditch. I clambered up the far side, leapt over a perfidious tangle of barbed wire, and arrived at the charred remains of the first chicken house at the same moment Dahlia pulled into the flat expanse in front of it and cut off the engine.

The resultant silence was unsettling, to say the least. In the wagon, Matt and Katie were motionless, too alarmed to even look at their driver. The fans waited in the road, tensed to fling themselves into the ditches if gunfire broke out. After a moment, the media people looked at me for some sort of cue. I listened to my lungs heave as if I'd finished a marathon in record time. And Dahlia Buchanon sat like a statue on the seat of the tractor, her eyes shut and her mouth puckered so tightly I wasn't sure she'd ever get it open again.

Before any of us could produce the obvious question, the door of the undamaged chicken house banged open, and out marched Raz Buchanon, a shotgun cradled in his arm.

"Git off my property afore I pepper ever' one of you trespassers with buckshot," he said, then frowned as he took in the rather formidable number of trespassers (we're talking more than two hundred within buckshot range), spat into the dust, and aimed his shotgun at Dahlia. "I reckon to count to ten, and if that contraption's still on my property, you kin bend over and kiss yer ass good-bye!"

I was sure this situation had been covered somewhere in my police training manual, but the precise paragraph escaped me. "Now listen here, Raz," I said, "you can't—" I broke off as I heard Dahlia's voice.

"You might as well," she said. "Dying now ain't no worse than wasting away in prison. I murdered a man in cold blood, and I deserve to be punished."

"Ye did what?" demanded Raz. The barrel of the shotgun wavered and tobacco juice dribbled out of the corner of his mouth as he studied her with a dumbfounded expression. "Ye murdered some feller?"

She held out her arms in preparation to be executed, if not crucified. "You heard me the first time, Raz Buchanon. I wrasseled with my conscience all night, but there's no getting around the truth. He's deader 'n a doornail—and I did it.''

"Wait just a minute," I said, surely as perplexed as Raz, if not more so. Tobacco juice did not dribble out of the corner of my mouth, however, and the only thing I aimed at her was my trembling finger. "Who's deader 'n a doornail, Dahlia?''

The self-proclaimed murderess covered her face with her hands and began to sob. The fans moved in closer and the media people surreptitiously raised their cameras and positioned their microphones in hopes of a real bang-up of a segment for the six o'clock news. Matt grabbed Katie's hand, and the two hopped out of the wagon and took refuge behind a stout couple in matching plaid slacks and windbreakers. Raz lowered his gun and gestured for Marjorie, who'd been hovering in the doorway, to come out. She glowered from the shadows. At least one camera shifted in her direction, thus ensuring our absolute and total humiliation at the hands of smirky, narcissistic newscasters.

"Dahlia," I said, "are you sure about this?"

Tears dribbled down her cheeks and her voice was so ragged that I could barely understand her. "I took a skillet and murdered him. I did it in my bedroom, but I was too scared to leave the body lying there on the braided rug, so I brought him down here. I don't know why I did that, except I was thinking nobody'd find him for a while and that'd give me a chance to figure out what to do."

"When did this take place?" I asked . . . and on what planet?

"Long about nine last night. I sat for mebbe an hour, but his eyes kept looking at me and I finally just zipped him up in Kevvie's sleeping bag, put him in the wagon, and drove out here. I stuck him in there so"—she gulped and grimaced—"the animals wouldn't bother him."

I turned to Raz. "Is there a body in a sleeping bag in there?"

"Ain't nuthin' in there," he muttered. "And don't you go poking yer nose in there, neither. I bought this piece off Adele Wockermann two years back and I got a deed to prove it. You jest tell ever'body to get their butts off'n my private property."

I tried to ignore the hum of the cameras. "Raz, if you don't shut up, I'm going to take that shotgun out of your sorry hands and tie it around your neck."

Raz looked back at Marjorie for help, but she lumbered away. "G'wan," he said grudgingly.

I heard a patter of applause as I stomped past him to the door, shoved it opened, and stepped over the threshold. I was sneezing when I reappeared. "There's nothing in there," I announced, "except petrified chickenshit and the rotted remains of a red flannel shirt."

"No body?" yelled one of the reporters.

I shrugged eloquently for the camera's benefit (and for Harve's amusement when he caught the news). "No body that I saw, no bloodstains, and no fresh graves. As Raz said earlier, this is private property, so we all need to go back up the road to the Wockermann house and let Matt pose for the photographers." I looked at Dahlia and lowered my voice to a snarl. "Drive this damn thing back and park it where you were supposed to park it twenty minutes ago. After you do that, I'd like to have a word with you in private."

Raz's renewed threats helped hurry everybody along. The celebrities came out of hiding, hopped back on the wagon, and after a moment, I decided to sit on the end of it in order to fend off the overly enthusiastic members of the infantry. The woman who'd been describing the "hostage situation" made a face at me as if I'd personally destroyed her chances for a slot on the network news team, but most of the fans seemed more interested in getting back to the business of idolization. We chugged up the road and into the driveway. Ripley swooped in to escort Matt and Katie onto the porch, then stationed himself as a buffer on the bottom step as the crowd surged forward to take photographs and beg for autographs.

I waited in the side yard until Dahlia joined me. "Okay," I said angrily, "what was all that?"

"I thought about it on the way back here, and now it's clear. I beaned Mr. Dentha hard enough to knock him out for a long spell, but I must not have killed him. He woke up in the chicken house, wiggled out of the sleeping bag, and staggered to his car and drove home. I ain't saying he didn't look and act like he was dead, but the only dead person I ever saw was a ninety-seven-year-old cousin who had such rubbery skin that she didn't look any worse in her coffin than she did in her bed. Granny thought she looked a sight better.''

''Exactly how dead did he look?''

She put her hands behind her back and gazed guilelessly over my head. ''Well, come to think of it, not more than half-dead, and he might well have been playing possum the whole time. He was probably so mad on account of the way I beaned him with the skillet that he wanted to teach me a lesson by letting me think I'd killed him.'' She gave me a blessedly terse version of her previous night's thought processes (they would not play in Peoria) and subsequent actions (*ibidem*), culminating with her drive down moonlit County 102 and the deposition of the contents of the sleeping bag/shroud. I regret to say it all made perfectly good sense, which was a grim reminder that I'd been in Maggody way too long.

''Jesus H, Dahlia,'' I said, shaking my head, ''I don't know what to do. If you're positive this prowler was Mr. Dentha from the Vacu-Pro office, maybe you'd better wait here until I call and make sure he got back safely to Farberville.'' Or if he ever left, I added to myself as I went to find Ripley and take a shot at explaining the incomprehensible before I found a telephone.

He was on the porch. He ostentatiously consulted his watch, slapped Matt on the back, and said, ''Sorry, folks, but Matt's great-aunt is inside waiting to see him after all these years. He sure does love letting y'all take his picture, but he doesn't want to keep that sweet old lady waiting any longer.''

Matt grinned apologetically and went inside, and after a moment, Katie Hawk rose from the porch swing, waved at the fans, and followed him. I was burning with curiosity to find out how the committee had handled the Adele Predicament, but I did as dictated in memo number seven thou-

sand or so and spent the next ten minutes shooing fans off
the lawn and arguing with the press. Photographers from
two magazines had been selected to immortalize the cozy
family reunion, which did not sit well with their competi-
tors. I was nearly hoarse when I finally got everybody on
the road and went into the Boyhood Home, noting for the
first time a brass plaque beside the door that proclaimed as
much.

Ruby Bee and Estelle were in the hallway, their hands
clasped as if they were praying (and I could think of reasons why they should be). The children had been hushed,
and stood in formation at the edge of the living room. Ripley noticed me and touched a fingertip to his lips. The photographers were not visible from my perspective, but I
could hear shutters clicking and film advancing in a soft
bombilation. I tiptoed to the doorway and peered over the
local cherubim's heads.

Matt Montana knelt beside the rocking chair, his hat in
his hand and face tilted toward the white-haired woman in
a shawl. "And do you recollect when I picked all those
huckleberries and you made me a pie?" he asked with a
dimply grin.

"'Course I do, Matt. But when you were down by the
creek, you got into a patch of them little seed ticks. Lord
a-mercy, I must have used a whole bar of lye soap tryin'
to scrub 'em off your hide."

"How about when Uncle Jesse took out that old banjo
that his pa had given him, and by suppertime I could play
all the way through 'Wabash Cannonball'? He got his fid-
dle, and we sat on the porch and played up a storm till you
made us go to bed. Remember that, Auntie Adele?"

"How could I forget? The whole time I sat in this room,
in this very same chair if I recollect rightly, tapping my
foot and thinking about when Mr. Wockermann came
a-courtin' with that same banjo."

Matt smiled at her, but he adjusted his profile for the
benefit of the photographers. "I brought that old banjo with
me, and I may just see if I can wheedle it into tune at the
concert tomorrow night and play 'Wabash Cannonball' specially for you, Auntie Adele."

"Why, Matt, I cain't think of a single thing that'd make me happier."

Vaguely nauseous, I headed for the front door, mutely snagging Ruby Bee by the arm on my way. Once we were on the porch, I whispered, "Who the hell is that?"

"Why, Miss Detective, I'd think you might recognize Matt Montana. He's wearing his signature white—"

"In the rocking chair."

She had the grace to look just a bit uncomfortable, although I doubted anything I said would do away completely with her air of complacency. "Matt's great-aunt. Isn't it touching how they're able to share all those—"

"In the rocking chair!" This time I admit I snarled the words at my own mother. "Who is it?"

"Since you were unable to find one feeble old lady, we had to ask another resident at the county home to fill in for a day or two. We were all opposed to the deception, but Mrs. Jim Bob kept saying that we'd given our solemn promise that Adele would be here and we had no right to disappoint folks and ruin their visit to Maggody." In response to my glare, she sat down on the edge of the porch swing. "It's Dahlia's granny, if you must know. I'm a little surprised that you didn't recognize her, since—"

"There you are," said Estelle as she came out the door and sat down next to Ruby Bee. After they'd hissed at each other, Estelle rose and deigned to notice me. "You should have put on a fresh shirt this morning, Arly. That one's all stained with sweat and I do believe it's missing a button. I'm too busy to fix it now, but you bring it by next week and I'll see if I have a spare button in my sewing box." She hurried down the steps before I could concoct a scathing comeback.

Ruby Bee stood up and attempted to sidle around me. "I got to get back inside now. Ripley said he might want me to be a cousin when it comes time to trim the tree."

I cut her off in front of the door. "Why'd Estelle rush off like that?"

"She has to get some snow," Ruby Bee said over her shoulder as she went inside.

I stood there and battled against the omnipresent forces

of terminal insanity. The corpse in the chicken house had
come to life and driven home. Dahlia's granny was Adele
Wockermann. Estelle Oppers had gone to get snow. Was
she getting it out of her freezer, or did she have to drive to
the handiest outlet of Flakes 'R Us?

I remembered that Dahlia was waiting for me to call
the Vacu-Pro office. The nearest available telephone was at
The Official Matt Montana Souvenir Shoppe, and I needed
to go there in any case to deal with the alleged break-in. It
was challenging to imagine someone so desperate for a
Matt Map that he would commit a felony, but I was clearly
in the early stages of *non compos mentis*.

Dahlia was in the middle of the road, being interviewed
by the press. She appeared to be enjoying the attention, and
I had no way to intervene short of dragging her behind the
house to lock her in a shed. Wondering how Eilene and
Earl would react when they heard about their son's infidelity on the evening news, I turned my car around in the
side yard, nudged gawkers out of the way, and drove up to
the main road.

Free parking was at a premium these days, but I figured
I probably wouldn't give myself a ticket for blocking the
lot behind what had been a run-of-the-mill New Age hardware store back in the good ol' days. The lock on the back
door was broken, and the wood around it splintered from
repeated assaults with a crowbar or similar tool. I went
through a storeroom piled high with unopened cartons of
Matt memorabilia, pushed aside the curtain that had replaced strands of beads, and came into the main room. It
no longer smelled of incense and exotic herbal concoctions;
now the primary redolence was of cold, hard cash, and
based on the size of the browsing crowd and the shoving
at the cash register, plenty of it.

Mrs. Jim Bob rang up a sale, stuffed T-shirts and a
receipt in a bag, and expressed her gratitude with a tight
smile. "There you are," she said as she noticed me. "I was
beginning to wonder when you'd find time to investigate a
crime committed under your very nose."

"Not my nose," I said more loudly than necessary to
be heard over the taped Montana music. "My nose was

asleep last night. It's exhausted from sniffing at the trail left by Adele Wockermann when she disappeared three weeks ago.''

She told Darla Jean to take over the cash register, then hustled me into the back room as if I'd asked the price— or the flavors—of official Matt Montana condoms. ''If you'd conducted a proper investigation and found her, we wouldn't be in this pickle,'' she whispered. ''You're hardly the one to get all high and mighty about a simple substitution. I should have brought in the state police in the first place, instead of listening to the likes of Ruby Bee and Estelle. Right from the start I told Jim Bob you couldn't find a flea on a dog, and—''

''Did you pay her or what?''

Mrs. Jim Bob's tirade had been perfunctory, and she let it drop. ''A certain sum was mentioned. Then that nosy Twayblade woman started carping about how it interfered with the schedule and how she might have to complain to the health department, so we ended up obliged to pay her off, too. It smells of blackmail, if you ask me.''

''I'll be happy to file charges. Let me consult the county prosecutor and get back to you as soon as possible. Elections are coming up in a year, and he'd love the chance for all the publicity. I'll bet he can arrange for television cameras right there in the courtroom, and you and all the other Homecoming Committee members who will have to testify can—''

''Never mind,'' she said. ''I am a good Christian and I see no need to cause the woman to lose her job. Now, what are you gonna do about this disgraceful break-in?''

''You've already disposed of any footprints, but I can take fingerprints on the doorknob, presuming no one has touched it.''

''How was I supposed to open the door without touching the doorknob? I am not a magician, missy.'' She realized I was not impressed with her reasoning and waggled a finger at me. ''And don't be giving me that supercilious look because Darla Jean mopped the floor. Today's likely to be our busiest to date, what with Matt in town and the concert tomorrow.''

I muttered something about tracking down possible witnesses, then asked to use the telephone. We had an argument, in that I needed to make a long-distance call, but I made it clear I was going to persist until she relented. The lure of the cash register was too much for her, and after a starchy comment to keep it short, she went through the curtain.

I called information for the number of the Vacu-Pro office, then dialed the number. When a female voice answered, I asked to speak to Mr. Dentha.

She hesitated, then said, "Who is this?"

"Someone who'd like to speak to Mr. Dentha. Is he there?"

"It's against company policy to put through callers who refuse to identify themselves."

"This is"—I cast around for a name that captured the surreality of the morning—"Ms. Hieronymous Bosch, and I own a house on Beaver Lake with over seven thousand square feet of wall-to-wall carpet. I was told to deal directly with Dentha if I decide to purchase the deluxe Vacu-Pro system, but if you're not—"

"He's out of town, Ms. Bosch," she cut in smoothly, "but he will be delighted to demonstrate the system and all its attachments in person when he returns. If I could have your telephone number . . . ?"

Ms. Bosch was not in the mood to dillydally. "Where did he go and when will he be back?"

"He went to Little Rock yesterday for a sales meeting. He wasn't sure when he'll be back in Farberville, but I fully expect him in the office bright and early Monday morning. Now, if I could just have your home address and telephone number, Ms. Bosch?"

"Do you have a number for him in Little Rock?"

"I cannot give out that information, but I can pass along a message when he checks in with me."

I was making very little progress, but it didn't seem tactful to inquire if Mr. Dentha's sales conference included a short service at a cemetery. "Has he called in for messages since he left?"

"Let me think," she said, breathing more heavily than

one normally associated with cerebration. "Yes, he did, about an hour ago. He said he had seminars the rest of the day and the awards banquet tonight, so I don't expect to hear from him again until tomorrow morning."

"How did he sound?" I asked, despite the sheer inanity of the question. Did I expect her to say he sounded quite chipper for a corpse?

"Mr. Dentha sounded as though he and the other district managers enjoyed themselves at the bar until quite late last night. Could you explain your concern for his well-being?"

"Not at the moment. I'll call Monday and talk to him in person." I hung up and was examining the broken lock when loud voices erupted from the front room.

"He stinks!" squealed an unfamiliar child. "He stinks like a poopy diaper and I ain't gonna stand by him."

"Hell, lady, he kin pose next to me for a dollar," said a more familiar one. Hammet Buchanon, to be precise.

I pushed aside the curtain. Hammet, dressed in a dazzlingly white cowboy outfit, was leaning ever so casually against a table piled high with coffee mugs and plastic figurines. His hat was tilted rakishly, and he was doing his best to imitate Matt Montana's laid-back grin. He was doing such a disturbingly good job of it that a woman with a camera appeared to be considering his offer. Her child, a pudgy creature who been stuffed into a pale green cowboy suit, was holding his nose and pointing at the mannequin.

Mrs. Jim Bob stepped in front of Hammet, shot the child a withering look, then smiled at his mother. "Our regular price for posing with Matt is five dollars, but I'll make an exception this one time and charge you half-price. We don't want any of Matt's little fans to be unhappy, and I can see he wants to hurry down to the Boyhood Home and see Matt in person."

Hammet stood on his toes and peeked over Mrs. Jim Bob's shoulder. "Only one dollar," he reminded the mother, "and I'll throw in my autograph for nuthin'. I'm going to be on the stage at the concert tomorrow night, so I reckon I should be charging two dollars, mebbe three."

"He stinks, too!" said the brat. "I can smell him across the room."

Hammet's affable grin faded. "And I'll kick his baby green ass for free, all the way to the edge of town and back. How'd you like that, you lil' peckerwood?"

Mrs. Jim Bob raised her hand, saw me, and lowered it real quick. "I will not tolerate that kind of language, Hammet Buchanon. Brother Verber may have told you to meet him here, but you can just go outside and wait there for him to pick you up. While you do that, ponder the sins of profanity and disrespect to your elders."

"Tell that lil' peckerwood to ponder his prick afore I feed it to the turkey buzzards," Hammet countered crossly.

The woman with the camera was stuffing it in her purse with one hand and clutching her son's shoulder with the other. "I am not accustomed to this kind of language, and I'm of a mind to tell my husband about this and let him teach that—that foulmouthed creature a thing or two."

It seemed like time to intervene, alas. I zigzagged through the tables and racks, caught the foulmouthed creature in the middle of a lunge, and squeezed his arm until I had his attention. "Hammet, I think you need to go out back and sit in my car. I'll be there in a minute."

"He don't stink as bad as the dummy," the brat said, now suffused with charity toward his would-be assailant. "'Sides, if you take my picture with him, there's enough money for another ice cream sundae."

"Shit," Hammet said, proving himself equally magnanimous, "you kin do it for free iff'n you buy me a sundae." He wrinkled his nose. "Phew-whee! That dummy shore does stink like an outhouse in August."

Mrs. Jim Bob was steaming, but she got herself under control and said, "There is nothing wrong with the mannequin. You may take the photograph with it at no charge, as long as you take your child out of my store once and for all. I'll pay you a dollar if you'll take this heathen along with you."

I may not have been at my height of perspicacity, but I sensed there was something fishy going on. I released Hammet and approached the mannequin in the front win-

dow. The face was obscured by a cowboy hat and polyester
wig, but even from a distance I could tell the hands were
not plastic. They were tied to the guitar with transparent
string, most likely fishing line, and dotted with freckles,
dark hairs on the upper fingers, and on the left thumb, the
residual whiteness of an old scar.

And it did smell bad. I ordered everyone back, then
knelt down and looked up at the shadowy face. I was prepared for Dahlia's missing victim, so I was startled when I
saw features that brought to mind Ripley Keswick. The
nose was as thin and sharp, the blank, open eyes the same
faded blue. Ripley's complexion was rosier, however, and
I'd left him in good health less than half an hour earlier.

"What's . . . wrong?" gurgled Mrs. Jim Bob.

I stood up and tried to ignore the sour redolence. "Unless you got a hot deal at the morgue, this is not your
mannequin. I don't know who it is. Do you?"

"It's a dead man," the brat squealed, still holding his
nose and prancing around the back of the room. "Mama,
why doncha take my picture with a dead man? The kids at
school will have a cow when I show 'em!"

The woman took out her camera. "Well, go up there
and stand next to him, Bernie Allen. Hurry up, now; we're
supposed to meet your pa for lunch in ten minutes."

The other customers were crowding in, and the smell
was threatening to dislodge the contents of my stomach. If
Estelle had walked in with a box of snow, I would have
buried my head in it. As it was, I ordered everybody out
to the parking lot in front and went to the telephone to call
Harve to report that I'd lost one body—but not to worry,
I'd found another.

Hey, all in a morning's work in the Garden of Earthly
Delights.

Chapter Thirteen

Harve caught a whiff of the corpse and halted in the doorway, his thumb hooked in a belt loop and his lips pulled back to expose tobacco-flecked teeth. "A real ripe one, huh?"

Behind him in the parking lot, the customers had recovered nicely from their eviction and were photographing each other in front of the store. Mrs. Jim Bob paced in a tight circle, snapping at anyone who dared stray into her path. I was responsible for this noticeably un-Christian behavior; she'd wanted to rope off the area around the body and keep selling ashtrays and T-shirts, but I had not been amenable. Darla Jean sat on the top step of the porch and prevented the more adventuresome fans from peering through the window. Hammet was charging two dollars to pose and his pockets were bulging.

"I took a quick look at the body," I said. "There's blood in the left ear and a dark smear visible under the back of the wig, probably from a fractured skull. It looks as if the face was wiped, but there's coagulated blood in the nostrils and a small amount of blood froth around mouth. Lungs punctured by a broken rib, maybe."

"But no blood on the clothes?"

Harve seemed content to conduct his investigation from the doorway, but I was keenly aware of our audience. I curled my finger until he came inside and I could lock the door behind him. I pulled down the shade, but there was no way to block the view through the window. We might as well have been investigating the death of a guppy in the bottom of a well-lit fishbowl.

I moved away from the window. "Not on what he's

wearing now and none that I could find on the floor. Even
if the injuries are the result of an accident, someone brought
him here, dressed him up, and propped him in the window.
Someone with a real macabre sense of humor, that is. We
know the body's been here since Mrs. Jim Bob arrived
shortly after nine and discovered evidence of the break-in.
Neither she nor Darla Jean paid any attention to the mannequin, but once the room warmed up, a kid noticed the
smell.''

"It's getting harder and harder to miss. Any idea of the
time of death?''

"The local forensic pathologist eloped with the local
forensic psychiatrist, Harve. All I could do was confirm the
guy's dead, secure the scene, and call you. I've got my
hands full with the Nashville folks and a town overflowing
with tourists, and I don't have time to take on a homicide
investigation, even with a body.''

"You in the middle of one without a body?'' Despite
strict procedural guidelines to the contrary, he lit a stubby
cigar. I didn't protest, because its stench was preferable to
the one emanating from the body hunched over the guitar.
At the moment of death, the body relinquishes any pretense
of dignity. Now I could only hope neither of us followed
suit.

I related Dahlia's ludicrous story, then pointed out that
Dentha had called his office from Little Rock a couple of
hours ago. "Also,'' I added, "she claimed her victim was
sixty-ish with brown eyes and silver hair. Our friend up
front has blue eyes, dark hair, and he's closer to forty.''

"You check for a wallet?''

"No, Harve, I didn't check for a wallet. I just explained
that this is your baby. I am a one-person department, and
I'm ass-deep in tourists, celebrities, reporters, traffic
jams—''

"Keep your tail in the water. Today's the final day of
deer season, so my absentee rate's sky-high, but the team's
already on the way and the coroner will be here as soon as
he gets the message at his cabin over in Comfrey County.
I don't see any reason why you can't slip that fellow's
wallet out of his pocket so we can have a look through it.''

"This is not my case. Your department has jurisdiction over felonies in towns where the police department lacks resources to handle the investigation. I've already told you—"

"I heard you the first time." Harve ground out his cigar in one of the souvenir ashtrays and brushed ashes off his belly, watching me out of the corner of his eye like a wolf nonchalantly strolling through a flock of sheep.

"I can call in the state police," I bleated.

"They're as shorthanded as I am. Tell ya what let's do, Arly—we'll see if this victim has any identification on him. He may be nothing more exciting than a tourist or a vagrant who had a heart attack, fell over backward, and cracked his head. Some drunken crony decided to have a little fun. If that's the case, I'll take full charge of the investigation."

"And if he doesn't fit either of those categories?"

Harve picked up a Matt Map and studied it. "I didn't know Matt attended that old schoolhouse over near Emmet. Wasn't it shut down back in the late sixties? Last I heard, the Klan bought it for their monthly potluck suppers and cross burnings. You ever wonder if they wear pointy caps on account of their pointy heads?"

There were times when I suspected Harve and Ruby Bee shared a common ancestor. "Would you stop worrying about Matt Montana's school days and the county coneheads and worry a little more about that dead man in the window? What if he's not a tourist or a vagrant?"

Harve put down the map, but he kept on browsing so he wouldn't have to look at me. "Well, if it turns out he had some connection with the group from Nashville, it makes a helluva lot more sense for you to take the case. You already know 'em, and they're more likely to confide in you than in a stranger."

"That is a detour on the highway to the garbage dump! I've had a couple of short conversations with the advance man, and Matt came by the PD last night for a few minutes. As for the others, we've exchanged nods and that's it. We are not bosom buddies, Harve."

"But your own mother is one of the organizers, so she'll know all kinds of things about them. Mrs. Jim Bob out there owns the store. Brother Verber has three racks of postcards in his vestibule. Don't forget about Elsie McMay and Eula Lemoy and Jimson Pickerell. All of 'em will do everything they can to help you.''

I was too pissed off to point out the holes in his glib reasoning, which was probably the response he'd hoped for. ''All right,'' I said as I went stomping toward the window, ''we'll just play your little game of Russian roulette. You're gonna be goddamn sorry when it turns out he's a salesman from Kalamazoo and you spend the next three days trying to explain this long-distance to his grieving widow. I hate to think about all the paperwork involved in transporting the body across state lines. He's wearing white just like the Klan, Harve. Hope you don't have to deal with the FBI, too.''

I ignored the flutter of excitement from the crowd, felt the corpse's rump, and realized someone had put the white cowboy suit over a more mundane outfit. There was a bulge, however, of the right size and shape. ''I'm going to have to disturb the body to get to the wallet,'' I yelled at the manipulative cigar-smoking son of a bitch in the back of the room. ''You going to make the apologies to the coroner?''

''McBeen won't even notice, 'specially if he got a big buck.''

I noticed all sorts of unpleasant things, but eventually I wiggled my hand under the belt, got my fingernails on the corner of the wallet, and eased it out. My audience applauded, but I failed to curtsy and went stomping back to join Harve next to the cash register.

''You want to open it?'' I growled, then slammed it down on the counter and flipped it open. The driver's license, the dozen credit cards, the Social Security and group insurance cards, the business cards, and the wrinkled receipt from a dry cleaner all bore the same name: Pierce G. Keswick. Unlike Adele Wockermann, he had so many cards that we had enough identification for two or three corpses. We could have picked up his laundry, made reservations for a racquetball court, written or called him at his office, or even faxed him a message—if he weren't tied to a chair in the window of Matt Montana's Official Souvenir Shoppe.

"Shit," I said as I stared at the photograph on the driver's license. "Put a pinch of thyme in the lamb stew, Harve."

★

Miss Vetchling sat alone in the Vacu-Pro office. The day's mail had been readied for attention on Monday morning. The plants were watered. The upturned coffee pot was drying on the counter, as was her mug. Her keychain lay on the desk, but Miss Vetchling continued to sit long past her designated hour to lock the office and depart for the remainder of the weekend.

She had always prided herself on the orderliness of her personal life. She had her cat, Pussy Toes, her apartment in a quiet neighborhood, her meetings of the genealogical society, her knitting projects for nieces and nephews, and her annual vacation to a family-run hotel in Mexico where she remained drunk out of her mind for ten days straight (and was affectionately known throughout the village as *Nuestra Señorita de las Margaritas*).

Rather than shopping at the grocery store or visiting the public library, Miss Vetchling was contemplating the telephone call. She had studied art history at college and doubted the call had originated from the curator's office at the Prado in Madrid. What maleficence was Mr. Dentha in the midst of? What cryptic chain of events had sent him off on a mission fraught with pseudonymous callers and the need for mendacity?

Miss Vetchling did not regard the world through rose-tinted bifocals. She eavesdropped on her boss's calls as a matter of course, steamed open his mail when the opportunity arose, corresponded with lonely gentlemen via personal ads, and read true crime articles as if they were recipes ("remove the eyeballs and set aside, then simmer the tongue . . .").

Something was afoot. Miss Vetchling had looked through Kevin Buchanon's folder long before Mr. Dentha had asked for it, but she'd found nothing to set her nose atwitch with the scent of intrigue. But he had, and that irritated her.

She went into his private office, sat down behind his desk and searched through the drawers, but his appointment book revealed nothing she hadn't known from the previous Saturday's ritualistic perusal. She used a hairpin to open the metal box where he kept papers, but again, nothing had been added to explain his mysterious trip. Once she'd extricated twenty dollars from his emergency fund, she conscientiously locked the box and replaced it.

She halted her investigation long enough to fetch her mug from the bathroom and pour herself an inch of scotch, then sat back in the leather chair, lit a menthol cigarette from the crumpled pack she'd found in the middle drawer, and considered Kevin's brief tenure as a Vacu-Pro salesman. A polite young man, cursed with pustules and more enthusiasm than intelligence, blindly believing in the integrity of the product and in Mr. Dentha's impassioned pep talks, eager to display wedding photographs that Miss Vetchling felt might bring a tidy sum from the tabloids.

Unlike many of the disillusioned salesmen, Kevin had come to the office to return his demonstrator kit. He'd been a good deal more emotional than she or Mr. Dentha, both of whom were accustomed to such resignations. What precisely had Kevin said? Miss Vetchling sent a stream of smoke into the air and watched the motes roil in the light from the desk lamp. Another job, he'd said, with a chance to make more money. That ruled out very little; Vacu-Pro salesmen usually qualified for food stamps.

She replenished the scotch in her mug, lit another cigarette, and foraged further into her memory. On the eve of his resignation, Kevin had come by the office late in the afternoon, joking half-wittedly about a disastrous demonstration, and she'd given him one . . . no, two appointment slips for the evening. The next morning, before the other salesmen dragged in for the meeting, he tearfully tendered his resignation.

She returned to her desk and thumbed through the log until she found the last page that included Kevin's name. Two appointments during the day, neither resulting in a sale. Then one at six o'clock and one at nine. It was impossible to determine if he'd shown up at any of them; salesmen were known to seek solace at a bar after a particularly brutal reception. However, she had something to go on that Mr. Dentha did not.

Once she'd copied the four names and addresses and placed the slip of paper in her purse, Miss Vetchling restored the log to the bottom drawer, turned off the lamp, put on her coat, and left the office. As she started down the sidewalk, she wrapped her coat more tightly around herself, wondering if she might need an umbrella before the afternoon was over. Not an umbrella, she corrected herself with a toss of her chin. *Brolly* was the term used by proper spinster sleuths.

★

It took two deputies and a solid hour to get everybody arranged to my satisfaction, and by then I felt as if I'd supervised the unloading of a circus train in the dead of night—in a blizzard. The Wockermann house seemed the logical choice to question the group; the PD was too small, and the bar, which I'd utilized in the past, was packed with tourists. I'd banished Ruby Bee and Estelle to the kitchen and the teenage guides to an upstairs bedroom (risky, but I needed to question them) and told Tinker to shoot to kill if the press attacked. Dahlia's granny had locked herself in the bathroom and, from what we could hear, was taking a bath.

The second deputy was due back any minute with the remaining members of the Nashville party. Ripley, Matt, and Katie knew only that Pierce's body had been discovered in the souvenir shoppe and that we'd confirmed the ID with his driver's license. Now we sat in awkward silence in the living room.

"I don't get it," Matt said suddenly. "Why the hell would Pierce be in Maggody? I mean, there ain't any reason for him to be here. This is *my* homecoming thing, the kickoff for *my* tour." He went to the window and waved. "Look at all those folks out there in the road. They came to see me back here celebrating Christmas like a true blue country boy. You think there'd be so much as a dead armadillo out in the road if I weren't inside this house?''

"Or a dead executive in the souvenir shoppe?" Katie asked in a husky voice.

"Aw, Katie," he said as he squatted beside the rocking chair. He tried to take her hand, but she pulled it away and rubbed her neck. "Come on, honey, none of this is my fault. You want me to get you a nice cup of tea?"

I cleared my throat. "The kitchen's closed for the moment. As soon as Les comes back with the others, I'll question everyone as briefly as possible and have you all escorted back to your rooms. The sheriff's promised enough deputies to make sure none of you are disturbed by the press."

Ripley leaned back and crossed his legs. "What have you told the media, Arly? I need to at least call the office and let them know before they hear it on the radio."

"His identity hasn't been released. The coroner arrived just as I left, and the boys from the lab will crawl all over the store for several hours. At some point, Harve will have to hold a press conference. I'll let you make your calls to family members before then."

"You're looking at the last of the Keswicks. Our mother, one of the Savannah Grahams, died while Pierce was in the army and I was in graduate school. Father was so distressed that he drank himself to death within the month. I'd submitted my dissertation proposal the day before his body was discovered in the library. He'd fallen across the maidenhair fern that Mother brought back on the train all the way from Atlanta. She'd gone to rescue Grandfather Ponder, who'd been put in the state asylum by mistake. To this day I remember what she said to me when she arrived home. She said, 'Ripley, imagine a world in which you can go fifty miles away and people don't know who you are!' The fern that Father crushed never did recover, and I told my advisor I simply could not continue with the influence of indigenous flora on Faulkner's early works."

I looked sharply at him, but he was lost in thought and mumbling to himself (or to his advisor) under his breath.

Odd noises came from behind the kitchen door. Neither
Matt nor Katie seemed inclined to comment, and I was
relieved to see Les pull into the driveway. Tinker was
forced to fire a couple of shots in the air, but at last Lillian
came into the living room.

She was teary, her lipstick smudged and her face etched
with pain. "My god, Ripley," she said, sinking down next
to him. "I can't believe it. Not Pierce. He can't be dead.
Somebody confused him with someone else, found his wallet by mistake. Pierce can't be dead." She fell against his
shoulder and began to cry. Ripley put his arms around her
and bent his head to whisper in her ear.

I waited for a few minutes in case someone wanted to
share secrets with me, then said, "I realize this is a terrible
shock, and I'll do what I can to be brief." I stopped and
frowned at Les, who was admiring Katie from the hallway.
"Where are the boys in the band?"

Lillian sat up and took a tissue from her purse. "My
fault, I'm afraid," she said, wiping ineffectually at the
smears of mascara on her cheeks. "They never get up until
late in the afternoon. I'm not sure what would happen if
any of them set foot outside in direct sunlight. They may
have seen Pierce at the studio, but I doubt they've ever
even met him. There's nothing they could tell you."

Ripley nodded. "Lillian's right. They're just hired help.
Pierce could hardly tell them apart."

"Imagine that," I said. "Okay, I'll talk to them later if
I need to. Do any of you know when or why Pierce Keswick came to Maggody?"

The ensuing eruption was remarkable only in its lack
of consequence. Ripley was sure Pierce had never heard of
Maggody until Matt's relationship surfaced. Lillian admitted she'd talked to him on the telephone in the bus, but
he'd said nothing about coming. Matt said Pierce had displayed no curiosity about Maggody beyond strategic photo
opportunities. Voices from the kitchen contributed that he'd
never called anyone on the committee. Dahlia's granny
broke into a song about a rubber duckie. Lillian began to
cry, but Ripley was too engrossed with the ramifications of
Faulkner's flora to provide a shoulder. Katie went to the

bathroom door and begged to be allowed to use the facilities. Someone in the kitchen mentioned a second bathroom at the top of the stairs. Someone else asked if there really was a telephone on the bus.

I finally put up my hand. "We can't do anything until I get a preliminary report from the coroner so we'll have an idea of the time and the cause of death. In the interim, the deputies will take you back to your rooms. Please don't make any comments to the press."

They all limped out except Ripley, who stopped and said, "What about that woman's claim that she put a corpse in the chicken house? Couldn't there be a mix-up?"

"I'm sorry, but that has nothing to do with this. The driver's license has a recent photograph. Unless there's a third Keswick brother . . ."

He shook his head and left.

I went back to the kitchen, told Lucy and Ethel to do something about Dahlia's granny before she disappeared down the drain, then remembered I'd left six hot-blooded teenagers in proximity to a bed for better than an hour. I hurried upstairs. For the most part, they were on the bed, but fully clad and playing cards. I'd told them earlier that there'd been a fatal accident at the souvenir shoppe, and they appeared to be disguising their fear of the specter of eternal nihilism with accusations of cheating at poker. All of them, that is, except for the two who were making out in the closet.

"Who was the first to arrive this morning?" I asked.

"Me," said the dealer.

"When was that?"

"Mrs. Jim Bob said to get over here by eight to turn on the space heaters, pick up trash in the yard, that kind of shit. Nobody else had to show before nine, since tours don't start till then."

"I came at eight-thirty," contributed a mousy girl with braces. "I brought Billy Dick some doughnuts and a carton of chocolate milk from the supermarket."

"That's nice. Billy Dick, did you notice anything out of the ordinary when you arrived?"

"Like what?"

"Like I don't know. I'm asking you."

"I noticed the living room was colder than a well digger's ass."

"And . . . ?"

"There was popcorn scattered all over the porch."

"Anything else?"

"The front door was unlocked, but I figured one of these other burgerbrains forgot to lock it."

In response to my look, the accused burgerbrains denied any carelessness. I forced myself to continue pulling insights out of Billy Dick's head with questions as small and precise as tweezers. "Was anything missing?"

"I didn't notice."

"Moved?"

"Nah, I don't think so. I mean, somebody could have switched the candy dishes with the candles, or the pinecones with the holly, but nothing like that jumped out at me."

The girl touched his shoulder. "What about the sign?"

"Oh, yeah," he said, smacking his head as if to dislodge a stray thought. "That sign that says welcome to Maggody used to be right out front by the edge of the driveway. I dint ever pay it any mind, but Traci here"—he squeezed her thigh hard enough to elicit a whinny of protest—"noticed that it'd disappeared. I went out to the road to see if it was lying in the ditch, and then I saw it. How the hell did it git all the way down by the low-water bridge?"

They all stared expectantly at me.

★

"Bernie Allen, you stop poking that stick in there. You're gonna be real sorry when a big ol' copperhead comes outta there and bites you and you're dead before I can drag you out of the woods."

He stood up and reluctantly joined his mother, who was sitting on a log while studying a map. "Ain't no snake in there," he said, thinking about poking her to see how high she'd jump. It'd be a lot more interesting than hunting for a stupid creek. "I wanna go back to the camper, Ma. My stomach hurts. I think I'm gonna throw up."

"Suit yourself." She ran her finger along a line that was supposed to be the path that started out behind the church and ended up at Matt Montana's Baptism Pool. The map made it look like it was right handy, but she and Bernie Allen had been wandering for the best part of an hour and hadn't so much as seen a mud puddle. Of course Bernie Allen had insisted they take a shortcut and had raised such a fuss that she let him lead the way.

She glanced up at the sound of retching from behind a pine tree. "Stop that, Bernie Allen. This isn't the time for your playacting. If you're throwing up, it's because you got your fingers stuck down your throat. Now come out from there so we can find this Baptism Pool before dark."

He didn't obey her, but this was so unremarkable that she went back to trying to figure out the map. At least they were moving downhill, so they'd find the creek sooner or later. Bernie Allen had chocolate syrup stains on his shirt, but he was gonna stand right on the edge of the creek where Matt Montana was baptized and he was gonna give her a nice, wide smile. They'd come all the way from Joplin to visit Matt Montana's Boyhood Home, and she was going home with the slides to prove it.

"Bernie Allen," she said more loudly, "I said to stop making those disgusting noises and come out from behind there. I don't want to have to tell your pa about this, but I will if I have to."

"You might ought to tell somebody," called Bernie Allen before he resumed retching.

Chapter Fourteen

"That's the third camper to leave," Earl grumbled as he came into the kitchen and tossed his cap on the table. "At this rate, the field's gonna be empty by sundown. It ain't like it was Matt Montana who got hisself killed in the window of Mrs. Jim Bob's shoppe."

Eilene hung his cap on the peg by the door. "I wish you'd remember to wipe your feet, Earl. I just finished mopping the floor."

He waited for her to get him a beer, but she walked right out of the room. "Are you sick?" he called in a real solicitous voice. "I can run over to the deli at the supermarket and pick up some tamales and beans for supper."

"Don't bother," she said from the front room.

Harrumphing under his breath, he got himself a beer and sat back down. She was acting awful peculiar, he thought as he popped the tab. Here he'd offered to go get the tamales and she hadn't even said, "Thank you for being so considerate, Earl." She was the one who was big on his being "considerate" and "sensitive to her needs" and was all the time taking quizzes in women's magazines. He'd found one on the counter that told you how to measure how much sexual magic there was in your bed. The score she'd circled said they needed a postmortem, but he wasn't about to let any wife of his order something kinky from a catalog. "You talk to the kids today?" he asked, trying to sound like Phil Donahue.

She came to the doorway, her arms crossed and her mouth not so much frowning as set like she was trying real hard not to frown. "I called this morning, but Kevin'd already gone to work. Dahlia was in a hurry because she was supposed to have the Matt-Mobile at the high school at ten, and she wanted to hose down the wagon because some tourist spilled a soda pop on the floorboards. She was afraid Matt Montana might end up with a sticky purple stain on his white britches. I'm real worried about her."

"We got any pretzels or chips and dip?"

She gave him a funny look before she drifted back to the front room. "She hardly ate any supper last night."

"Won't hurt her," Earl said, determined to keep trying to have a normal conversation. "You know, I'm kinda glad to get those trucks and RVs out of the field. If it rains tonight, their tires will tear it up and it'll take weeks to get it plowed next spring."

She came back to the doorway. "Did you hear what Dahlia said this morning down by the low-water bridge?"

"That hogwash about murdering some old guy and rolling him up in a bag? She must have gone home last night and eaten a couple of frozen pizzas, or stopped by Raz's place to buy some shine. Indigestion or a hangover—one or the other of them was making her crazier than ol' Typha Buchanon. Remember when he burned down his own house 'cause he thought he had Mormons in the basement?"

"I wonder," Eilene said as she once again disappeared.

"You wonder what was making Dahlia crazy—or are you starting to wonder if we got Mormons in the basement, too? For pity's sake, Eilene, just call her and ask." He looked at the doorway and almost choked on a mouthful of beer as he saw her standing there. "If you want to, I mean. It can't hurt to ask her why she was spouting off like that."

"I spoke to Eula this morning. She was at the supermarket yesterday evening, and a man with silver hair asked her for directions. All he had was the rural route and box numbers, but they got to talking and it turned out he was looking for Kevin and Dahlia's house. He claimed he was interested in buying a vacuum cleaner from Kevin, but Eula said he looked more like someone trying to sell time-shares in a cemetery."

"So?"

"So Dahlia didn't make up everything. There was a

man with silver hair who was looking for the house. What if he found it?''

"Why, she murdered him like she said, but then somebody happened into the chicken house and brought him back to life so he could go home. Problem is, nobody's seen the Messiah walking around Maggody, and Brother Verber ain't up to that kind of miracle yet. Besides, if he brought a fellow back from the dead, you can bet he'd be crowing about it from the roof of the Assembly Hall. You sure we ain't got any pretzels?"

Eilene took a cellophane bag from the bread box and came to the table. "All I said, Earl, was that someone ought to be thinking about what Dahlia said happened last night."

"Maybe you ought to be thinking more about fixing my supper," Earl said with a smile. He'd opened his mouth to suggest spaghetti when she poured the pretzels on his head, folded the empty bag, and put it in the wastebasket. He took a pretzel off his ear and stared at it. "What the hell's gotten into you, Eilene? I've been messing with those fool tourists all day and I'm hungry. If all you're gonna do is stew about this, call Dahlia and ask her straight out what happened."

"I can't. She came by an hour ago and borrowed my car."

"She did what? Damn it, I told Ira I was bringing my truck in so he could fix that busted headlight. It won't be ready till Monday. I figured we could use your car the rest of the weekend. Where'd Dahlia go?"

"I didn't ask," Eilene said as she left the kitchen. This time she went to the bedroom and locked the door.

★

I drove to the motel parking lot, where my two recruited deputies had been told to wait for me. "Tell me about last night," I suggested. "The comings and goings."

They solemnly assured me no one except Ruby Bee had entered or left the parking lot. I let them finish, then asked, "What about Matt Montana?"

One of them (and it doesn't matter which) said, "Never so much as peeked out of the bus the entire time. It was a good thing, 'cause we sure as hell wouldn't have known what to say to him if he wanted to take a walk.''

I gave them a knowing grin. ''Got pretty cold last night, didn't it? If I'd been here, I wouldn't have thought twice about sitting in my car while I watched the lot. I'd have run the heater just so my toes wouldn't freeze, and if Ruby Bee'd brought me some coffee, you can bet I'd have poured an inch or two of something in it to keep me warm.''

We all agreed I'd hit it square on the head, that what I'd described was the only way to survive a long, cold, boring night in an empty parking lot. I told them to talk to Harve about their paychecks, politely asked the real deputies to station themselves at both ends of the lot, and went to the souvenir shoppe to see if the coroner had made any progress.

An ambulance had joined the cars from the sheriff's department and a truck with a well-stocked gun rack and an orange cap on the dashboard. A tablecloth had been taped across the store window. The tourists, deprived of a view of the corpse, were gone, and the media had regrouped across the street at the parking lot. They looked unhappy, but there wasn't much I could do about it.

Inside, deputies were sprinkling fingerprint powder on the souvenirs. The coroner supervised the ambulance attendants, who were struggling to fit the curled body into a bag designed for a recumbent one.

''Do we have an estimated time of death?'' I asked.

The coroner looked up peevishly. ''Rigor's established, so he's apt to have been dead at least twelve hours, but that's all I can say until we know if he was outside any length of time. It was damn cold last night. Depends, too, on the circumstances preceding his death. Maybe the state medical examiner can do something with the stomach contents.'' He gave me a smile I found ghoulish. ''Too bad it ain't summer, Chief. The maggot count can be real accurate.''

''Come on, McBeen,'' I begged, ''give me a ballpark figure.''

''More than ten hours, less than eighteen,'' he said, then paused to scowl at a photographer who was getting in the way. "And I ain't even touching the corpse before it goes to Little Rock. There's something perverse about the way he was dolled up in these clothes and set like that. This kind of tomfoolery may be fine for those silly mystery novels my wife reads, but I'm not having any part of it. Soon as the paperwork's ready, he's off to the state lab."

I looked at Harve for help, but he was busy pricing a Matt Montana duck caller. "McBeen, we all know the lab down there's staffed with a bunch of yuppies with telephones in their cars and silk neckties under their one hundred percent cotton lab coats. You've had more experience than all of them rolled together, and you don't waste time counting toes and fingers before you identify the cause of death."

McBeen picked up his notebook, tucked his pen behind his ear, and, with a weary sigh, prepared to follow the gurney out the door. "Get yourself a cellular phone, Arly. It'll give you something to do when you're stuck in one of these local traffic jams I've been hearing about lately. Give me a ring and we'll have a chat about livor mortis."

"Internal hemorrhage and a fractured skull?" I said to the back of his neck. He nodded perceptibly as he left.

Harve tested the duck caller (*non quack pas en francaise*), then set it down. "You already knew that. Get anywhere with the Nashville folks?"

I considered how much damage I could inflict with a short length of hollow wood. "I haven't had time to question them individually. This far, no one admits to having any idea when the victim came here, or why. Yesterday afternoon he didn't mention any intentions of coming, but he obviously changed his mind. I'll call his secretary and see if she knows anything." I did a bit of arithmetic. "McBeen said death occurred ten to eighteen hours ago. That puts it between seven last night and three this morning. That's a lot of help, isn't it?"

"It was dark by half past five yesterday evening. When did Mrs. Jim Bob close the store?"

"She left early because of her guests, and Darla Jean locked up at seven. The bar and grill and the pool hall close at midnight, so there would have been traffic until then.

Mrs. Jim Bob leaves an overhead light on to discourage burglars.'' I realized we were missing a player. ''Has anybody found the mannequin?''

''Uh-uh. I had the boys look out back and on the adjoining property in case our smartass dumped it nearby. I guess we need a description of it from Mrs. Jim Bob. She's waiting in the back room.'' He took a cigar butt from his pocket, then put it back and grimaced. ''Sounds ridiculous, don't it?''

''Yep,'' I said as I went past him and pushed back the curtain.

''Just bring home something for supper, you hear?'' Mrs. Jim Bob said into the telephone receiver, saw me, and hung up as if she'd been talking to the KGB. ''Is the body gone?''

''Just now, but it's going to be some time until everything in the immediate area is fingerprinted. It won't do any good, but I suppose they'll do the same around the back door. Did you ever have any communication with this Pierce Keswick?''

''Never heard of him until he had the audacity to be found in my front window, and on a day when the store was packed with customers. Jim Bob said folks at the supermarket are talking about leaving on account of a murderer loose in town. The parking lot's half-empty. The Christmas Boutique isn't doing any business to speak of. Brother Verber hasn't sold a single postcard this afternoon, and not one soul has signed up for a guided tour down to the creek. I'm beginning to think we never should have . . .'' She hung her head and began to sniffle. ''Jim Bob doesn't know this,'' she said between gulps, tears welling in her eyes, her cheeks turning fiery, ''but I borrowed close to seven thousand dollars for inventory and fixtures like the tables and postcard racks. If the store goes broke, I don't know how I can pay the bank and replace the money from the . . .'' She began to root through her purse for a tissue, all the while mumbling about her precipitous foray into debilitating debt and disgrace.

I knew how to deal with her sanctimoniousness, but not with this admission of vulnerability. I couldn't bring myself

to pat her shoulder, but I did nod sympathetically and say,
"You should be able to open the store in the morning. I
don't know how this will affect the remainder of Matt's
visit, but it's possible the concert can go ahead as scheduled."

"The T-shirts alone cost me one thousand four hundred
and fifty-nine dollars, and that's not including freight. I
only ordered two dozen embroidered jackets, but they were
almost thirty-five dollars apiece wholesale. The caps were
nine hundred and twenty-five dollars. There are sixty dollars worth of pencils in that carton right there. One hundred
and twenty-eight dollars worth of coffee cups. The novel-
ties company gave me thirty days, but that was three weeks
ago."

"Maybe they'll give you—"

"I allowed myself to be blinded with a vision of saving
the community. Satan was whispering in my ear, but I kept
picturing the faces of innocent little children on Christmas
morning when they came downstairs and saw those empty
stockings. I knew better than to heed the devil. 'But they
that will be rich fall into temptation and a snare, and into
many foolish and hurtful lusts, which drown men in destruction and perdition.' "

"The gospel according to J. C. Penney?"

Mrs. Jim Bob stuffed the wadded tissue into her purse
and stood up. "First Timothy, missy. If you'd make it a
habit to attend church on a regular basis, you might just
learn something. Are you planning to stand here the rest of
the day, or is there a murder you might want to investigate?"

I asked for a description of the mannequin and with
great seriousness recorded her answers: molded blond hair,
flesh tone #4 (moderate tan), six-foot even, forty pounds
roughly. Left foot missing, chipped nose, and a broken right
forearm now held together with duct tape, all why she'd
gotten it cheap.

Harve agreed it was premature to put out an APB, fid-
dled with a cigar butt until it was lit to his satisfaction, and
went to the front of the store to watch the photographer

capture the lack of bloodstains on the wooden floor and chair.

Hammet came across the road as I parked in front of the PD. He was back in overalls, a patched flannel shirt, unlaced sneakers, and my army surplus jacket from distant college days. "Did ya catch him yet?" he asked as he followed me inside. "Is the sumbitch locked up in the pokey—or did he pull a gun and force you to splatter his brains on the ceiling?" He aimed an imaginary assault weapon at my chair. "Get 'em up or you're dead meat, slime bucket."

"What happened to your fancy white duds?" I asked as I went into the back room and got a cup of coffee.

"That ol' fart said I cain't wear 'em unless I'm gittin' my picture taken. He wuz sposed to take me down to the house so I could be in some pictures, but then he said weren't nobody gonna do anything else today 'cause of the dead man. I kin question folks for you, 'specially that piggy lil' kid."

"Better let me do that, Hammet. I might lose my job if the town council found out I was making you do the tough stuff. There is a way you can help me out, though, if you're not too busy posing for photographs."

"You jest name it." He sat down across from me, his back rigid, his eyes popping with eagerness, his trigger finger itching, and his grin a damn sight more infectious than Matt Montana's would ever be.

I felt like a latter-day Fagin as I told him about the missing mannequin. He demanded a description, and once he was clear about the *left* foot versus the *right* arm, he promised to "git busier than a guide on a riffle" and shot out the door. The colloquialism was beyond me, but his intentions were unmistakable.

I took Ripley's business card out of the drawer and dialed the office telephone number of Country Connections, Inc. After ascending through the corporate hierarchy, I was passed to Pierce Keswick's private secretary, Amy Abbott. She sounded genuinely upset when I told her the bad news and said they'd been worried all morning when he had not come into the office as usual.

"Mr. Pierce was a really nice man," she said in response to my question. "He was strict, and he could get furious when people lied to him or made dumb excuses, but everybody respected him. He was always up front with you, not like . . . other people in the office."

I presumed she'd heard about Faulkner's flora. "What did he do yesterday and when did he leave the office?"

"Let me check his appointment calendar." She put me on hold but returned within a minute. "He had a meeting yesterday morning with the legal department, and then lunch with an agent. He just worked the rest of the afternoon."

"What about calls?" I asked.

"Oh, he made some and people called him. He spends a lot of time on the telephone. Spent, I should say. Golly, this is so awful." She put down the receiver to blow her nose, then continued hoarsely. "At three o'clock, he had me get Lillian on the phone to make sure they arrived safely. That's why I was surprised when Katie called an hour later."

"How do you know she called?"

Amy sighed. "She called collect. The switchboard finally put the operator through to me so I could accept the call because it's against our rules. Katie was calling from a pay phone at a laundry or something, and all these machines were clanging in the background and people kept telling her to get off the phone so they could use it."

"Did she say why she was calling?"

"No, and I left while Mr. Pierce was in his office with the door shut. I guess he was still talking to her. He wanted me to take a box of demo tapes to one of the studios and told me to go on home afterward."

"Did that happen often?" I asked, feeling as though I was in the general proximity of a vital clue, if not in danger of stumbling over it.

"All the time," said Amy. "When traffic's heavy, it takes almost an hour to get out to that studio. My apartment's right down the street."

Apparently, the only thing I was stumbling over was

my appetite for red herrings. "Would anyone else in the office have spoken to him yesterday afternoon?"

"I don't think so, but I'll ask. When his door's closed, you'd better have Wynonna Judd or Emmylou Harris with you if you knock. That's the first thing I tell the temps. When Mr. Keswick's door is closed, you'd better have Wynonna Judd or—"

"How about when he went through the office at the end of the day?"

"He might have gone that way if he had contracts to put on someone's desk or something like that, but most of the time he uses the stairs right outside my office."

I heard voices in the background. Amy asked me if she could tell the others. I gave her permission, then said I might call her again and replaced the receiver. Pierce Keswick had been in his Nashville office at four o'clock and had died in Maggody within the next eleven hours. It was a long haul to Nashville, at least ten hours. If he'd driven, he hadn't wasted any time admiring the scenery.

I made a note to have Harve call the Tennessee authorities and ask them to check with the airlines—and with the state police to see if any speeding citations had been issued to Pierce Keswick. I could do the same with the Arkansas State Police, who were cooperative if approached with proper deference.

It was nearly four o'clock. The heavy clouds that had moved in earlier in the day hung over the valley, apparently satisfied to remain indefinitely. Rain was more likely than snow. It rarely snowed before January, and I could recall exactly one white Christmas in all my childhood years of listening to carols about winter wonderlands and sleigh-bells. You can't build a snowman out of drizzle.

Witnesses were waiting, and by now half the town had experienced Hammet's unconventional investigative techniques. Some of the tourists had packed up and were rolling out of town in search of other stars shining in the east. They may not have come bearing frankincense and myrrh, but the local merchants would be sorry to see all those gold credit cards leaving.

I was on my way out the door to have a chat with Katie

Hawk when one of Harve's deputies came running down the road. "Chief Hanks!" he called, "Sheriff Dorfer says for you to come back to the souvenir shoppe."

"Did the duck caller nip him?"

He leaned against my car and caught his breath. "No, he was just leaving when some lady charged into the shoppe, dragging this little boy with her. She was carrying on something awful, but she finally calmed down long enough to say they'd found a man's body down toward the creek somewhere. Sheriff Dorfer's waiting for you."

"I'm busy."

"You want me to go tell Sheriff Dorfer that, or should I stick my gun in my mouth and save him the trouble?"

"The person he ought to be waiting for is Dahlia Buchanon. Unless this body has a chipped nose and duct tape on his arm, this lady undoubtedly found the body Dahlia was toting around town last night. He must have regained consciousness and staggered into the woods . . . to use the pay phone to call his office and check for messages."

"There aren't any pay phones in the woods," the deputy said with a pitying look.

"But there is one at Aunt Adele's Launderette, and that's the one I'm interested in at the moment. Tell Harve to give my regards to McBeen."

"Whatever you say, Chief Hanks."

"I'll give you a ride back to the souvenir shoppe," I said as I got in the car, since we both knew that's where I was going despite my piddling outburst of bravado.

"I prefer to walk," the deputy said. He turned sharply and headed back up the road.

He was a prime candidate for roadkill, but I drove sedately past him. Harve was waiting by his car, doing his best to talk to a woman who was doing her best to collapse in his arms. The kid in the green cowboy suit was eating a candy bar.

"What is wrong with this town?" the woman demanded as I rolled down my window. "I have never been in a town where there are so many dead bodies just lying around! Haven't you all heard of funeral homes? In Joplin we have all these funeral homes where—"

"Who is it?" I asked Harve.

"She didn't stop to ask him his name," Harve said gruffly. "She has a point about all these bodies, you know. Is anybody else missing?"

"Sure," I said. "Adele Wockermann has been missing for weeks, and although Patty May's not technically missing, I can't seem to find her either. Did you get any kind of a description of this latest body?"

"No, and we'd better get started. If we wait around for McBeen to get back here, we'll never find it in the dark. They strayed off the path and were lost back in there for at least an hour."

"I don't know how we found our way out," the woman contributed shrilly. "Bernie Allen was so upset that he twisted his ankle and I had to carry him half the way."

Harve glanced at Bernie Allen, who probably weighed well over a hundred pounds. "He can wait here while we—"

"We? You don't think I'm going back into that jungle, do you? Bernie Allen saw a snake, and—"

"Tell you what, Harve," I said as she continued to describe the ordeal, "you give me a ring when the body's been brought back to civilization and I'll see if I can find Dahlia. In the meantime, I've already got my body."

"He has a beard," Bernie Allen announced through a poorly masticated mouthful of chocolate and caramel. "My Uncle Bootie had a beard, too. He got killed by a bus."

Sobbing, the woman crumpled to the ground. Bernie Allen wadded up a candy wrapper and tossed it at her. Harve folded his arms and stared at me.

★

Ruby Bee and Estelle stood on the flagstone patio in back of the Wockermann house. The guides had left as soon as they'd been questioned, and Billy Dick had been paid off to drive Dahlia's squeaky-clean granny back to the county home. Now that just the two of them were lingering, the house seemed empty and kinda spooky, and not much warmer than outside.

"I reckon he's even more handsome in person," Estelle

said, her hands buried in the pockets of her heavy sweater. She squinted at the clouds, wondering when it would rain. There were still some slivers of broken glass underfoot that must have been overlooked during the cleanup, but a heavy rain would wash them away. The last thing she wanted to do was drag out the broom and the dustpan.

"But he looks older," Ruby Bee said. "They do something to the photographs so you can't see all those little fine wrinkles around his eyes. Maybe you couldn't find his birth certificate at the courthouse because he's older than the magazine claimed. You were looking in the wrong year."

Estelle was too dispirited to get riled up. "He's got a few gray hairs, too. But I still say he's more handsome in person. When he grinned at me, I felt like I was sixteen and had just been kissed for the first time. I had to go into the kitchen and drink a glass of water before I dared so much as glance in his direction."

"He glanced plenty of times in Miss Katie Hawk's direction. She's a cold thing, and I'm beginning to regret naming the chicken 'n dumpling special after her. I may just scratch it out on the menu."

"Think how she'd feel if she found out," gasped Estelle, her eyebrows disappearing under the row of rigid ringlets on her forehead.

"Oh, I suppose I'll leave it as long as they're in town, but I don't know what to make of her." She was going to expound, but a movement way across the pasture caught her attention. "Down there by the chicken houses. You see something?"

"I see chicken houses."

"Behind the one that's not burned down. I distinctly saw something."

"If you distinctly saw it, you ought to know what it is."

Ruby Bee wished she had her bifocals in her coat pocket, even though she never wore them in front of Estelle. But even without them, she knew darn well she'd distinctly seen something. "What'd you think about Dahlia's claim that she murdered a man and put the body down there?'' she asked.

"I thought it was time for her to get her batteries checked. Arly went in there to see for herself. Are you saying that just because Arly couldn't find Adele, she can't even find a corpse in a chicken house?"

"No," Ruby Bee said, still looking across the pasture at the dim outlines of the two structures, one a mess of charred timbers and the other more substantial. "So Raz bought that parcel of land a few years back, did he? Why would he do that? It's clear on the opposite side of town from his place, and the land ain't good for anything but making mud pies in the spring."

Estelle stamped her feet to keep them warm. "I don't pretend I can explain Raz Buchanon's behavior. Dahlia's, either. Maybe they're getting their drinking water from the same spring. That'd account for Kevin's having an affair with a Farberville floozy. Everybody up that way, including Marjorie, is acting downright peculiar."

"I don't think we ought to dismiss Dahlia's story as a fairy tale. Lottie said that Eula said there was a man in the supermarket yesterday evening that was quizzing her like a game-show host. She ended up drawing him a map so he could find their house. Dead men don't wake up in the middle of the night and go home any more than Raz Buchanon throws away money on property he's got no use for. We ought to go down there and see what he's up to."

"And get our heads blown off, Miss Purple Heart?"

"We're not gonna get our heads blown off if he's not there," Ruby Bee said with a smug smile. "And I'll bet you dollars to doughnuts he won't be there at midnight."

Chapter Fifteen

Miss Vetchling went to the front door of the small frame house and rang the bell. Inside, a dog started barking and she had to wait several minutes before the door opened a scant inch. "Yes?" the woman said, wincing as something clattered behind her.

"I'm the regional supervisor of the Vacu-Pro Home Cleaning Systems, Mrs. Borland. We're doing a survey. Could I take just a minute of your time to ask a few questions concerning the Vacu-Pro demonstration conducted in your home approximately two weeks ago?"

"Some boy came to the house, but I'd forgotten that the baby had a doctor's appointment. I told him to call back later but he didn't. I forgot about it until now."

"Thank you." Miss Vetchling made a check next to the first name on the list. "Would you like to schedule an appointment in the future with one of our salesmen?"

"Is it true the vacuum cleaners cost seven hundred dollars?"

"Seven hundred fifty-three dollars, plus shipping and handling."

"We got a lot of doctor's appointments coming up," Mrs. Borland said as she closed the door.

Miss Vetchling returned to the curb, got in her car and consulted the street map, and then drove off toward the second of Kevin Buchanon's appointments on what she had awarded the sobriquet of "His Fateful Day."

Ten seconds later a car pulled away from the curb and followed her at a distance carefully calculated not to arouse her suspicion.

★

"This one is all yours," I said to Harve, allowing myself the pleasure of chortling as we trudged along the path back to the Assembly Hall. "He's just a tourist who stumbled and fell into the official Baptism Pool. What a shame little Bernie Allen upchucked all over what evidence there might have been."

Harve gazed disapprovingly at me. "Carlos L. Tunnato of Chattanooga might not find it all that funny."

"Everybody would be a sight healthier if the hometown boy had chosen another hometown. Adele would be at the county home, stringing cranberries, and Patty May would be threading the needle for her." I tore a branch off a bush and stripped it of its leaves. "Mrs. Jim Bob was bawling about all the money she invested in souvenirs. Eula and Elsie are likely to be in bad shape, not to mention Ruby Bee and her shelves of crap. Brother Verber has taken to dressing up as if he ought to be leading a pony at a birthday party. We should have yanked up all the . . ."

"All the what?" Harve muttered, not sounding all that eager to find out.

I was so overwhelmed with my theory that I had to sit down on a rock and wait for the adrenaline to ebb. "The town limits signs. The county survey map may lay out the town to the last foot, but nobody's going to get a tape measure and argue with the sign. That sly ol' geezer . . ."

"Which sly ol' geezer are you getting so rapturous about?"

"Raz," I said. "He thinks that, as long as those chicken houses are outside the town limits, I won't take an interest in them. Maybe he thinks they're outside my jurisdiction. Hell, they may be, but so's Cotter's Ridge. Surely he's aware that I've been up there on countless occasions to look for his still. Shit, I've told him so."

Harve pulled me to my feet and said, "We need to keep going. We've got a corpse back at the creek that needs to be moved before dark." He gallantly held back a spindly bush for me, then let it whip past and nudged me into step. "Are you saying Raz has his still in the chicken house?"

"No, he wouldn't risk that. But it's getting near the holiday season, and he may have decided to use the chicken house as a warehouse. I wouldn't be surprised if on certain nights there were cases covered with tarps in there. No wonder he was pissed when the sign was moved."

"The sign was moved?" Harve said blankly.

"Because the Wockermann house was not within the town limits," I said, so pleased with my deductions that I was waving my arms at Harve and walking backward while I elaborated. This is not always wise in the woods, and only his split-second grab saved me from sprawling over a log. "The Homecoming Committee decided to redefine the boundaries of the town so that they could claim Matt was born in Maggody. Don't you love it? Other towns go through an arduous process to annex adjoining land, but we just get our shovels and do it in the middle of the night."

Harve was looking confused, understandable in that I hadn't gotten around to mentioning the midnight stalkings. After I explained, he said, "All right, but what does that have to do with the bodies that keep turning up—or not turning up?"

"How should I know? I was merely solving one minor puzzle, not auditioning for a role on *Mystery*. As soon as the Nashville people are gone and things quiet down, I'm going to stake out the chicken house and nab Raz with a truckload of moonshine—and not even Marjorie the Wonder Pig can save him."

"I'm sure you'll get a letter of commendation from the revenuers. I'm gonna wait here for McBeen and the boys. I don't suppose you want to go over to this guy's motel room in Farberville and poke around?"

"Sorry, Harve," I said, not even making an effort to sound sincere. I left him in front of the Assembly Hall and walked back to my car in front of the souvenir shoppe. The tablecloth across the window reminded me of how Pierce Keswick had looked when he'd been found, hunched over the guitar, his hands tied in place, the wig hanging over his face. I sat down on the hood of the car and for the first time asked the glaring question: Why?

To implicate Matt? It hadn't, thus far, or anybody else

(Darla Jean did not qualify as a suspect). I muddled for a long while, almost able to make a connection but unable to bring it into focus. First there was Matt, then the mannequin dressed to look like Matt, then Keswick dressed to look like the mannequin dressed to look like Matt. Except, of course, Matt Montana was a package designed and produced in Nashville.

I finally gave up the antediluvian issue of man versus mannequin and returned to a more concrete realm. It seemed likely that Pierce Keswick had come to Maggody as a result of one of two telephone calls. I wanted to talk to Katie Hawk about hers—which she'd failed to mention earlier. But first I decided to talk to Lillian Figg and find out in more detail what she and Pierce Keswick had said to each other. And swing by the Dairee Dee-Lishus on the way to the motel parking lot. Country music fans may survive on a diet of broken promises and harrowingly bad puns, but I thought I'd squeeze in a corndog and a cherry limeade.

Twenty minutes later I tapped on the door of the bus and was admitted with a sinister hydraulic hiss. Lillian suggested we sit at one of the tables in the middle of the bus, explaining Matt was in the shower and liable to pop out into the back room without so much as a towel. Modesty, she'd added with a small shrug, was not among his talents. She offered me a cup of coffee and, when I declined, sat down across from me. Her eyes were red and her eyelids swollen, but she'd repaired her lipstick since I'd last seen her in the Wockermann living room.

"I still can't believe it," she said. "Pierce and I met a good twenty years ago, when we both were so damned determined that we thought we'd invented the word." She rubbed her face hard enough to peel off a layer of skin. "I don't know if I'm gonna get by without that son of a bitch."

"Tell me about Country Connections."

"Fifteen years ago, give or take, Pierce and Ripley inherited everything from their parents. Pierce was the executor, naturally, and he bullied Ripley into selling the house and the farmland in the delta and investing the whole bundle in a seedy little label company that was about to sink into obscurity. It's not exactly a major force in Nashville these days, but it's respectable. Pierce puts in eighteen hours a day, and his reputation for honesty is a rare thing in the business. Was, I guess.'' She knotted her fingers and looked away.

"Why did you say that Pierce bullied Ripley into investing in the company?

"You've met Ripley, right? He claims that back then he was lost in such rigorous and demanding intellectual pursuits that he had no time to read the legal papers Pierce shoved under his nose. He was crawling around yards in northeast Mississippi in search of botanical specimens and pallid young southern intellectuals.'' She caught my questioning look and shrugged. ''I don't think so. His kind are so obsessed with analyzing literary passion that they're too exhausted to indulge in it themselves. I find them curiously asexual.''

"Quite a contrast with what you've told me about Pierce,'' I said impassively.

"Pierce spent his childhood fishing and hunting. Ripley used to go to the attic, dig old clothes out of trunks, and reenact scenes from *A Streetcar Named Desire* to entertain his mother's bridge club.''

My expression slipped just a tad. ''It's hard to see him as Stanley Kowalski, survivor of the stone age.''

"Try Blanche DuBois, depending on the kindness of strangers,'' Lillian said drily. ''Pierce left when he finished high school, joined the army, and ended up in Nashville. God, it's gonna be a lonely town without him. He held my hand at funerals and kept me company during my low-budget divorce. You ever been divorced?''

I nodded, surprised. ''Yes, once.''

"Take my advice and hire a lawyer to make sure everything was filed properly, notarized . . .'' She looked over my shoulder. ''Arly was asking me about Pierce.''

Matt wore a terry-cloth robe, although it was belted loosely and most of his chest was exposed. He sat down across from us and propped his bare feet on the back of the seat. This exposed enough to give his most tepid fan a stroke.

"Lillian and Pierce," he chanted in a cruel parody of the schoolyard rhyme, "sitting in a tree, F-U-C-K-I-N-G; first comes the contract, then comes the screw, and now they're fuckin' Matt and Katie, too."

Lillian winced. "Why don't you get back in the shower and turn it on cold?"

"Aw, I was just joking. I owe everything I have to you and Pierce. You discovered me, and he was generous enough to offer me an exclusive contract that'll keep me tied up for four and a half more years. I know Katie's grateful, too, now that she's in the same situation."

It was cold outside, but the temperature was plunging in the bus. I'd learned at the police academy that marital disputes were a helluva lot more dangerous than armed robberies, ticking bombs, and pit bulls. My experience to date consisted of going out to a rusty trailer at the Pot o' Gold and lecturing two teenagers on how to resolve arguments about her lack of expertise in the kitchen. The only time I'd been in real danger was when she'd tried to get me to taste the chili.

"That contract was in your best interest," Lillian said defensively. "Your single happened to hit the charts and win the award, but the label company took a big risk when they put up well over a quarter of a million to cut the new Christmas album. Would you have preferred to keep performing at those dinky amateur-night clubs?"

"What I'd prefer," he said, grinning at me, "is to be released from the contract so I can go over to MCA or Arista and make the sort of money a star deserves. I'm stuck not only with pissant Country Connections, but also with Lillian here, who's promised to deliver me at the back door of the poorhouse if I'm not a good boy."

"Richer or poorer, till death do us part," Lillian said as she went into the bedroom and closed the door.

"Till death do us part," echoed Matt, licking his lips as if he could taste each word.

If Lillian turned up dead in Mrs. Jim Bob's front window, I'd have a good idea where to begin the investigation. I tried to remember what bits of gossip I'd heard from Ruby Bee and Estelle. Katie Hawk's name had been mentioned.

"Does Lillian represent Katie's professional interests, too?" I asked.

Matt spoke more loudly than necessary. "If you wanna call it that. The agency signed her up, arranged for her to cut a few singles at Country Connections, and every now and then they book her at a crappy club. Slavery is alive and well in Nashville."

"How does Pierce's death affect your contract?"

"Depends on what Ripley does, but there's hope. He ain't what you call a true aficionado of country music. I went by his place one night to pick up a press release, and he was listening to a CD with some woman screeching like she was being poked up the butt. In Italian, too. I hope he'll sell out to Breed, who'll sell my contract to one of the big companies. Next year I'll be playing in Las Vegas between tours in Europe. When I get tired of that, maybe I'll open myself a country music house up in Branson, Missouri—right between Willie Nelson's and Barbara Mandrell's. I'll have 'em over for supper on Sundays."

"Perhaps you can persuade Auntie Adele to keep house for you," I suggested, watching him carefully.

"She's too old for that. I'll fix her up with an apartment of her own just like Elvis did for his aunt. After all she did for me, I ought to take care of her till the angels take her away—long as they don't take their own sweet time about it."

His consideration for Dahlia's granny was touching. I wondered if he was so egotistical that he hadn't stopped posing for the press long enough to take a hard look at her earlier in the afternoon. "She looks fairly healthy for her age. How old is she, Matt?"

"Old as the hills, I reckon."

"Do you think she's taken a turn for the worse since you were here two years ago?"

"Shit, I dunno. I just said what they told me to say. I guess she said what they told her to say. I thought the old bag did a better job of acting like Aunt Adele than she would have done herself—if you'd found her."

"Maybe so," I said as I stood up. "When's the last time you spoke to Pierce?"

"I don't know. Couple of days ago in his office, I suppose. He was real fond of lecturing me." Matt grinned at me, possibly because he knew I was floundering like a fish out of water.

"He didn't say anything to indicate he might come to Maggody?"

"Nope. After he got off his high horse, we reviewed my new album. Come Christmas, it's all you're gonna hear on every radio station in the whole damn country. Hey, you wanna hear 'The Maggody Blues'?"

"I don't think so." I went to the door of the partition and knocked. "Lillian, a couple more questions before I leave you in peace."

She opened the door. "Yes?"

"What time did you speak to Pierce yesterday?"

"He called me at about three," she said. "He wanted to make sure we'd arrived safely and everything was set for the concert. He was going to call today. Guess he won't."

"Did you leave the bus last night?"

"I went for a walk, and then I went to the bar and sat there until it closed. And no, I didn't talk to anybody."

I lowered my voice. "Were you and Pierce . . . ?"

"He was my best friend, not my lover. Matt has trouble conceptualizing a relationship in which one person's not screwing the other physically, emotionally, or financially." She glanced over her shoulder at a chirrupy sound. "Another call, probably from Amy. She's in a dither, and Ripley won't even talk to her."

"Why is Amy calling you?" I asked bluntly, my ignorance of such matters well-established by now. I wasn't overcome with embarrassment; after all, not one of them had my expertise in such matters as following school buses or mediating over chili made with turkey sausage.

"I'm a partner." She shut the door.

Matt had found a bottle of wine and was tippling as I headed for the front of the door. "Some might say," he said, ignoring the red wine that ran down his chin and splattered on his white robe, "that she has a conflict of interest, being my agent and manager on the one hand and a partner in the label company on the other hand. It's sort of like having your hands in both ends of the cookie jar, but I checked with a lawyer and it's legal.''

"Where did you go after you left the PD last night?"

"I bought a jar of field whiskey and went up to the place where Katie's staying. I sat below her window, listening to her sing, till my toes froze. I got back here about midnight.''

"Can Lillian confirm that?"

"I dunno. I was too cross-eyed to git any farther than this seat right here."

I left the bus, considered questioning the boys in the band, and decided to leave it as an act of total desperation. The possibility that I might arrive at that point shortly did nothing to lighten my mood as I drove out Finger Lane to our local bed and breakfast.

Ripley answered the door and led me into the living room, where Katie sat on the sofa. "Our hostess," he said, "is on the telephone, and our host is in the attic. May I offer you tea?"

Only for the very briefest second did I allow myself to imagine Jim Bob in a feather boa, prancing around the trunks. "I need to speak to you," I said to Katie.

"Speak," she said listlessly.

"In private."

Ripley leaned toward me, his fingertips under his chin. "We don't have any secrets, Arly. You just ask Miss Katie Hawk anything you want, and I'll help her answer."

It occurred to me that he was beginning to annoy me. "I need to speak to you," I repeated to Katie, who, for the record, was also beginning to annoy me. "We can go out on the porch or we can go up to your room."

Katie led the way to her room. Once we were inside, I sat down on the ruffly bedspread and said, "When is the last time you spoke to Pierce Keswick?"

"A week ago. He had some new material he wanted me to listen to. Something called 'Your Death Put a Damper on Our Love.' I wasn't real excited." She stood in front of the mirror and began to brush her waist-length hair, but she was watching me furtively.

"Pierce's secretary said you called yesterday at four o'clock. She said you called collect from a launderette."

"Well, I didn't."

"If you want to lie about it, that's up to you—but there are two or three dead bodies in town, depending on whose tales you believe, and this is a police investigation. Did I mention that the telephone company will have a record of the call?"

Katie's aloofness vanished, and she looked as if she wanted to stamp her foot or snatch up the brush and fling it at me. She seemed to be leaning toward the latter, but instead narrowed her eyes and said, "Okay, so I went to call Pierce. I wanted some privacy—"

"You wanted privacy so you went to a public phone?"

"I had to because the woman who owns this place is the type to eavesdrop in the hall or listen in on an extension. Matt's driving me crazy. He wouldn't leave me alone on the bus, and I thought Pierce ought to know."

"And what did Pierce say?"

"Nothing."

"Did anyone see you leave the house?"

"I climbed down the drainpipe outside the window. Back home there was a walnut tree that was mighty useful when my pa wouldn't let me go out at night. He never did figure out why I had scabs on my elbows and knees all the time. Ma had her suspicions, but she never said much."

"Let me get this straight," I said. "You climbed down a drainpipe and walked to the launderette to call Pierce collect and tell him that Matt's been bothering you. Pierce says nothing, but drops everything and comes dashing here within a matter of hours. What was he going to do—slap Matt on the hand?"

"I told you," she said, getting more agitated and glancing at the door with every word. "He didn't say he was coming here. He just said he'd talk to Lillian about keeping Matt away from me." She went to the window, pulled back the drape, and looked down at the yard as if terrorists were creeping up the hill through Mrs. Jim Bob's loblolly pines. "You don't know what it's like to have someone after you all the time. When I perform, he comes to the club and sits

at the front table. He brings champagne backstage. He
hangs around my apartment door. He calls all hours of the
day and night and sends flowers two or three times a
week!''

"A nightmare," I said evenly. "I mean, you have to
find vases for all those flowers."

She finally cracked and stamped her itsy-bitsy foot.
"And Lillian is doing everything she can to destroy my
career because she's jealous. She flat out told me to either
keep Matt away or go on back to West Virginia and marry
a coal miner. It's so pathetic the way she thinks she can
hang onto him by threatening everybody. If she'll just agree
to a divorce, Matt can get a big contract and he and I
can—'' She chomped down on her lip.

"Can what?"

"I don't know! I didn't want to come here in the first
place. I should have listened to my instincts and refused to
come. At least there are places in Nashville where Matt
can't find me."

"Did he find you last night?"

"No, but only because I was in here with the door
locked. Ripley went off somewhere, though. I heard 'em
talking about it in the hall, first when he was supposed to
have supper, and later when they were arguing about
whether to leave on the porch light."

I didn't doubt the argument, and I didn't doubt who
won. "Why did you stay in here with the door locked?"

She stood up and gave me the terribly sincere smile of
a slick little liar. "Matt might have tricked that woman into
letting him in the house. When he gets to hell, he'll start
grinning and the devil will give him a desk in the reception
room and a key to the executive washroom."

I noticed a cassette player on the bedside table next to
a Bible. "Recording scripture verses?" I asked, also notic-
ing several cassettes on the floor.

"I'm a professional singer," she said, maintaining the
smile. "I listen to myself so I can perfect the material."

Her tone made it clear she was no longer going to indulge in temper tantrums for my enlightenment. We started

downstairs, not exactly chatting amiably, and then froze as we heard a voice in the living room.

"There's no L in our lovin' anymore," Jim Bob sang loudly, enthusiastically, and very atonally, "but Christmas ain't the season for frettin' 'bout the reason, why there's no L in our lovin' anymore."

"Interesting," murmured Ripley.

"You think it's got potential?" demanded Jim Bob, less loudly but with the same enthusiasm. "I knew it was in a notebook up in the attic. Like I told you, Mrs. Jim Bob gave away a whole goddamn box filled with songs just as good as this, but I remember most of 'em. Should I sing this for Matt before the concert or come to Nashville and have a tape made at a studio?"

"By all means, come to Nashville. We'll work things out to everyone's advantage, and I think you'll be pleased with the deal. You do remember what I said yesterday, don't you? This is between you and me."

"And Matt Montana," said Jim Bob.

"Yes, indeed."

Jim Bob began to sing his song once again. I slipped out the front door and stood on the porch, trying to make sense of what I'd heard. In one small way, it did make sense. Katie had been in the house yesterday, too, and might have overheard the conversation between Jim Bob and Ripley (an unlikely alliance, granted, but anything was possible). Whatever it was sent her to the pay phone at the launderette.

The one thing it was not was the discovery of the hottest new country lyrics since "You're a Detour on the Highway to Heaven."

★

Miss Vetchling approached the second house with her brolly clenched in her hand. It was a duplex, and the side on the right was the one to which she'd sent Kevin Buchanon on his Fateful Day. Both sides were equally disreputable. On one porch was a disemboweled washing machine surrounded by stacks of yellowed newspapers and magazines; on the adjoining one were several boxes filled

with empty whiskey and beer bottles. The shared yard was
a hodgepodge of weeds, raw earth, orange rinds, and flattened eggshells. It was difficult to conceive of either tenant
being worried about life-threatening germs in the carpet.
The property itself was a biological warfare battlefield.

But she was a woman with a mission, Miss Vetchling
told herself as she knocked on the door, and she would see
it through to the bitter, or in this case malodorous, end. She
knocked again, then turned and stepped carefully over the
decaying remains of a pepperoni pizza that not even the
neighborhood scavengers had touched.

"Yo," called a voice. "You selling Girl Scout cookies?
I got a hankerin' for those chocolate patties."

"A mission," she said to herself, tightened her grip on
her brolly, and turned back. Her smile faded as she took in
the potbellied man dressed in boxer shorts and a dingy undershirt, his mouth slack and wet, his sparse hair greasy,
his nose quite rosy enough to rouse feelings of rivalry
in Rudolph. "I am," she said, "looking for a gentleman
named Arnold Riggles. Are you he?"

"At your service."

She gave him her prepared spiel. He looked so blank
that she came a bit closer and said, "His name was Kevin
Buchanon, and he would have been carrying a—"

"Oh, hell yes!" Arnie said, slapping his knee and cackling with such fervor that Miss Vetchling prudently re-
treated. "He's a great guy, that Kevin feller. He came
inside and spread out so many tubes and odd-shaped
brushes and mysterious gadgets that I thought he was gonna
assemble a Stealth bomber. I told him that'd be a waste of
time 'cause we wouldn't be able to see it!"

He found this so amusing that he staggered out of view,
and all Miss Vetchling could do was hope he ceased braying and emerged from his dwelling, since she had no intention of pursuing him into it. When he finally did, his
shoulders still shaking and his eyes blurred with tears, she
said, "Then you found the demonstration to be interesting
and effective?"

He considered this with great seriousness. "It would
have been. I mean, it had potential, if you follow my drift.

Kevin, he says this vacuum cleaner can suck stains right out of the rug. Any stain at all, he says. I say it can't suck up catsup, and he says it can. So I go get a bunch of those little packets you get with your fries and he and I rip 'em open and squirt catsup all over the rug. Then we dance all over it and squish it in real good. I wish you coulda seen us!''

Miss Vetchling did not share his wish. "And was the Vacu-Pro everything that it was promised to be?"

"Well," Arnie said, coming to the edge of the porch and shaking his head, "there was a problem. I been so busy for the last few months that I haven't had time to pay the electric bill. Kevin said to be sure and call when I get the electricity turned on and he'll come back to show me how those stains are sucked up in a flash. He's also gonna scale some catfish I got in the freezer. Maybe you can come with him and we'll have us a fish fry. You like hush puppies?''

Miss Vetchling thanked him for the invitation and went to her car as briskly as she dared without offending him. With a gay wave, she drove around the corner, then stopped and drew a line through Mr. Riggles's name. After further consideration, she erased his address.

Two names remained. Miss Vetchling decided to go by her apartment and feed Pussy Toes, have a cup of soup, and then resume her investigation with replenished zeal.

The driver of the car lurking at the corner was equally zealous.

★

"No, you stay in the house!" Joyce Lambertino snapped at her little niece Saralee. "Do you want to get your leg chewed off?"

Saralee didn't bother to answer, that being the stupid kind of question adults asked. Yesterday morning Aunt Joyce had asked if she was the only one in the house who could carry dirty dishes to the kitchen (it sure looked like it), and an hour earlier she'd asked Saralee why she'd smacked her cousin on the head with a flashlight (because the ax was out in the carport).

"It's just a pig," said Saralee.

Joyce stood on her toes so she could see better out the kitchen window. "It's that sow of Raz's, that's what it is. Did you see how she attacked poor Poochie?"

Another dumb question, since they'd both been looking out the window. "I can go out and scare it away."

"I'm going to call your uncle Larry Joe. That sow's acting mighty strange, don't you think?"

Like either of them were experts in sow behavior. Saralee went off to find the flashlight and her cousin, in that order.

Chapter Sixteen

I found Hammet sitting on the landing outside my apartment, his investigation unsuccessful and his mood no more jovial than my own. He agreed that drowning his sorrow in Ruby Bee's cream gravy would be acceptable, and we were walking down the road when Les pulled up.

"McBeen wants to talk to you before he leaves," he said. "He's waiting at the Assembly Hall. And Sheriff Dorfer said to tell you that we found Pierce Keswick's rental car parked behind the old Esso station."

I sent Hammet on to the bar and grill, then got in Les's car so he could drive me back to this unanticipated assignation with the coroner. "What'd you find in the car?"

"His airplane ticket was stuck under the visor. He flew into Farberville last night on Northwest, arrived around ten o'clock, and got directions to Maggody from the girl at the car rental desk. According to her, he was real curt and in a hurry."

"Anything else in the car?" I asked optimistically.

"A couple of music magazines and a newspaper. No luggage and no indication that he rented a motel room."

"Was it a round-trip ticket?"

"Yeah, back through Memphis to Nashville first thing this morning. Kinda queer that he wouldn't stick around for the concert, ain't it?"

"Nothing these people do strikes me as queer. If they don't go home, I'll go crazy," I said as he let me out.

McBeen was sitting in his truck. "You were going to call me," he said as I got in the passenger's side.

"I'm waiting for Santa to bring me a cellular phone.

Did you bring me back here to give me yours? If so, I'm going to feel guilty because I didn't get you anything.''

"There'd better be a bottle of brandy on my desk by Christmas Eve. I took a look at the body before I sent it to Little Rock. Couple things might interest you. The cause of death is liable to be a combination of injuries that resulted from a fall. The impact left material embedded in the back of his head and his shoulders. The state lab will give you a detailed list, but I spotted gravel, mud, and a lot of fragments of glass." He held up his hand before I could get out a word. "No, I don't know how far he fell. It doesn't take much, but the material was embedded darn deep.''

"A couple of things, you said.''

"The only hemorrhaging came from the head injury, so you don't need to go searching for extensive blood stains. He hit hard and died fast." McBeen paused for dramatic effect, or, more likely, to allow his dyspepsia to ease. "But his body remained supine long enough for lividity to develop. You can operate under the assumption he laid there for a couple of hours, but was moved before rigor became a factor—say, three to four hours. He was in the chair for at least six hours.''

"McBeen, I'll send you a case of brandy," I said. "What about the man who was floating in the creek?''

"Why did I think you'd be so overwhelmed with gratitude that you wouldn't start pestering me about that one? Discoloration and a lump on his head, but more than likely the cause of death will turn out to be water in the lungs with some hypothermia thrown in. The water's so damn cold it's hard to say when. Could be as much as twenty-four hours." He gestured impatiently for me to get out of his truck. "No more corpses today, okay?''

"I hope not," I said, sighing.

Les had driven off, so I walked down the road toward Ruby Bee's. The tourists had thinned out considerably since the discovery of the body. When news of the second one spread, the merchants and ticket scalpers would find out how much of a damper death could put on their profits.

Unless Pierce Keswick had fallen out of a tree, he'd

gone out of a second- or third-story window or off a roof and had landed on a surface less accommodating than a shrub. No one had implied he'd been inordinately clumsy or deeply depressed and suicidal, but defenestration is a risky way to murder someone, messy and very unreliable. If he'd been pushed, why had he been left there for so long, then taken to the souvenir shoppe?

He could have arrived in town as early as ten-thirty. If he'd gone to the bus to talk to Lillian or Matt, they'd lied about it. It didn't seem likely that he'd stopped by The Mayor's Mansion for a cup of tea. He certainly hadn't come to my apartment and politely asked if he could fling himself out the living room window.

There was one place in town that met two criteria: it had a third floor and it was uninhabited after dark. It was also the birthplace and boyhood home of one Matt Montana (in theory, anyway). Ripley Keswick had gone to his attic to dress himself in tea gowns. Jim Bob had gone to his attic to find a notebook filled with lyrics. An unknown person had gone to the attic of the Wockermann house and dropped a handkerchief. Now it seemed possible that Pierce Keswick had gone there, too.

I'd been there a couple of weeks ago, and Les and I had opened the wardrobes and trunks, pulled back the flaps of boxes of dusty books and hymnals, made sure the hatboxes held hats and the rafters nothing more portentous than cobwebs and bat guano. Billy Dick had found the door unlocked when he arrived less than twelve hours ago.

Earlier in the afternoon it hadn't occurred to me that the house was the scene of a crime, so I had simply walked and assumed Ruby Bee and Estelle would lock up when they left. I needed a key. Luckily, I knew where to find one.

Hammet was perched on a stool, regaling Ruby Bee with the details of his search for the missing mannequin. From what I could overhear, he'd grilled Bernie Allen with such dedication that he'd been obliged to flee from the wrath of the suspect's parents. "But if that fucker ain't guilty," he concluded, "then bears don't shit in the woods."

"He's finished with his supper," Ruby Bee said to me. "Feel free to take him out of here as soon as possible. He's already run off half a dozen customers."

I sat next to Hammet. "Did you know Ruby Bee is at least partially responsible for you being here? She's on the committee that had to find someone to go up on the stage with Matt Montana during the concert. You ought to thank her, Hammet."

"You ain't funny," Ruby Bee said as she snatched up the empty plate from in front of Hammet and started for the kitchen. "I told you that was Brother Verber's idea."

Hammet frowned thoughtfully. "Maybe he ain't such an ol' fart after all."

When Ruby Bee returned, I asked her for her key to the Wockermann house. She wanted to know why, of course, and so did Hammet and most of the customers at that end of the bar. Estelle came out of the rest room in time to throw in her two cents. The detective in the movie Hammet and I had seen the previous evening did not have to present his proposal and get a show of hands before he continued his investigation. He simply drove up and down steep city streets at a hundred miles an hour, splattered crates of produce, averted collisions with buses, and ultimately watched his pursuers drive through a barrier and sail into the bay. He had it easy.

After all this, she admitted that they kept a key on the ledge above the front door.

"What's in the attic?" demanded Hammet once we were outside and I'd quit grumbling. "Ghosts? Skeletons?"

"I'm not sure," I said, "but at least two people have been up there looking for something. I wonder if maybe we ought to get the owner's permission before we go there."

"How we gonna do that?"

I told him.

After a detour by the PD to make a call, we drove into Farberville and parked in front of the lobby of the motel where Patty May Partridge had vanished. This time I told Hammet he might as well come along, since I was going to disrupt the ambiance in any case and he might as well have the opportunity to observe a professional in action.

The manager was as peevish as McBeen. "We're even busier tonight," she said. "There are four private parties, including the county bar association in the Razorback Room, and the club is always packed on Saturday nights. If you'll excuse me, Chief Hanks, I must attend to business."

"Officer McNair, Larry, and I will try our best not to disturb your guests." I beckoned to the two figures outside the door. "Here they are now. Larry is also trained to find illegal substances, so we may have to bring in more police officers if . . . well, I'm quite sure none of those lawyers and their spouses in the Razorback Room would be in possession of drugs, not even the designer ones."

"That's a dog," the manager said in a horrified voice.

I nodded. "I have a handkerchief with the missing woman's scent. We'll start here in the lobby, or maybe in the restaurant, and hope he can pick up the trail. If not, we'll go up and down the halls. Unless, of course . . ."

"Unless what?"

"If I'm correct, these women have been here for almost three weeks. Someone on the staff has seen them, talked to them, taken them extra towels or trays of food. And while you're at it, calls may have been placed to Nashville from their room. The area code is six-one-five."

She made one last stand. "Do you have a warrant?"

"I have a dog. His name is Larry."

"Just don't bring him in here," she said, heading for the desk. "I'll try the long-distance records, and my assistant will start questioning the staff. Leave the dog in the parking lot, all right?"

I went outside to thank Officer McNair for coming to the motel. When I came back in, Hammet was scooping pennies out of the fountain and the manager was shrieking in her office. Within five minutes, she came out and said, "There are two women in 223, one young and one elderly, registered as the Misses Germanders. On six occasions, calls were made to a number with a six-one-five area code. Is that adequate, Chief Hanks?"

I thanked her, grabbed Hammet by the back of his belt,

hauled him out of the fountain, and propelled him out of the lobby.

"I got seventy-three cents," he crowed, showing me his drippy treasure. "Coulda got more, too. Why do you reckon folks throw money in there? Don't they figger somebody's gonna fish it out?"

I admitted I didn't know as we walked past the frozen pool and up the concrete steps to the balcony. Room 223 was next to an alcove with ice and soda machines, convenient for either Miss Germander should she feel the need of a cold drink. Lights were on, and through the door I could hear the sounds of a television game show. I hesitated, recalling all the time and energy I'd spent trying to find Adele Wockermann and all the exasperation I'd experienced because of it.

Hammet leaned over the iron railing. "Do they throw money in the swimming pool, too?"

"You can go look, but don't fall in." After he'd gone back down, I knocked in the manner of a maid with an extra blanket.

Patty May opened the door, saw my badge, and tried to close it. I pushed my way inside. "Where is she?" I demanded, eschewing inquiries into her health.

Her mouth went limp. "Where's who?"

"Adele Wockermann." I made sure she wasn't in the bathroom or the closet, switched off the television, then sat down on the nearest of the two beds. On a table was a tray with the remains of a meal, although it appeared that only one person had utilized room service. "Come on, Patty May, I know what happened the day Adele disappeared. There were no unfamiliar cars in the parking lot that day —only yours and the ones that belong to the other employees. If no one saw any strangers, heard any strangers, or even recalled any strangers in the area, then there weren't any strangers. The dog did not bark in the night."

"I don't know what you're talking about," she said as she sank down on a chair across the room and stared at me, more stunned than hostile.

"The cook goes outside to have a cigarette during the dessert course. You carried a tray into the kitchen, cut the hose on the dishwasher, and went back to the dining room. Twenty minutes later water was spurting onto the floor, Mrs. Twayblade was mopping madly, and you were helping Adele out to your car. It was cold, so I hope you covered her with a blanket. She might have been forced to stay there until your shift ended at four, but fortunately Mrs. Twayblade told you and Tansy to take your cars and drive along the road."

"She did?" breathed Patty May, who apparently had no experience with drawing room denouements and therefore had not yet burst into tears and admitted her guilt.

I wasn't in any hurry. "So at three o'clock you drove away with Adele on the floor in the back. You needed to stash her somewhere for an hour, didn't you?"

"I did?"

"Asking questions in response to questions is a very irritating habit, Patty May. It's almost as irritating as failing to return calls." I went to the window and looked down at the courtyard, where Hammet knelt by the pool wielding a long metal rod with a net on the end. He'd collected several beer cans and a black brassiere. I let the drape fall back. "Maybe all this talk about the old homestead made Adele feel nostalgic. You dropped her off there, went back to the county home, and picked her up again once your shift ended. Is that right?"

She struggled to come up with a lie, but she lacked Katie Hawk's experience. "It was her idea to go there, and like you said, it was cold and I hated for her to have to huddle on the floor of the car for another hour. Her arthritis has been acting up lately."

"Did she mention going up to the attic?"

"Yeah," Patty May said with some reluctance. "It could have been awful if she fell on the stairs, but she didn't. She said all this talk about her great-nephew reminded her of what all was up there. I asked her what, but she told me to mind my driving because she wanted a jalapeño pizza as soon as we got to Farberville."

"Then the two of you came here and checked in under a pseudonym. Why'd you do all this, Patty May?"

"He told me to. He arranged to pay for the room and

all our meals and told me to keep her here until it's safe. Nobody is supposed to know where we are.''

"Who is this benefactor?"

"Why, Matt Montana, of course. He found out about a scheme to kidnap Miz Wockermann because she's his great-aunt. An ordeal like that would be awful hard on her. He's cooperating with the FBI, but until the kidnappers are in jail, Miz Wockermann has to hide out.''

I wish I could say I was so astounded by this unexpected turn of events that I was tongue-tied, but I'd had no theories whatsoever about why Patty May had helped Adele escape and this was plausible. More plausible than extraterrestrial involvement, anyway. "Where is Mrs. Wockermann?" I asked.

"She's out on a date."

This was less plausible. "Out on a date with whom, Patty May?"

"A man named Merle Hardcock. He's from Maggody and they're old friends. When she and I first got here, we went out to eat a few times and went to matinees, but I ran out of money pretty quick. Once we'd watched all the pay movies, she got bored and called him to come over and play pinochle. Two different times they locked me out of the room and I had to sit in the lobby, and another time they were in the nightclub until two in the morning. Matt Montana's private secretary promised he'd send some money, but that was most of a week ago and nobody answers at the number he gave me.''

"And this private secretary's name is Ripley Keswick?"

She nodded so vigorously that her glasses slid down her nose and into her lap. "How you'd know that?" she demanded as she squinted at me.

"Just a wild guess," I said. "Have you ever spoken to Matt Montana?"

"No, he's been real busy finishing his Christmas album, but he sends messages through Mr. Keswick and is going to thank me in person when it's all over. I get all tingly just thinking about him shaking my hand. I finally remembered when he came a couple of years back to visit

Miz Wockermann. He was just a regular person back then, so I barely paid any attention to him except to tell him when it was time to leave. He's a lot more handsome now that he's famous."

I returned to the window to check on Hammet, who'd perfected the art of pool retrieval and now had a sizable pile of undergarments on the deck, to the amusement of the motel guests, who hung over the railing and shouted encouragement. "Why did you call me when Adele disappeared?"

"I thought maybe she'd be safer if the kidnappers found out that they couldn't get their evil clutches on her. If they heard on the news or read in the paper that she was gone, then they'd give up. They haven't, though. Last night they followed me, and one of them was hanging out the window trying to shoot me. I lost 'em, but it was so scary that I threw up something awful when I got back here. I don't reckon I ever hugged the porcelain that long in my whole life."

"I doubt the kidnappers will bother you anymore. When are Adele and Merle Hardcock supposed to be back?"

Patty May's face turned the precise shade of the carpet, which, unfortunately, was avocado green, and she appeared to be in peril of a repeat of the previous evening's gastric extravaganza. "They left yesterday evening while I was visiting my family, and they haven't come back. I been trying all day to get hold of Mr. Keswick and find out what I should do, but like I said, nobody answers. It's not my fault. Miz Wockermann wasn't a prisoner or anything. I was just supposed to protect her until it was safe for her to go back to Maggody."

I felt as if I'd fallen into Hammet's pool. "She left last night and hasn't come back?"

"She wrote a note that they were going to have Mexican food at a place called Matamoros. I looked in the telephone directory, and even called information, but there's no restaurant with that name. My ma says there's no town with that name anywhere around here."

"The only one I can think of is about a thousand miles

away, but the food is authentic.'' I saw no point in further distressing Patty May by telling her that Merle Hardcock owned a motorcycle the size of a Brahman bull. Oddly enough, he has no known links to the Buchanon family.

Patty May finally made the connection. ''You mean Miz Wockermann's going to Mexico? You got to stop her. Can't you call the Texas Rangers or somebody like that?''

''And have her brought back in chains to the county home? No, she can do whatever she damn well pleases, and she and Merle will undoubtedly have an intriguing time of it. Now stop worrying about Mrs. Wockermann and listen to me. I want to hear every conversation you've heard—or overheard—concerning Matt Montana's return to his boyhood home. Every word.''

Patty May complied.

★

Miss Vetchling stuck out her tongue at the dog barking furiously on the opposite side of the car window. Its paws made muddy splotches, and drool flew from its mouth and dripped down its fangs. It was tempting to roll down the window and poke the brute in the eye, but there was no time to indulge in such frivolity. Later, there might be time to drive by and toss a doctored dog biscuit out the window.

She lit a cigarette from Mr. Dentha's rapidly dwindling pack, then checked off the third name on the list. Kevin had been to the house and demonstrated the system to Mrs. Karpik's satisfaction. Once again it was time to consult the street map.

The driver of the car parked half a block away would gladly have eaten a dog biscuit. There were no provisions on the seat, and the candy bar fortuitously discovered in the glove compartment had long since been consumed. Fingers had been sucked clean. The driver was beginning to feel downright crotchety.

★

Mrs. Jim Bob sat in the living room. The fire in the fireplace had sputtered out, and the lights on the Christmas tree were dark. Her tea was cold. Jim Bob had claimed he was going to the SuperSaver, but she knew where he was and with whom. She was too good a Christian to envision the specifics of what they were doing, but even her sanitized version was disgusting and wicked. If he'd paid attention to business instead of chasing after loose women, the store would have done better and she would not have been driven to glean and reap in another field. She would not have been seduced by Satan. Love of money would not have replaced her love of the Lord, who, now that she thought about it, could have sent a signal back in the beginning that she shouldn't open a souvenir shoppe. She wouldn't have needed a bolt of lightning to get the message. Surely He could have created an insurmountable problem with the lease or burned down the novelty company.

But He'd let the sun shine on her endeavor. Now it was dark and cold, and sleet would fall by morning. It would fall on the empty spaces at the campgrounds and on the vacant parking lot beside the bank. It would fall on the yard of Matt Montana's Birthplace & Boyhood Home, but not on more than a few tourists waiting in line for a guided tour. It would fall on the roof of an almost empty Official Matt Montana Souvenir Shoppe. Worst of all, she thought with a shiver that ran clear down to her toes, it would fall on the Voice of the Almighty Lord Assembly Hall, where there was a room used exclusively by the Missionary Society. Where they kept their trays, their coffee and tea pots, their packages of forks, napkins, and paper plates, their spiral notebooks with meticulous minutes of each meeting, and their checkbook that indicated to the last penny how much had accumulated in the treasury. In that the extent of their mission thus far consisted of meeting weekly for refreshments, the treasury had grown steadily.

A knock on the door startled her, and it took her a minute to unclench her fingers from the cushions and go to the door. She opened it, then gasped as she found herself regarding a sheriff's deputy in a khaki uniform.

He pulled off his hat. "Sheriff Dorfer is conducting an investigation into an accidental death down by Boone

Creek. We're asking folks if they saw the man around town or were down there in the last twenty-four hours.''

"I heard about that." Mrs. Jim Bob took the photograph of a bearded man, studied it briefly, and handed it back. "If he came into the shoppe, I didn't notice him. Why would Sheriff Dorfer think I have time to go waltzing around the woods?''

"I'm supposed to show the picture to everyone in your house, so if you could . . .''

"Ripley Keswick has gone off to the high school gym and Jim Bob's not here. I'll fetch the woman." She grudgingly told him to come inside, then went upstairs and knocked on Miss Katie Hawk's room. "There's a deputy to speak to you," she said, aware she was delivering the message in a manner that might alarm those with guilty consciences.

Katie didn't look all that guilty as she came out the door, but Mrs. Jim Bob was still seething over how she'd refused to come down for supper, so she went back downstairs without another word of explanation. The deputy repeated his request to Katie and handed her the photograph.

"That's—that's the fellow I talked to yesterday in the launderette. You say he drowned in the creek?''

The deputy wasn't expecting any positive replies to his inquiries and therefore had no idea how to proceed. "You'd better wait here until I find Sheriff Dorfer and see what he says, Miss Hawk," he said at last.

Mrs. Jim Bob went to the breakfast room to call Eula and tell her how risky it was to open your own home to strangers. It didn't matter if they were famous. The next thing you knew, the silver'd go missing, there'd be coffee stains on the place mats, and they'd get drunk and scatter cigarette ashes on the bedspreads.

She felt much more cheerful.

★

Hammet, who'd not been allowed to bring home the catch of the day, sulked in silence on the way back to Maggody, which allowed me to think about everything Patty May had told me. It fit in with what I'd learned from the interviews with the Nashville people and even with what I'd seen and heard—and failed to appreciate. Pure and simple greed seemed to be the primary motive behind everyone's behavior, from Matt Montana right down to Raz Buchanon. There was room in between for a lot of folks, including the local entrepreneurs. If my theory was correct, Hizzoner headed that list. It remained to be seen if the evidence remained to be found in Adele Wockermann's attic.

I stopped in front of the antique store and said, "Go upstairs and watch television until I get back, okay?"

"Yeah, I 'spose," Hammet said, his tone making it clear that I was asking a lot of him. "What's gonna happen after this concert tomorrow night?"

"I don't know if there will be a concert. I'm beginning to understand some things, but I still don't know who's responsible for Pierce Keswick's death."

"Is it Matt Montana?"

"It could be," I said. "He had a reason, and he was roaming around town last night. Then again, so were plenty of other folks. I'm going out to see if I'm right about certain things. I'll be back in half an hour."

He wasn't pleased to be excluded from the investigation, but he slouched upstairs to my apartment. I drove back down the road and turned on County 102. It wasn't all that late, but it was dark and there was no light in the attic. I could have waited until morning to test my theory, but I knew I wouldn't be able to sleep despite the fact that it had been, as I'd predicted with the precision of a Delphian oracle, one helluva day.

I parked beside the house and took a flashlight from the glove compartment. Rather than charging up to the attic, however, I went to the patio behind the house. There was a vague discoloration on one of the flagstones, but Harve would have to send out the lab boys to determine if it was blood. A few splinters of glass glittered in the light. I turned the flashlight toward the attic and located a broken window almost directly above the patio.

I couldn't tell if the window had been broken the previous night or the previous decade when numerous other windows had suffered from rock-flinging vandals. I went around the house to the front porch. The key was where Ruby Bee had said it would be, above the door and therefore in the very first place anyone who grew up south of the Mason-Dixon line would try (if there wasn't a doormat). I went inside and paused in the doorway of the living room to shine the light on the unadorned Christmas tree. What a cozy scene it had been—the fake heirlooms, the fake relatives, the fake memories shared by those present. An artificial tree would have been more appropriate.

I went upstairs and continued up the squeaky steps to the attic. It had not been ransacked by any means, but several boxes had been pulled away from the wall and a wardrobe door was open. Bread crumbs were scattered on the floor, as if Hansel and Gretel had passed through on their way to the witch's house. A greasy bag indicated they'd also stopped by the Dairee Dee-Lishus; it looked as if it had been put through a food processor.

Congratulating myself on my brilliant deductions, I went to the back of the attic. An empty box sat under the window, surrounded by stacks of books. A briefcase had been knocked over. I righted it and took out a Methodist hymnal with a warped cover and brittle yellow pages. Also inside the briefcase were documents with the letterhead of Country Connections and some correspondence addressed to Pierce Keswick. Nothing seemed to relate to Maggody or to Matt Montana, and I replaced them to read in a less hostile environment. The thick layer of dust on the windowsill had been disturbed. I looked more closely and found two crescent marks that very well could have been made by the heels of shoes—if someone had stood on the sill while facing the interior of the attic. The edges of the broken windowpane were clean. Thirty feet below was the discolored flagstone.

I sat down on a box and regarded the room from a perspective eight or ten feet lower than someone teetering on the windowsill. Katie Hawk had called Pierce with information that sent him racing to the Nashville airport and ultimately to Maggody. The signs on the main road would have led him to the house, and even the most architecturally impaired among us can find an attic. It was impossible to tell if he'd found anything more entertaining than a Methodist hymnal before he climbed onto the windowsill and fell backward to his death.

If he'd arrived around eleven, Dahlia might have been chugging past, although he certainly could not have seen her by standing on the sill behind me. I went down the trunk-lined passageway to the front of the attic and looked out at the road. She'd knocked out poor Mr. Dentha at nine, she'd said, then sat in the living room and considered what to do for most of an hour before she put him in a sleeping bag, carried him out to the Matt-Mobile, and drove out to the chicken house. There are no great distances within the town limits of Maggody (unless someone had gotten real carried away with sign relocation), but she'd come a couple of miles at a turtlish pace.

I went to the side window, rubbed a circle in the dusty glass, and stared until I could make out the oblong shapes of the chicken houses by the creek. A third shape was discernible, a shape suspiciously like that of a truck that belonged to an ill-tempered moonshiner who thought he was so damn clever. How damn clever would Raz have been if he'd arrived with a load of whiskey and found a body? Even love-besotted Dahlia had realized it would be difficult to explain the presence of one in her bedroom. Raz would have faced a similar problem. He hadn't killed (or even beaned) anyone, but he would be forced to explain what he was doing in the chicken house after dark—and why'd he bought the property to begin with. Even if I couldn't prove he was using the chicken house for illegal purposes, I'd keep an eye on it and he'd be out of a warehouse and whatever he'd paid for it.

So what had he done? He'd moved the body, then cleared out the whiskey temporarily. Now it looked as though he was bringing the whiskey back. I waited. Light flashed as a door opened for a moment. A figure moved toward what I was sure was a truck, disappeared, and shuffled back slowly, carrying a load with the care of a grave robber.

If Pierce Keswick had been in the attic, heard the Matt-

Mobile pass by, and then come to this window in time to see Dahlia unload a body and carry it inside, or even taken a break an hour later and seen Raz Buchanon load it into his truck . . . what had he thought? Could he have been so bewildered that he'd not heard a squeak as someone came up the steps to the attic?

I say this because I heard a squeak.

Chapter Seventeen

I climbed over a trunk, dropped to my hands and knees, and crawled down the narrow space below the eaves until I was jammed behind a wardrobe with a canoe paddle stuck in my side. A hatbox fell on my head. Dust swirled into my eyes and nose, and airy strands brushed my face. I'd turned off the flashlight while watching Raz out the window. Now my hand was so sweaty that I could barely hang onto it, but doing so was high on my list of priorities. Real high.

Two more squeaks were followed by profound (as in when you can hear your hair growing) silence. I listened intently, forcing myself to breathe through my nose and battling not to sneeze as decades of dust and mold tickled my sinuses. At the last second I clamped my nostrils together and imploded a sneeze that reverberated through my ears and made my head throb.

Another squeak indicated the intruder had not heard the muffled sound—or was coming to investigate. One of these days I'd learn to bring along my gun, I thought, as I peered futilely around the edge of the wardrobe. There was no utility pole near the property, no moonlight, no hazy diffusion of light from the big city in the distance. I'd been in caves that were better lit.

I became aware of wheezing as the squeaks became more frequent. The intruder was asthmatic or sadly out of shape, I told myself, as if this were information that would be invaluable when I battled for my life. I realized I was reacting as Dahlia had when she found Mr. Dentha in her house, allowing my imagination to run hog-wild. Just because the squeaks were twice as loud as the ones I'd made coming upstairs, and just because the intruder raled like an incubus (or a succubus—gender was not yet established), there was no cause for alarm.

The squeaks were now coming from the floorboards of the attic, not more than fifteen feet away from me. The wheezing was interspersed with low growls. An earthy, fetid smell found its way to my hiding place. The squeaks continued toward the window, passing by the opposite side of the wardrobe with such tentativeness that I suspected I too was putting out a tattletale smell that announced my presence.

A new sound was added to the cacophony of squeaks, wheezes, and thuds from my heart. This one was best described as a plop punctuated with a sputter. Abruptly the smell was so gawdawful that my eyes watered and my stomach convulsed. Acid shot up my throat. Breathing through my nose was impossible, but I was afraid that I'd retch if I removed my hand from my mouth. All in all, this was not a scene from a genteel traditional mystery novel, where fragrant sherry mingled with the aroma of scones baking in the oven.

"Shit!" I said, standing up so recklessly that I banged my head on a rafter. I switched on the flashlight and straddled the trunk beside the wardrobe. There it was in all its organic glory: plump, moist, steaming on the floor. Its producer had lumbered away at the sound of my voice, but to another part of the attic rather than down the steps to the second floor.

I continued over the trunk, careful not to place my feet in a regrettable location, and swung the flashlight as if it were a gun. I certainly wouldn't have minded pork chops for dinner and ham for breakfast.

"Marjorie?" whimpered a voice from the second floor.

"She's up here!" I shouted. "Hiding in disgrace behind a trunk, I guess. Come get her before I"—no explicit threats came to mind, obliging me to make a generic one—"before I think of something to make both of you sorrier than you already are!"

I turned the flashlight toward the top of the steps. Raz's face appeared, his eyes screwed up as the glare caught him and his cheek bulging in alarm. Droplets of sleet dotted his greasy hair and whiskers, but he looked more like something from a Himalayan mountainside than from Santa's workshop. "Is that you, Arly?" he said as he tried to block the light with a shaky hand.

"Just get your damn sow."

"Ye might oughtta not rile her," Raz said, still whimpering and looking as panicky as I'd felt earlier. "Mebbe ye should jest come down here and let her leave when she's of a mind."

"I am conducting a murder investigation. I am not going to allow a damn sow to snuffle around the scene of the crime until she gets bored or deposits another load of evidence." I walked toward the window, shining the light into the crevices between the trunks and boxes. "I don't know what the hell she's doing up here," I continued irritably, "but I'm not about to . . ."

Marjorie charged out from behind a trunk, her pink eyes flashing savagely. Her wheezing had been replaced with snarling, slobbering, and grunting. Four hundred pounds of fury thundered across the attic at me.

"Watch yerself," Raz called helpfully as I leaped onto a trunk, lost my balance, and scrabbled to hang onto a rafter, my feet skittering because I'd misstepped in my haste. I still had the flashlight; it bobbled and jerked, adding to the madness of the moment.

Marjorie snapped at my ankle, and for the first time I realized how powerful her jaws were. This was not the sort of pig that tricked huffy-puffy wolves or went wee-wee-wee all the way home. This was a pig possessed with a lust for blood. I kicked out at her head, then decided I was in danger of losing the piggy that went to market, if not the ones that stayed home and had roast beef. I resumed my slippery tap dance on the top of the trunk as splinters dug into my hand.

"Do something, dammit!" I called to Raz, managing to point the flashlight at him as if he could pull out a police manual and read the directions for a rescue mission. As if he could read.

"I tol' ya not to rile her. When she gets in a mood like

this, the last thing ya want to do is rile her. I reckon she'll come to her senses here in a minute and let you be. She shore ain't been her sweet self lately.''

I scrambled on top of a wobbly wardrobe, again bumping my head, and peered down like a minor griffin on the side of a cathedral. It was not a dignified position, particularly since I'd misstepped as mentioned earlier and was now conveying miasmatic matter on the bottom of my shoe. However, it seemed to be a relatively safe position until Marjorie gave up her quest for fresh, juicy flesh. Raz seemed content to wait on the steps, bleating about his sow's delicate sensibilities.

There were other topics he and I needed to discuss.

★

Earl had fallen asleep on the sofa by the time Eilene was done with the dishes. She stood in the doorway, looking at him but wondering what to do about Dahlia and Kevin. It was awful to think they might not be celebrating their first Christmas as newlyweds. Dahlia'd been acting crazier and crazier every day, mumbling to herself while she drove the Matt-Mobile, lashing out at folks in the supermarket—and she'd been driven that way by the disgraceful behavior of one Kevin Fitzgerald Buchanon. He wasn't the brightest thing to come down the pike, but he'd been raised to be honest and forthright, not to lapse into the sinful ways of someone like Begonietta Buchanon, who'd wept at the gravesides of five husbands and three gentleman callers (two of 'em funeral directors) before anyone tactfully inquired into her recipe for strawberry-rhubarb compote.

There was only one thing to do, Eilene decided. She put on her coat, took Earl's keys, and went out to his truck. She was going to their house. This whole business was going to be brought out into the open and resolved before the night was done. There might be tears. There might be angry words of accusation. There might even be pots and pans flying and dishes shattering. Half the town might hear the fracas from their porches, but Kevin and Dahlia would iron out their problems by dawn.

The Matt-Mobile was parked beside the house, but no cars were parked in the driveway. Eilene sat in the cab of the truck for a moment, her resolve weakening as she contemplated the dark house. She probably should have left a note for Earl in case he woke up.

It was too late for regrets. She would go inside and fix a pot of coffee and be sitting in the middle of the sofa when the kids came home. If the door was unlocked, of course, because it was one thing to mend a marriage and another altogether to break a window. That was an act of desperation.

The latter was not necessary. Eilene turned on the overhead light, started coffee in the kitchen, and returned to the living room just as Elvis pointed his short arm at the numeral eight on the clock. Dahlia wasn't much of a housekeeper, she thought as she took dirty dishes into the kitchen, then gathered up some of Kevin's shirts and shorts and went into the bedroom to put them in the hamper.

It took her a few attempts to find the light switch. As soon as the light went on, the clothes fell out of her arms and she staggered back through the doorway, unable to keep from gaping at the bed. She bumped into the edge of the sofa and sat down hard enough to rattle her teeth.

How could she have doubted Dahlia?

★

"This," I said, "is Raz Buchanon. Some of you saw him this morning when he threatened to fire his shotgun at those of us who were trespassing on his property."

We were in the high school gym rather than a Bethlehem barn, but I had a reasonable cast assembled. The role of the shepherds had gone to the boys in the band. If you've seen a pageant, you know they don't do anything more challenging than sit with the sheep, and they never have any lines. The angel was to be played by Katie. The three kings consisted of Harve, Les, and Tinker, who'd traveled afar from Farberville.

Two of the coveted leading roles were going to Lillian and Ripley. If they did not exactly regard themselves as Matt's parents, they behaved as if they were his keepers,

and that was close enough for me. Which brought us right
to the babe in the manger, little Moses Germander, now all
grown up and blessed with a new name, pretty white
clothes, and an award for best original song of the year.
Now he awaited further acclaim when his album of original
Christmas songs hit the market. Who would have dreamed
that a boy from Maggody could grow up to be a renowned
country songwriter? My, my.

Raz Buchanon had no place whatsoever in the script.
None. I just needed him nearby as I tried to sort through
the last twenty-four hours. Marjorie had been lured out of
the attic with a jar of hooch and was locked safely in the
chicken house. I could have used Dahlia, but she wasn't
home. The Homecoming Committee members were not
present. If any of them had walked into the gym, I might
have borrowed Harve's gun and introduced a level of
violence heretofore unseen in your standard Christmas
pageant.

Relying on the prerogative of the director to seize center
stage, I did so. "This may well go back to the birth of a
baby, but we're going to skip ahead to when Pierce Keswick got the bright idea to send Matt back here to rescue
his image as a hometown boy. No one could even remember him, but some of us spotted the potential to exploit the
Nashville folks while they exploited us. A perfectly reasonable symbiotic relationship, born and fueled by greed."
I waited until everyone nodded, even Raz, who wouldn't
know a symbiotic relationship if it bit him on the butt.
"But, as I said, no one in town remembered Matt. Essential
to the picture was Matt's white-haired great-aunt, who
could tell lively stories of his summers here in Maggody
and give credibility to the scenario. However, Adele's stories were not at all what the image makers wanted. She
remembered what a hell-raiser he was, drinking beer and
going after—"

"Boys'll be boys," Matt interrupted, grinning as if I
were about to present an award of an entirely different nature, "and girls'll be girls, 'specially in the moonlight down
by Boone Creek."

I waited politely until he shut up. "Adele mostly remembered how he went up to the attic and pawed through his great-uncle's boxes and trunks and cartons. In them were letters that had been collected, notebooks from school days fifty or more years ago, books and hymnals, original poems of unpublishable quality, and some that could be converted into lyrics for country songs."

Matt laughed and said, "You're outta your mind. All that was up there was broken fishing poles, boxes of musty old clothes, and stuff like that. If there were any of these so-called lyrics, I sure as hell never saw 'em."

"How about a poem concerning a sweet angel named Jaylee at the top of a tree?" I suggested helpfully.

Ripley and Lillian were watching without expression. I hadn't expected to surprise either of them with my revelation. Katie wasn't exactly bowled over, either. Les and Tinker poked each other and whispered, while Harve puffed contentedly like a Buddha. The boys in the band wandered away, perhaps to keep watch over their flock by night or to compare tattoos. Raz scratched his chin.

"Never heard of anyone named Jaylee," Matt said, having a little trouble with his grin. He was doing his best to imbue it with warmth and sincerity, though, and I was impressed. "Accusations like this are real common, you know," he continued. "You have a hit, then some asshole claims he wrote the song and sent it to you the year before. Lawyers get to slinging letters at each other, and it turns out the asshole really did write a song—it just happens to be completely different except for two words and three chords. Country music is about women and whiskey and love. I wrote Christmas material. Yeah, there's an angel and a Christmas tree. I couldn't seem to get the Easter Bunny to come hopping down the trail."

I shook my head. "You even came back two years ago to see if you could find some of those notebooks that you found so diverting as a teenager. One would almost suspect this 'Detour on the Highway to Heaven' song came as a result of that expedition, but if it did, surely the source has been destroyed."

"It had better have been!" yelped Ripley. Lillian whispered something to him and he smiled benignly at Matt.

"But there was this problem about Adele," I said, resuming my lecture to the cast. "She's not the sort who can be fed lines for a press conference or told what to remember and what to forget. So there was Pierce, all excited about reuniting Matt with his great-aunt, and there were others who realized the potential for disaster. The last thing any of them wanted was for Adele to make remarks to the press and ruin Matt's career, especially when it was possible that Country Connections could be sold for a tidy profit. The only solution was to remove Auntie Adele from Maggody —and I'd like to say it was in keeping with the Christmas spirit to do so without any undue physical discomfort or unpleasantness."

Katie looked as confused as Les and Tinker, who were redefining the term. "What are you talking about?" she asked. "I saw the old lady this morning. She was sitting in a rocking chair in the living room."

"That was a substitute," I said. "The real Adele Wockermann was whisked away to a motel and tended to by a sincere if overly imaginative nurse's aide. I was convinced this had something to do with Pierce Keswick's death, but it did so only indirectly. He came to Maggody because Katie called him yesterday afternoon and hinted darkly that Matt had been writing his lyrics in the Wockermann attic. Pierce was the honest one among you. He would have canceled the tour, killed the album, and exposed Matt's plagiarism, even if it ruined the company."

"Plagiarism?" Matt began loudly and indignantly, then stopped as every last one of his companions glared at him. "Okay, okay, so maybe I got some ideas from a notebook or something. Inspiration, rhymes, stuff like that." It took him a moment to realize what else I'd dropped. "Katie, my sweet angel, did you really call Pierce and tell him that?"

"I wanted to make sure he kept his promise about my album. I made it clear I wasn't going to tell anyone else, but he got awful upset and hung up on me." Licking her lips, she tried to smile at Ripley. "Pierce mentioned hunting for some new material right away. I do hope you're gonna honor his promise."

Ripley studied his cuticles.

I grabbed Raz's gnarly arm and dragged him in front of the bleachers. "What happened next is this old fool's fault. He drove down to his temporary warehouse, a load of moonshine in the back of his truck and his demented sow in the cab, and found a body. Rather than inform the authorities like any law-abiding citizen would do"—I stared at the conspirators in front of me in case they missed the irony—"he got the brilliant idea to move it to another location so no one would link it to his property."

Harve came out of his stupor to ask, "Are we getting to that body Dahlia was talking about? I thought he called from Little Rock this morning."

"I don't know where he is right now," I said, still clutching Raz. "Tell them what happened."

"Well," he said, yanking on his whiskers and pretending to be a prime example of American Gothic, all glassy-eyed with virtue and about to take root in the amber waves of grain, "it seemed to me all this bother about the ol' Wockermann place was the cause of the troubles. Goddamn cars and trucks on the road all the time, folks wanting to take my picture like I come off a flying saucer, making Marjorie fractious. So there's this feller in the chicken house and I decide I'm jest gonna take him up the road apiece and let somebody figger out who it is. I git him on the porch swing, and then all of a sudden I hear glass break in the backyard. Marjorie comes tearing outta the house like greased lightning, we toss the feller back in the truck, and git outta there."

To Harve, I said, "Raz finally admitted that he kept the body in his barn all day and took it back to Dahlia and Kevin's house earlier this evening. I have no idea who it is, but perhaps one of your deputies could check this out. There's liable to be a wallet in the body's pocket. If you call McBeen, please don't mention my name." I waited until Tinker left, then related my experience in the attic, omitting only the detail about where I'd stepped. I kept everyone's attention to the end, then gave them a while to assimilate it.

Lillian was the first to try. "Are you saying that this pig frightened Pierce so badly that he fell out a window?"

"She's a pedigreed sow," Raz said churlishly, then scuttled away and sat down near the door, his eyes shifting from me to the empty hall as he considered his chances.

I told him I expected to find a whole lot of chickens in the chicken house by morning, and let him leave. I sat down next to Harve and waved away some of the smoke. "I don't seem to have the proper equipment to take the pig into custody, nor do I intend to have my leg chewed off while trying to do it. You want to arrest Marjorie, it's okay with me. If she gets the electric chair, Ruby Bee makes a tasty barbecue sauce."

"Seems to me these folks stirred her up," Harve said.

"That's not all they did," I said as I stood up and confronted Ripley. "Jim Bob recognized some of his lyrics when the bus arrived yesterday, and he told you his notebook was likely to be in the Wockermann attic. You went over there to make sure there was no evidence, and found Pierce's body on the patio, didn't you? I kept asking myself why someone wanted to draw attention to the souvenir shoppe or send some sort of metaphorical message about Matt. Your reaction was as simple as Raz's: move the body to draw attention away from the scene. The souvenir shoppe was the closest place, and the switch with the mannequin would only confuse things further."

Matt turned around to stare at him. "You put Pierce in the window dressed like that? How's that supposed to make me look?"

Ripley gleefully considered his response, but Lillian dug her fingers into his arm until he shrugged and said, "Perhaps just a tiny metaphorical message, as Arly so nicely put it."

"That's creepy," Katie said.

Matt scooted across the metal seat and patted her knee. "Yeah, it is. Thinking a dead person could take the place of a mannequin dressed like me." He realized what he'd said and slumped forward, his head propped in his hands. He may not have been thinking deep thoughts, but he appeared to be trying.

I looked at Lillian, who was shaking her head as she looked at her husband on the seat below her. "I can't see

Ripley doing this on his own," I said to her. "Let's hear what you did after the bus was parked at the motel."

"I told you that I took a walk and ended up at the bar," she said.

"Did you go past the PD?"

"Is that the funny-looking red brick building? I walked by it, but I didn't pay it any mind."

"You did laundry," Katie contributed. "I saw you while I was talking to Pierce. You had a magazine and were sitting by one of the dryers."

"Oh, yeah," Harve said, rising to his feet and taking an interest now that I'd done all the hard work. "Les here says you saw Carlos Tunnato in the launderette, Miss Hawk. Could you tell us what happened?"

"Back in Nashville he called me a bunch of times before we left. I mean, the messages on my answering machine were always that Charlie called, but he came up to me in the launderette and told me that was his nickname. Charlie the Tunnato. I told him that was as cute as a butchered hawg."

"Charlie?" Matt echoed. "Where've I . . . ?"

"What else did he tell you?" I prompted her.

"He said he had some information that would interest me. I told him I'd meet him later. He had this silly map, so I pointed to some place on the creek and said for him to meet me at midnight."

I gazed evenly at her. "A stranger in a launderette says he has some interesting information, so you arrange to meet him in the woods at midnight? Doesn't that seem overly trusting?"

She glanced nervously at Lillian, then pushed her hair back and gave me a defiant smile. "I had no intention of going, of course, and you already heard that I stayed in my room the rest of the night. I figured he'd freeze his butt off out there and maybe stop calling me in the future. I never dreamed he'd fall in the water the way he did."

"Did you hear any of their conversation?" I asked Lillian.

"It was too noisy, and I was busy reading."

"Why were you there?"

"Why does anyone go to a launderette?"

I was not in the mood for sarcasm. "You'd left Nashville less than a day earlier. It's hard to imagine that you already needed to do laundry. Did you follow Katie—or Charlie?"

Matt made a face. "I jest know I heard that name before. Was it at your office, Lillian?"

"No," she said coldly.

"You might as well tell us who this Carlos Tunnato is," I said when she failed to continue. "The Tennessee authorities will go to his house, question whoever else lives at the address, and find the connection, although it may take a week or two. Do you all want to wait in Maggody until they call us?"

"He was my second husband," Lillian admitted. "We were divorced eighteen years ago. He's been trying to borrow money from me, and I guess he heard we were coming here and followed me. I didn't see him in the launderette. I didn't even know he was in Maggody until I heard about his death."

"That's right," Katie said with that same terribly sincere smile I'd seen earlier. "Lillian was way off in the corner, reading a magazine. She didn't talk to him, and there's no way she could have overheard what I said to this Charlie man. Nobody could have known about our meeting."

"Divorced eighteen years ago . . ." I said, sitting down on the bottom row of the bleacher and thinking about what she'd said about making sure everything was done properly. I could almost smell Marjorie's majestic offering as I thought how I'd feel if I learned my divorce had not been finalized. I'd raise hell with the lawyer, threaten malpractice, hand-carry the documents to Manhattan, and if I had to, drag the judge out of bed. But I hadn't remarried. If Lillian's divorce wasn't legal, neither was her marriage to Matt. He was free to marry Katie Hawk.

I looked up, ready to say as much, and faltered. Lillian and Katie looked as if they were listening to each other breathe. There was enough bonding going on to bring Wall Street to its knees. As a corporate entity, they turned and sent the same message to Ripley. He positively rippled in response.

"Lillian did not hear the conversation in the launderette," Katie said abruptly. "Couldn't have. No way. And I was in my room singing right up until midnight. Those folks what own the house heard me."

I shook my head. "They heard something, and you couldn't have climbed back up the drainpipe until after midnight. Matt said he was sitting below your window. He didn't see you."

"Was he drunk?"

The accused gave her a mournful look. "Not the whole time, Katie. It takes a couple hours to get warmed up, and besides, I would've noticed if you put your foot on my head."

"That'd be a first," she shot back. A more perceptive person might have taken it in the heart, but Matt grinned and ruffled his hair.

"And Lillian was helping me with Pierce's body at midnight," Ripley said. "I found her at the bar and we went to the house together."

"It took well over an hour," Lillian said. "Breaking into the store, undressing the mannequin, dressing poor Pierce, trying to get that guitar set just right."

Harve threw up his hands and stomped off to yell at Les, who hadn't done anything worthy of a tirade but might well in a day or two.

"Charlie was your ex-husband?" said Matt. "Didn't I meet a guy named Charlie at your office?"

"Oh, shut up!"

It was impossible to attribute this final statement to one particular speaker, since it came from all three of them.

★

"Grab me! I'm fixin' to fall!" screeched Ruby Bee, hanging onto the branch above her head. The one she'd been standing on continued to bend under her weight until it snapped like a firecracker.

"Gimme your hand," Estelle said from a higher roost. She caught Ruby Bee's hand and helped her relocate to a branch sturdy enough to hold her.

Ruby Bee tried to find a spot that felt secure, comfortable being out of the question. It was a spindly tree, chosen out of necessity. She was still amazed at how quickly she and Estelle had arrived up in its branches. Terror could do that. "I cain't believe this," she grumbled. "Women our age sitting in a tree, and most likely stuck here all night. I ain't climbed a tree since I was ten years old, and I only did it then to get down my cousin's kite on account of his bawling. It's not dignified."

"Then shinny on down."

There was a moment of silence while they pondered their predicament. Sleet pattered on the pasture and rustled the few leaves on the branches around them, and up on the main road a car door slammed and an engine came to life. Water gurgled across the low-water bridge. Way across the field, Christmas tree lights sparkled in a window.

Estelle risked life and limb to lean forward so she could see the ground underneath the tree, then sighed and wrapped her arm back around the trunk. "You got us into this, Rubella Belinda Hanks, you with your bright idea of spying on Raz Buchanon. I hope you'll be proud of yourself if and when they find our frozen bodies in this tree like two turtledoves."

"I told you not to open the door," Ruby Bee said promptly, not willing to take the blame alone. "I clearly said that I heard Marjorie inside there, snuffling and snorting, and you said that no one over the age of six was afraid of pigs."

"And who said she'd take a stick and smack the pig on the nose if she bothered us? Whose idea was that?"

"I had to say something when you insisted on opening the door."

They carried on like this for a while longer, but then

branches creaked as they settled in and took to listening to the restful sounds in the blanket of darkness.

★

Loud music blared from inside the house. Lights shone from the living room windows, and the Christmas tree in the window glittered in tiny explosions of colored lights and tinsel. A plastic Santa posed on the roof, his arm raised to encourage eight plastic reindeer to dash away, dash away into the sky.

Miss Vetchling observed the scene from inside her car, the windows rolled down far enough to allow smoke to escape as she finished a cigarette and made sure she was at the correct address. It was far too late to drop by someone's home without an invitation, but there were at least two dozen women inside who'd received theirs. They carried cocktail and wineglasses and plates of food, and they milled about with a great deal of laughter.

To drive away would be craven, Miss Vetchling told herself as she got out of her car. No dogs came howling out of the darkness, but she took her brolly along as she went up to the front door and knocked firmly enough to be heard over the music.

The door swung open and a woman with wildly crimped blond hair and scarlet lipstick grabbed Miss Vetchling's arm. "Glad you could make it, darling! You haven't missed a thing, but we're getting ready to start. Come on in and let me take your coat and umbrella."

Before she could demur and present her spiel, Miss Vetchling was pulled inside, stripped of her coat and only weapon, and handed a cup of what she was told killer eggnog. The first sip was enough to cause her to shudder, but the second was really quite tasty. Miss Vetchling allowed herself to be presented with a plate of canapes and placed on the sofa between a hard-faced woman with black hair and a young woman with an anxious expression.

She put a meatball in her mouth to forestall attempts at conversation while she assessed the group. All women, all dressed casually but not cheaply, all seemingly having a delightful time in what Miss Vetchling knew was the home of Miss Cherri Lucinda Crate. Miss Crate seemed to have abandoned her guests for the moment. None of them allowed this to adversely affect their spirits; all were indeed consuming spirits with enthusiasm.

After finishing her eggnog, Miss Vetchling decided she could not remain at the party under false pretenses and went into the kitchen to seek out Miss Crate. There were cookie sheets of food awaiting their turns in the oven, plates of cookies, bowls of red and green candies, and bottles jammed on a counter that served as a bar. Glasses were lined up nearby.

Miss Vetchling made herself a martini (eggnog was high in both calories and cholesterol) and continued her search for Miss Crate. The carpet was in need of a good shampooing, she noticed with disapproval as she went down a hallway. Miss Crate should be presented with the opportunity to see how effective a Vacu-Pro could be.

"No peeking," said Miss Crate, popping out of a room and closing the door behind her. "Let's refresh your drink and then we'll get started right away. Have you ever been to one of these before, darling? I can tell you're going to love it. It's so much easier to shop like this than to battle those crowded malls. Free gift wrapping and delivery up until Christmas Eve."

Miss Vetchling could make no sense out of Miss Crate's babbling, nor could she get in a word edgewise. Once her martini had been enhanced with a hearty dollop of gin, she obediently followed her hostess to the living room and resumed her seat on the sofa. Accepting the reality that her investigation was temporarily halted, she lit a cigarette and sat back to await developments and contemplate a career in private detection. It really was more scintillating than phone sales, she thought with a tiny hiccup. One met so many congenial people.

The other guests found seats or sat on the floor, and the music stopped. Miss Crate's head appeared around a corner. "You ready, ladies?"

Everyone assured Miss Crate that they were, including Miss Vetchling, who did so with a merry flick of her finger. The lights dimmed and sultry music filled the room like mysterious and exotic perfume. Miss Vetchling watched the doorway with a sense of anticipation that was not unpleasant.

Miss Crate stepped into the room. She wore a shimmery white nightgown gathered demurely at her neck with a red velvet ribbon and falling inches short of panties made only of a wisp of lace. "Picture yourself as a Christmas present," she cooed at her audience. "What would the man in your life do if he found you under the tree like this?"

"Climb up the chimney," said a stout woman with a hint of a mustache.

Miss Crate giggled. "Oh, come on, Lynne, he'd drag you off to the bedroom for a night of passionate love. And just how does this passionate lover come dressed on Christmas Eve? In an undershirt? In worn flannel pajamas? Hell no! He comes in the sexiest, skimpiest briefs so you can both see what he's got in mind. Right, darling?"

Into the doorway stepped a gangly young man, and indeed he was dressed in the . . . well, skimpiest briefs Miss Vetchling had ever seen. They appeared to be dotted with tiny reindeer, but there were very few of them, certainly not the standard allotment for a sleigh. On his head was a red cap trimmed with white felt. On his face was an embarrassed smile.

Miss Crate stroked his arm. "Why, here's Santa."

"No," said Miss Vetchling, "actually it's . . ."

"Kevvie!" screamed a figure pressed against the living room window. "Kevvie!"

Chapter Eighteen

"So why'd you let them go ahead with the concert?" asked Harve, who as usual was safe at his desk in Farberville where Maggody was nothing but a bad memory, at least for the moment.

It was Monday afternoon, and I'd finally had time to sit down in the PD (where Maggody is an omnipresent menace day and night), lean back at the preferred angle in my chair, get my feet settled just right on the corner of the desk, and call him to exchange information.

"I wasn't going to," I admitted, "but Ripley and Lillian came by yesterday morning and told me how the cow ate the cabbage, as Dahlia would say. It wasn't exactly blackmail, but there were some overtones. We dickered back and forth and finally agreed. It's not like any of them shoved Pierce Keswick out the window, Harve. I'm satisfied that he was there when Marjorie came charging at him, and I can tell you it's not the time to consider the safest place to retreat."

"I grew up on a farm," Harve said. "I know how dangerous those old sows can be. Got a five-inch scar on my leg to prove it. But they did drag the body to the souvenir shoppe and dress it up like that. I dunno what the charge should have been, but we might could have come up with something to entertain ourselves."

"Sure we could have, and I could have called a press conference and told everyone that Matt Montana lied about his original lyrics and that Hizzoner is in line for a Country Sound Award for sleaziest songwriter of all time. The story might not have made the front page of the *New York Times*, but it would have been hot stuff in the tabloids and country music publications. The tour would have collapsed. The label company wouldn't be worth the price of a CD—or even a cassette. I could have done all that, Harve, but I didn't.''

Harve grumbled as he lit a cigar and told LaBelle to bring him some coffee. He wasn't a dedicated chauvinist, but he wasn't averse to letting someone else fetch and carry. ''So why didn't ya?''

''What Ripley and Lillian told me is that this little town of Maggody broke a zillion copyright and trademark laws. We are talking more infringements than on Dahlia's uniform. They put Matt's name and face on ashtrays, coffee cups, T-shirts, caps, place mats, maps, pencils, pens, duck callers, and so forth, and every one of them is a violation. They printed songbooks of copyrighted lyrics and reproduced photographs from magazines. They used his name, which is registered. Katie Hawk's, too.''

''I didn't see her name.''

''On the menu at Matt Montana's Hometown Bar and Grill. Country Connections has an entire legal department to deal with this, to see that the miscreants are dragged into court and fined into oblivion. They don't mess around because it's a very lucrative source for the company. They come down like a block of granite. And I can't think of a single business in town that didn't use Matt's name, from the obvious ones on the main road all the way to the Satterlings' produce stand out toward Emmet. They were selling Matt's Homegrown Pecans. What was I supposed to do? Tell 'em to sue everybody in town?''

''Reckon that might cause a problem,'' Harve acknowledged with a sigh. ''What did ya do?''

''There were still some tourists in town, and I didn't much want a repeat of the earlier riot. I told 'em to have the concert and then go back to Nashville and do whatever they could for a week. It's going to leak out by then, anyway. Jim Bob was swaggering around at the concert, talking about *his* songs, and a couple of folks at the launderette overheard Katie's so-called private conversation and yelled some crude remarks at Matt while he was on stage. Only about a hundred people showed up, which makes me think the grapevine is back in business, even if certain establishments are closed real tight. Once I explained the problem, you've never seen signs come down so quickly. The town limit sign is back in its original spot, and the only signs on the highway claim there are seven hundred fifty-five of us and that we've got a Kiwanis Club somewhere.''

"Out behind the Methodist church, maybe."

"Hammet was so disillusioned that he turned in his cowboy suit and refused to attend the concert. He hung around the apartment all day yesterday, then went off earlier this afternoon. Brother Verber is supposed to drive him back to the foster home in the morning.''

"Then everything'll be back to normal, heh?'' Harve said, chuckling. "As normal as it ever gets over there, anyway.''

"As normal as it ever gets,'' I said as I stared glumly at the ceiling. The water stain did not have ears.

Harve rumbled uneasily, took a few puffs, and finally said, "About that guy that drowned in Boone Creek . . . ?''

"That one's still yours. He was a tourist and we had a deal, Harve. He may have been married to one of the Nashville people, and it may have been more than a coincidence that he appeared in town, but there's no proof that any of them went down to the creek and shoved Charlie Tunnato into the water. I'm not saying it wasn't in all of their interests not to let him talk to Matt Montana. None of them want Matt to realize he might be a free agent in both marital and professional matters.''

We chatted a while longer, then I hung up and went to the window to look at the darkening town. The streetlight was on and the one stoplight was keeping everybody from getting too rowdy. The town had survived the onslaught, and if we weren't wiser, I'd like to think we would be a good deal warier in the future.

There were a few things I hadn't told Harve. One was that Adele had called from Padre Island. With Merle Hardcock cackling in the background and urging her to hurry on account of the wet T-shirt contest, she'd said she was well and asked how had little Moses Germander's visit turned out. Fine, I'd mumbled. She'd gone on to say how disappointed she was not to have been there to hear little Moses sing the song about the detour to heaven that Mr. Wockermann had written on their tenth wedding anniversary. I'd said it was shame. Her last remark was the clincher. She'd finally recalled the details of the baby's birth all those years ago. Adele, the expectant mother, and Mr. Wockermann had been visiting kin in Cassville when the baby came a week early.

Seems the manger was in Missouri all along.

★

"Therefore," Mrs. Jim Bob said, "it's clear that the Good Lord wants me to donate all the profits from the shoppe to the Missionary Society. If you'll give me the key to the Assembly Hall, I'll just go get the checkbook, take it home, make sure it's balanced nice and neat, and bring it back. Of course I'm busy these days, but it shouldn't take too long."

"Praise the Lord," said Brother Verber. He lifted his face to give her a perplexed look, then let it drop and gave his feet a perplexed look. Lots of things were perplexing, he thought as he took a drink of wine. Even that was perplexing.

"We missed you at the concert," she continued, "but it went well enough, considering the sort of characters those Nashville folks turned out to be. Miss Katie Hawk was supposed to go first and sing two songs, but Ripley Keswick came right onto the stage and said she was going to do a full set. It's kinda funny they'd change the schedule like that, just to do her a favor, isn't it?"

Brother Verber knew he had to say something—that much he could tell from the way she was glaring at him. "Praise the Lord, Brother Barbara."

"Perhaps I'd better just get the key later," she said, her mouth real pinched as she stood over him. There was an empty wine bottle on the kitchen cabinet and half a dozen next to his garbage can. Later, she thought, when her own position was . . . less vexatious, she'd remind him of his sacred duties as pastor of the flock of the Voice of the Almighty Lord Assembly Hall. She'd remind him at length and in a loud, clear voice that would drive demon rum from his gullet and cleanse his soul.

He fell over on the couch and began to snore, bubbling at the mouth like a spring. It occurred to her that she might just take the key right then and there, fetch the checkbook, and be about her business. The key was likely to be on the dresser, so she picked up her gloves and purse and went down the short hallway to the little bedroom.

She couldn't find the switch, but she could see the dresser over by the bed, and she stepped gingerly through a mess of clothes and dishes on the floor. She was feeling for the key when she realized someone was sitting on the edge of the bed, and she screamed so loudly that if it were Satan himself, he'd have flown straight out the window.

Once she realized it wasn't any sort of manifestation of the devil, but was instead a woman with long dark hair and dressed in a cowgirl outfit, she let out a little self-deprecatory laugh. "Excuse me," she said, "but you startled me sitting so still like that. Brother Verber didn't mention he had a guest. I suppose you're a relative from out of town, and that's why he's sleeping on the couch and you're in here?"

There was no response. Mrs. Jim Bob was miffed, but she didn't have time to do anything more than sniff, find the key, and start back to the door. "I'll just be on my way . . ." she began, then looked a little harder. There was a chip on the woman's nose and she was missing a foot.

Mrs. Jim Bob began to scream with all her might.

★

"Aw, Kevvie," Dahlia said, holding out her hand so her in-laws could see the diamond ring. It wasn't gonna blind anybody, but it was definitely a diamond. "I cain't believe you got me this for our very first Christmas. Ain't he a sweetie?"

Earl agreed in a grumbly voice. He wanted to watch the basketball game, but decided maybe he'd better not. Eilene had fixed his breakfast for two days running, but she was still acting kind of spooky. Before the kids arrived for supper, he'd been out changing the oil in the truck and turned around to find her standing in the doorway, looking at him like he was a used car out at Hobart Middleton's lot. There hadn't been a '64 Mustang glint in her eye, either.

"And I forgive you," Dahlia was saying, slobbering all over Kevin and managing to admire the ring all the while.

Kevin squirmed. "I jest couldn't make enough money selling those durn vacuum cleaners to buy you this for our first Christmas together. It had to be something real special, not just a box of candy and a bottle of cologne. Miss Crate had me delivering packages all day and then, well, modeling at her parties. I just reminded myself it was all so I could get my love goddess the best present in the world."

Earl felt his blood pressure shoot up on account of his son being a model, which meant he'd probably decide next to be a florist or a hairdresser or a ballet dancer. "Just don't show up here in leotards," he said, then glanced at Eilene. "Ain't no son of mine gonna dance on a stage. That's all there is to it. He can clean septic tanks or git a job with the Mafia, but he ain't gonna dance. Now I'm going in the other room to watch the game. Are you coming, son?"

"Sure," Kevin said as he untangled his sweetcake's arms from around his neck and whispered something in her ear that turned all of her chins bright pink.

"Is everything okay?" asked Eilene when Kevin had stumbled away to watch basketball and drink beer and do other manly things like belch and scratch, just so his pa could sleep knowing there was no *pas de deux* in Kevin's future.

"Yeah, I suppose," Dahlia said. "I still worry about beaning Mr. Dentha. Mebbe I should call him and apologize." She thought about it, then brightened up and said, "Or mebbe I should send him a fruitcake. Whattya think, Ma?"

"A lovely idea," she murmured, "and so appropriate."

★

Miss Vetchling gazed down at the expanse of blue water below her. Little whitecaps dotted the surface like a sprinkle of snowflakes, but of course it was all sunny and warm down there, just like it would be at her final destination. It was very cold where Mr. Dentha was, but there'd simply been no time to call someone to repair the broken window at the office. Or to notify the regional manager that the Farberville office was closed indefinitely. Or to arrange for someone to remove Mr. Dentha's body in preparation for his successor. There was Pussy Toes to deliver to a friend, and the hasty trip to the travel agent, and all the last-minute shopping and packing. Only now was Miss Vetchling able to sit back, enjoy a glass of gin, and speculate as to why Mr. Dentha had returned to the office to have his fatal heart attack. Perhaps he'd desired to die in a room where his lips would match the wallpaper.

"Pretty down there," said the man in the seat next to her. He leaned forward, pressing her arm as he tried to get a better view of the island they were approaching.

"Cozumel," she told him. "A tourist trap, from what I've been told. Very, very expensive and horrible service. I have a tight budget, so I'm always careful to avoid places like that and find something with the authentic feel of the real Mexico."

"So where are you going?"

Miss Vetchling decided that she did not care for his shifty eyes any more than his bad breath. "Oh, a little town with primitive facilities. Nothing worth visiting, I'm sorry to say."

"Why go? You a missionary?"

"No," she said as she looked down at the golden sand and the toy hotels so far below, "I'm a private investigator. Now if you'll excuse me, I must . . ." She gave him the chagrined look of a spinster too prudish to even allude to bodily functions, and he smirked as he rose to let her out.

Toward the back was a gentleman with a balding head and a sloppy mustache, but there was something she liked about his smile. The seat beside him was empty. She put her hand on the arm rest and struggled to look out the window. "Is that Mexico down there?" she asked, wondering how he would react at the sight of her dressed in a red teddy and a garter belt adorned with little green bows.

She'd been foolish and extravagant, but after all, it was almost Christmas and Mr. Dentha was beyond begrudging her the contents of his metal box—and his wallet.

★

"How about supper?" I called to Hammet, who was sitting on the landing. "We can drive into Farberville afterward and get ice cream. Maybe go to another movie or hunt for fountains."

He didn't react. I went across the street and stopped at the bottom of the steps. I knew what was wrong, and I knew what he'd say if I asked. His answer was the problem. He represented a tie to Maggody, another reason that would keep me here until my hair was as gray as Ruby Bee's was reputed to be. At the moment, the only thing keeping me from leaving was my own sense of uncertainty. I couldn't let myself use him as an excuse to justify my behavior to myself or to anybody else. There was too much of that going on already.

"Got somethin' to show you," he said.

"Can it wait until we eat? I was so busy talking to people all day that I skipped lunch."

He lifted his face and gave me a full dose of the starving orphan, even sucking in his cheeks and widening his eyes as if he were expiring from malnutrition on the spot. "If it has to, I guess it can," he said morosely. "Don't much matter anyways, seein' how I'll be gone come tomorrow. It's a present for you."

So what's the big deal about allowing yourself to be manipulated by a pint-sized con man? "Okay," I said, "show it to me and then we'll eat. You want cobbler at Ruby Bee's before we go for ice cream?"

He opened the door and gestured for me to go in. I took a step and stopped, too surprised to go any farther. In the middle of the room was a misshapen pine tree, no more than five feet high, branches at odd angles, and sticking out one side as if trying to keep from pitching over. It was decorated with dozens of glass balls, strands of lights, wooden soldiers and animals, loops of tinsel—the whole bit up to the fat silver angel who'd slipped but was hanging on by a halo.

Heaped around it and over most of the floor was powdery snow, or powdery something. Mounds and mounds of undulating white covered the furniture and the countertops. Your basic winter wonderland right there in my apartment.

"Where'd you get all this?" I asked.

"Oh, I dunno," he said, beaming at me as if he hadn't ever heard the word *thief*.

I squished through the flakes and looked more closely at the tree. "Is this a loblolly pine?"

"I reckon it's a Christmas pine."

"Do you?" I sank down on the sofa and stared at him. "Loblollies don't grow wild. Did you cut this down from someone's yard?"

"Not me. I jest found it lying in the alley right out back and figgered somebody threw it away on account of it being runty. Folks shouldn't throw things away on account of them being runty. This little tree needed somebody to take care of it and make sure it has a happy Christmas, dint it?"

The child had more weapons than a battalion of marines. The haggard face, the big eyes, the deft way to turn a phrase and stick it in me like a bayonet. And don't think for a second he hadn't rehearsed half the afternoon. Hammet Buchanon was no amateur. Then again, I told myself as I flopped back on the sofa and struggled not to laugh as white flakes fluttered around me, maybe I'd let the Nashville madness extinguish my holiday spirit. Maybe it was time to get in touch with my inner-elf.

"But you're going back after Christmas," I said as we started down the stairs. "Understand?"

"Hey, whenever you want. Don't matter none to me."

"That's good to hear. Hey, Hammet, about that fake snow?"

"Miss Estelle gave it to me for free. She had six whole cases of it in her living room. She said it were ivory snow, but it looks white to me."

"And the decorations?"

He pulled my jacket more tightly around him and looked up, grinning. "I heard Ruby Bee tellin' you the key was above the door. It weren't no problem gittin' the decorations downstairs and it only took three trips to carry 'em, but the tree in the living room was too goddamn heavy for me to drag. 'Sides, it was so straight and green and perfect that it looked kinda fake to me.''

You are invited
to preview
Joan Hess's
hilarious new mystery
Martians in Maggody,
now available
in a Dutton
hardcover edition
at your local bookstore.

Chapter One

"It seems downright peculiar that all the alien babies are born in South America," Estelle was grumbling as I came across the tiny dance floor of Ruby Bee's Bar & Grill. She wasn't grumbling at me, or even at the comatose truck drivers in the back booth, but at the proprietress herself, who was wiping down the surface of the bar and visibly simmering over some unknown indignity. "This one here," she continued, jabbing her finger at a fuzzy photograph inside the tabloid spread in front of her, "was born in Brazil last year and already speaks seven languages and is learning calculus."

"Sez who?" countered Ruby Bee.

"Sez Dr. Raul Sancrispo, who's a child psychologist at a university in Rio de Janeiro. He took the baby to his clinic and has been observing it ever since it was born. According to him, the baby has all kinds of strange sexual organs. Poor little critter . . ."

"How 'bout a beer?" I asked as I slid onto a stool at a circumspect distance down the bar and smiled politely at Ruby Bee, who happens to be among other exasperating things, my mother. Her round face looks innocent enough, except for a few too many streaks of undulating pink eye shadow and unnaturally blond hair (courtesy of Estelle's Hair Fantasies). She always wears a crisp apron with her name embroidered on the pocket, and she can sound real sympathetic when someone's crying in his or her beer (and unwittingly making a substantive contribution to the grapevine). Then again, there are plenty of good ol' boys who've smarted off once too often and found themselves in the gravel parking lot, their legs crossed and their ears stinging.

She raised her carefully drawn eyebrows. "Ain't you still on duty, Ariel Hanks?"

"I'm always on duty," I pointed out mildly. "I am the entirety of the police force, which means there is no one else to come on duty should I go off duty. Hizzonor the Moron explained this to me only last week at the town council meeting, right after they voted to cut the budget so deeply you could look through the hole and see China." I glanced at Estelle. "Anything in there about alien rice forms in China?"

"Don't go smirking at me, Miss Priss. I only buy these fool things out of idle curiosity. I know darn well they're made up."

Ruby Bee banged down a beer in front of me, at the same time slyly scooting the basket of pretzels out of reach so I'd know she didn't approve of this blatant dereliction of duty. "I just hope there ain't an accident or something that requires sober judgment," she said.

"Or a holdup at the bank," Estelle added sternly.

"We don't have a bank," I said, wondering why they were both so cantankerous. Outside on the streets (the street, anyway) of Maggody, Arkansas, the sun was shining and the weeds were swaying in a warm breeze. Across the way, a goodly number of the seven hundred fifty-five residents were going in and out of Jim Bob's SuperSaver Buy 4 Less, and the Suds of Fun Launderette was doing a steady business as spring cleaning got under way. The bench in front of the barber shop was lined with grizzly old coots chawin' tobacco and gossiping worse than the Missionary Society. Ruby Bee's Bar & Grill was peaceful in midafternoon, but there were hungry crowds at noon and downright boisterous ones at happy hour, when draws were a dollar and the jukebox never cooled off. Rumor had it that rooms had been rented recently at the Flamingo Motel out back, but the molting neon sign still read: v CAN y, and Ruby Bee was too diplomatic to confirm anything.

This isn't to say that three quarters of the buildings weren't boarded up, or that the merchants were getting rich, but it was a pleasant change after a cold, hard winter that dragged on until cabin fever was epidemic, if not worthy of investigation by the Centers for Disease Control in Atlanta.

They'd have a tough time finding us in the backwoods of the Ozark Mountains. Maggody's all of a mile long, with a single traffic light and a singular lack of charm. Tourists might gape at the odd shape of the Voice of the Almighty Lord Assembly Hall, the charred timbers of the bank branch, the occasional drunk sprawled in the mud outside the pool hall, the blinding pinkness of the bar and grill, and ultimately at the skeletal remains of Purtle's Esso station, but that's about it until the Missouri line. Unless they're enamored of cows, scrub pines, and litter, of course. There's an abundance of all three.

Estelle tucked an errant wisp of bright red hair back into her beehive, took a delicate sip of sherry, and turned the page. "Listen to this, Ruby Bee. Down in Louisiana the police chased a 1990 Grand Am until it smacked into a tree. It turned out there was twenty buck-naked Pentacostals inside it, none of them hurt on account of being jammed in thicker than fleas on a wisp. They said their clothes were possessed by the devil."

Ruby Bee snorted. "Sounds like something Brother Verber might find of interest. He's all the time worried that folks are getting naked without his knowing—or without his being there to sputter about eternal damnation and Satan's handiwork."

"He ain't said much about that since he and Mrs. Jim Bob were caught up on Cotter's Ridge dressed in lacy lingerie." Estelle turned another page. "Did you know that a family in France has been living in a hollow log since the end of World War II? They have it fixed up real nice, although they sometimes have a problem with termites."

I finished my beer. "I guess I'll go patrol for Bigfoot, ladies. He was last seen at the Pot O'Gold, knocking on Eula Lemoy's trailer door."

"She probably invited him in," Ruby Bee said as she took my glass and swished it in the sink. "If you're in the mood to patrol, you ought to look for a black limousine that was all over town this morning. It was longer than two regular cars, and the windows were so dark nobody could see who was driving it. Dahlia said it went real slow by her house twice, and Joyce Lambertino said it was up their way. Slinky Buchanon said he saw it going across the low-water bridge, but of course he claims he sits with his grand-mother in the front pew every Sunday and she's been dead for nineteen years. Still, I can't imagine why this limousine would be creeping around town.''

''I'll bet that's how Bigfoot came to Maggody,'' I said as I headed for the relative sanity of the street. ''He's starred in enough movies to be able to afford a limo.''

''It went by my house, too,'' Eselle said, although dis-missively. ''Here's where a man took his wife camping in Canada and she exploded from spontaneous combustion right there in the tent. There's an actual artist's depiction.''

''Lemme see,'' said someone's mother.

I walked to the PD, which consisted of a brick building with two rooms, one desk, three chairs (one of them the repository for junk mail), yellow-and-white gingham cur-tains, and a telephone attached to an answering machine. The red light wasn't blinking, but it rarely did. I picked up my radar gun and went back outside to run a speed trap by the school zone. With any luck at all, I could bust Bigfoot, sell my story to *The Probe*, and make enough money to escape a humdrum existence in a ho-hum town where noth-ing much ever happens.

★

''Did you see that limousine this morning?'' Mrs. Jim Bob asked Brother Verber. They were standing outside the Voice of the Almighty Lord Assembly Hall, enjoying the sunshine and pondering what to do about the threatened rift in the Missionary Society. Out of deference to the weather, she wore a pale blue linen suit and was holding her white gloves in one hand. As always, her face was devoid of the devil's paint and her underwear was starched. Her lips were pinched, but that was on account of Elsie McMay's mul-ishness rather than her own mood, which was more mellow than usual. That very morning she'd managed a smile when Jim Bob announced he was staying late at the SuperSaver to inventory, even though she knew perfectly well that he'd stagger home stinking of whiskey and cheap perfume. He'd pay for it when the time came.

Brother Verber, who'd been lost in thought (or something closely resembling it), clasped his hands and beamed at her. She was nothing short of a source of inspiration and an obvious candidate for sainthood when her time came. She was looking particularly fetching in the Good Lord's golden glow. "See what, Sister Barbara?" he asked.

"A big black limousine went down Finger Lane this morning. I happened to notice it while I was straightening Jim Bob's dresser drawers."

"I'm afraid I didn't. I was down on my knees all morning, praying for guidance in the upcoming battle with Satan." He gave her a chance to nod approvingly, but she merely looked back at him. "Everybody knows that in the spring a young man's fancy turns to love," he went on, obliged to pull out a handkerchief to mop his neck. "I wish I could feel confident that our youth will express their love by picking posies and sipping lemonade on their front porches, but they're more likely to go sneaking down to the banks of Boone Creek to engage in lustful depravity right there in the moonlight. I shudder to think how many innocent young souls will be lost to Satan in the next few months."

"What do you aim to do about it?" Mrs. Jim Bob asked curiously. Boone Creek ambled through the middle of a national forest criss-crossed by logging trails. It was likely that moonlight shone on a whole passel of idyllic clearings, and those who frequented them weren't apt to be passing out maps.

He closed his eyes as he imagined all that lustful depravity. Why, he could almost hear Satan rubbing his hands together and chuckling over ripe young bodies writhing and groaning on the very banks of the river Styx. "I've been thinking about patrolling the creek, armed with a flashlight and a Bible. If I was to chance upon a couple of young lovers fornicating on a blanket, I could fall to my knees beside them and counsel them to avoid eternal damnation by joining me in prayer. If they resist, I'll denounce them from the pulpit the very next Sunday."

Mrs. Jim Bob debated mentioning that he was more likely to end up with a load of buckshot in his backside, since most of the males in Maggody had shotguns before they had primers. However, he clearly was smitten with his idea and she had more important things to do. "You might pray a little harder before you go tromping along the creek. I'm going to run over to Millicent McIlhaney's to find out where she stands on this problem with Elsie."

She drove away in her pink Cadillac. After a moment of thought, Brother Verber went back into the trailer that served as a rectory and started hunting through his kitchen drawers for flashlight batteries.

★

"It drove by your house twice?" Eilene Buchanon asked her daughter-in-law, who was on her third piece of pecan pie and showing no signs of losing enthusiasm. "It came by here, too. I yelled at Earl to come see if he could tell who was in it, but by the time he came out of the bathroom, it was long gone."

"This sure is tasty," Dahlia (nee O'Neill) Buchanon said as she licked her fingers. She paused in case another piece was forthcoming, then reluctantly set down her fork. "Kevin dint see it, either, on account of he was at work. I sure am glad Jim Bob gave him back his old job at the SuperSaver. He ain't nearly as tuckered out as when he was selling vacuum cleaners in Farberville. Kevin, I mean."

Eilene tried not to grimace as she recalled the bizarre string of incidents during Kevin's tenure at VacuPro. None of them had been his fault. The whole town of Maggody had gone flatout crazy for a month, and only now were certain people able to make polite conversation when they couldn't avoid each other. "So you're adjusting to married life?" she said encouragingly.

"I reckon so, but some days I just don't know what to do with myself. Ruby Bee sez she might hire me back this summer when business picks up. Even though Brother Verber says it's a sin for a wife to work, I miss the jukebox and the laughter, and the rednecks howling at me to fetch another pitcher and a basket of pretzels.'' She sighed so ponderously that all three hundred pounds of her quivered and flatware clicked in the drawer. ''I guess I just miss the bright lights, Ma, despite bein' a respectable married woman. Sure, I got my own little home, a loving husband, a vacuum cleaner with thirty-five attachments, and a sub-scription to *TV Guide*. I fix Kevin tasty suppers every evening and biscuits and gravy every morning. All the same, something's missing from my life.'' She sighed again, at length and with wheezy, heartfelt misery. ''When I saw that limousine, I started wondering what I'd do if it stopped out front and the back door opened and someone beckoned for me to climb inside it.''

Eilene resolved to have a word with Ruby Bee.

★

Jim Bob scratched his bristly head as he read the article concerning the twenty Pentacostals. Why was there two pictures of a squinty-eyed little alien baby and not one of the buck-naked pilgrims, some of whom were women? He moved on to the horoscope page, where he knew he'd find a clear shot of Madam Kristen's cleavage. After he'd studied it for a long while, licking his lips and savoring a warm flush to his privates, he found his sign. It turned out to be right inspirational, if you interpreted the promise of meeting new people to mean meeting new people with cleavage like Madam Kristen's. For the first time in years, Mrs. Jim Bob's suspicions were unfounded. Jim Bob hadn't screwed anybody (including her) for the best part of a month, and he was painfully aware of what was missing in his life. Just the other day he'd found himself appraising a heifer in a remote pasture beyond the low-water bridge.

The office door opened and the newest employee shuffled in, his throat bobbling and his hands flapping like dying fish. His eyes had the same yellowish tinge as Jim Bob's, but they were noticeably blanker and his beetlish forehead was a great deal more pronounced. Buchanons were scattered across the county like ragweed, but incest and inbreeding had taken its toll. Some of them could outwit a possum (on a good day, anyway), but Kevin Fitzgerald Buchanon wasn't among the lucky few.

"What?" Jim Bob barked, annoyed at being interrupted while he was working.

Kevin tugged at his collar. "Kin I ask you something, Jim Bob?"

"You just did."

This resulted in a momentary silence while Kevin tried to sort this out. He finally gave up and said, "About the new schedule, I mean. It says I'm supposed to work every day from four till midnight."

"Where'd you learn to read, boy? On weekends you're working from three till midnight."

"Oh, I dint see that. Anyways, now that I have a wife, I was hoping I could have some nights off so we could go to the picture show in Starley City or even just stay home and watch television together."

"Are you implying your television set doesn't work during the day? Mrs. Jim Bob turns on those gabby morning shows the minute she gets up, and her soaps are on when I go home for lunch. Maybe you'd better get yourself a new television set."

"That ain't what I mean, Jim Bob. Dahlia's kinda moping around these days on account of not having anything much to do except things like laundry and washing dishes and—"

"Spare me the details. I got a whole pile of paperwork to do by the end of the day. If I don't get it done, I can't start figuring the paychecks. Do you want to explain this delay to all the dumbshits out there who are counting on getting paid on Friday?"

Kevin shook his head and went back to the bucket and mop in the produce aisle. He thought mebbe later he'd sneak out to the pay phone in front of the store and call his beloved in hopes of brightening up her dreary day. He knew it was dreary because she told him so every evening when he got home, sometimes explaining for the better part of an hour before she gave him his supper. He had a feeling she wasn't gonna clap her hands when he told her about the night shift.

★

"Get this," Darla Jean McIlhaney said to Heather Riley, both of them flopped across the bed and so bored they'd painted their toenails three times. Now they were reduced to hunting for stories in *The Probe* about grotesque sexual practices. "This scientist in Germany has discovered a new diet that's guaranteed to make you lose ten pounds in one week."

Heather reached for the fingernail polish remover and a tissue. "Does it involve self-cannibalism?"

Darla Jean squinted at the print. She knew she needed glasses, but she was damned if she was going to get 'em and be the laughingstock of Farberville High School. Not one cheerleader or member of the pom-pom squad wore glasses. Last year's homecoming queen wore contacts, but there wasn't any way her own pa would pay for 'em. "No, it says all you're allowed to eat are hot dogs and ice cream, but you can have as much of them as you want. There's some enzyme that goes to work and explodes fat cells like they were little firecrackers. Read it yourself."

Heather obeyed, but she wasn't nearly as impressed. "What about that unit on nutrition last fall? Miss Estes made it real clear that none of these crazy diets work."

"Then why does this German scientist swear it does? Miss Estes is just a teacher. She can't keep up with every scientific breakthrough."

"Go ahead and try it," Heather muttered as she kept reading. "Now what kind of crazy woman would steal Elvis's body, have it cremated, and use the ashes for breast implants?"

Darla Jean was about to offer an opinion when the phone rang out in the hall. It turned out to be a sight more intriguing than breast implants.

"That was Reggie Pellitory," she said as she strolled back into her bedroom and pretended she was looking for something on her dressing table. "He broke up with Traci last night and he wants me to go out with him after supper. He's gonna borrow his cousin's four-wheel so we can go riding around."

Heather wrinkled her nose. "You better be careful, Darla Jean. When Traci let him do it, Reggie did everything but announce it over the PA system at school. She liked to have died."

"Who says I'm gonna let him do it?"

"Well, everybody in town knows it wouldn't be the first time," Heather pointed out tartly. "Last Saturday night Beau saw you and Dwayne heading toward the creek with a six-pack and a blanket. Did y'all go out there to count lightning bugs?"

Darla Jean decided she needed to wash her hair again.

★

Raz Buchanon was mulling over something real important. He was also scratching and spitting and doing other less fascinating things that involved bodily functions and infestations, but they can be left unspecified. He was doing all this in the cab of his truck, which was parked outside a cafe in Hasty. Inside, the waitress and the owner were discussing whether they should disinfect the booth or have it replaced altogether.

"I'll tell ya, Marjorie," Raz said to his companion sitting in the cab, "it might jest work. Bizness was mighty slow last winter, and that's my best time of year. Come hot weather, folks prefer cold beer over my 'shine, and I don't rightly blame 'em." He glanced timidly at her. "Now, Marjorie, don't git all fractious jest because you had to wait out here while I talked with that feller what's slicker than a preacher's ass. There weren't no way they were gonna let you inside."

Marjorie stared out the window.

Raz sighed. "Iff'n I pull this off, I was thinkin' we might look into one of those fancy satellite dishes that sucks in channels from all over the world. I hear tell ye can git movies all night long, and they don't cost you nuthin'. You'd like that, wouldn't ye?"

Marjorie's beady pink eyes blinked.

"What's more, we kin have our pitcher in *The Probe*, jest like that woman what had ever' last drop of blood sucked out of her body by vampire mosquitoes."

Marjorie relented, but only after he went back inside and bought her a candy bar.

★

Way down in Little Rock, which was only two hundred miles away but could have been on another planet, Cynthia Dodder checked in the bathroom mirror to make sure her gray hair was neat and her nose powdered. After further deliberation, she removed her broach and put it away in her jewelry box. As the featured speaker at the UFORIA meeting, it was important to present herself as a detached professional investigator.

She went to the kitchen table, currently covered with newspaper clippings and magazine articles, each marked with a date and ready to be filed. There were also journals and newsletters, letters begging her attention, and a list of telephone calls to be made when she had time.

Cynthia Dodder felt strongly about keeping her priorities straight, however, and her speech was in the forefront of her mind as she made sure the back door of the apartment was bolted and the porch light shining to ward off burglars. The neighborhood had deteriorated over the last twenty years to the point she hardly recognized anyone and spoke to no one. Had her budget allowed it, she would have moved to a nicer area, one inhabited by respectable folks like herself rather than whiny welfare mothers and impertinent young men of a different racial persuasion.

She watched them now as they gathered out in the parking lot, laughing and passing around a bottle in a brown paper bag. If any of them had dared set foot in the exclusive dress shop where she'd been a clerk for forty years, he or she would have been escorted out the door by a security guard.

It was nearly seven o'clock, and surely Rosemary was aware that it took more than half an hour to drive to the library. She needed time to review her notes before she called the meeting to order promptly at eight. Tonight's agenda would be brief because of the portentous content of her speech, during which she would prove conclusively that NASA officials had destroyed the Mars Observer spacecraft rather than allow it to transmit pictures of an ancient alien citadel. The real question was why NASA had sent the probe in the first place, since they and other government agencies (the CIA, FBI, USAF, and the top-secret Majestic Twelve commission, just for starters) possessed physical evidence of an alien presence and had covered it up for forty-five years.

Cynthia was on the verge of calling Rosemary when a familiar white compact chugged into the lot. She picked up her purse, manila folders, clipboard, and packet of blurry photographs, and let herself out, making sure the door was securely locked behind her. It was unfortunate that the hoodlums could watch her as she left, but there was nothing to be done about it.

"Sorry I'm late," Rosemary said as she maneuvered out of the parking lot. "I locked myself out of the car at the grocery store. The manager finally got it open with a coat hanger, but by then it was after six. I barely had time to eat a bite of supper and clean Stan's litter box before I came rushing here to pick you up."

"That stoplight was red, Rosemary," Cynthia said as the car lurched along the street like a three-legged dog. "Please pay attention to the traffic. I too am sorry you were late, but now it's more important that we arrive at the library in one piece. If you don't mind, I'd like to study my speech."

She took out a stack of index cards, but it was almost impossible to concentrate over Rosemary's atonal humming and occasional mumbles to herself about approaching intersections. Really, Cynthia thought with a sigh, it was so very challenging to imagine Rosemary Tant as one of ufology's most vital contributors. She was scatterbrained and forever late. She dressed with no attempt to downplay her thin shoulders and heavy hips. Her hair was a particularly drab shade of brown, her long face perpetually riddled with anxiety, her voice tremulous and uncertain, even when discussing the weather.

But she was.

SORRY TO LEAVE MAGGODY?

Well, come back for another visit in Joan Hess's rollicking new Arly Hanks mystery, MARTIANS IN MAGGODY!

GET $4.00 BACK
WHEN YOU PURCHASE
MARTIANS IN MAGGODY
IN HARDCOVER.

Just mail in the coupon below, along with cash register receipts with prices circled, and copies of UPC codes.

To receive your rebate, you must purchase both O LITTLE TOWN OF MAGGODY and MARTIANS IN MAGGODY (keep the receipts, please).

Then, simply send in:

1. Receipts for purchased books with prices circled

2. Coupon, completely filled in

3. Photocopy of book UPC codes

4. Send to: MARTIANS IN MAGGODY REBATE OFFER, P.O. Box 1019, Grand Rapids, MN 55745-1019.

5. You will receive your $4.00 rebate in 4 to 6 weeks.

NAME _____

ADDRESS _____

CITY _____._____STATE_____ZIP _____

Offer expires 12/30/94   Mail will be received until 1/21/95

PENGUIN USA

PRINTED IN THE USA

Signet • Dutton

$1.50 CASH BACK
on Maggody books!

Now that you've bought Joan Hess' O LITTLE TOWN OF MAGGODY you can get $1.50 back when you buy either of her hilarious mysteries, MALICE IN MAGGODY or MISCHIEF IN MAGGODY.

⊜ ONYX

To receive your $1.50 rebate enclose:

1. Sales register receipts for O LITTLE TOWN OF MAGGODY and either MALICE IN MAGGODY or MISCHIEF IN MAGGODY (prices circled)

2. This rebate certificate completely filled out with your name, address, and UPC numbers from appropriate books

3. Send to:
   O LITTLE TOWN OF MAGGODY REBATE OFFER
   P.O. Box 1013 • Grand Rapids, MN 55745-1013.

NAME_____

ADDRESS_____

CITY_____STATE_____ZIP_____

UPC #_____; UPC #_____

PENGUIN USA

Offer expires 1/31/95. • Mail will be received until 2/17/95.

This certificate must accompany your request. No duplicates accepted void where prohibited, taxed or restricted. Allow 4-6 weeks for receipt of rebate. Offer good only in U.S., its territories, and Canada.

Printed in the USA